Bob Langley was born in Newcastle-upon-Tyne
and started his career as an insurance clerk. After
a period of National Service and three years
travelling round North America, he joined Tyne
Tees Television, first as a scriptwriter and later as
a presenter and roving reporter. In 1969 he moved
to the BBC, becoming first a national TV
newsreader, and then going to work on *24 Hours*
and *Nationwide*. He is now best known as the
popular presenter of BBC-1's lunchtime magazine
show, *Pebble Mill* and of the late-night chat show
Saturday Night at the Mill.

Bob Langley is married and lives in the Lake
District, the setting for his second thriller, *The
War of the Running Fox*. He is also the author of
the highly-successful *Warlords*, also in Sphere
Books.

Traverse of the Gods
BOB LANGLEY

SPHERE BOOKS LIMITED
30–32 Gray's Inn Road, London WC1X 8JL

Glossary of Mountaineering Terms

Abseil
: Technique used for lowering oneself down a rockface by means of a rope.

Belay
: Technique of fastening oneself to rock or ice to safeguard against the effects of a fall.

Bergschrund
: The crevasse between a glacier and the mountain proper.

Couloir
: A gully.

Karabiner
: An oval-shaped metal link used for belaying and abseiling, etc.

Piton
: Metal spikes, used for hammering into rock cracks.

Serac
: Pinnacle of ice.

Snaplink
: Another word for a karabiner.

Traverse
: To move to right or left rather than straight up.

Prologue

Last summer, at eight o'clock on the morning of 11 June, three thousand feet up the North Face of the Eiger, Jörg Binder, twenty-three-year-old mountain guide from the village of Wengen, was nearing the series of rubble-strewn ledges known as the 'Traverse of the Gods' when he heard a soft hissing sound from above and peered up to see a great avalanche of snow and ice spewing out against the sky like the wings of some incredible bird. Binder knew his position was hopeless. He was nearing the top of a Grade V crack, its walls crumbling like brittle toffee at the sides, its belly packed with crisp hard ice. His companion, Eduard Arbenz, was somewhere below, hidden from sight, waiting for Binder to bring him up on the rope. The piton Binder had been hammering was only half-way in. There was no time to clip himself on, or any guarantee that the damn thing would hold even if he could.

Sweating desperately, he rammed his iceaxe blade deep into the pitted crystal in the crack's interior and gripped the shaft with both fists. A clatter of stones whistled by, bouncing off his helmet top, then a handful of ice granules, dropping like stars into the void beneath, and then, with a murderous roar, the full force of the avalanche burst through the snow-chute above and cascaded down upon his skull. There was no doubt in Binder's mind that he was about to die, and yet curiously, he felt no fear, only a conviction that death was imminent and a grim urge to hang on for as long as possible.

The snow thundered around him, working its way into his clothing, piling up beneath his body like layers of fine soft sand which pushed him outwards away from the limestone wall. His fingers, gripping the iceaxe, lost all feeling. He tried to concentrate on shutting out the din, on living just a few seconds more.

He had no idea how long the snowy bombardment continued, but suddenly and without warning, the thunder began to ease. One second he was in the centre of a raging cataract, the next he was clinging to his iceaxe, torn, bloody, but thankfully alive.

He held his breath, waiting for the second wave. None came. The racket died away, and the silence which followed seemed strangely painful to listen to.

His first thought was for his companion, Eduard Arbenz, trapped on a perilous belay further down the crack where the rock was particularly bad. Fearing the worst, Binder called his name. At first, there was silence. He tried again, and this time an answering cry came back, strong and clear. Binder felt a stab of joy. Against all odds, they had both survived. It seemed a miracle.

Dazed and breathless, but overcome with relief, Binder continued up the crack, picking his way with care until, just before the 'Traverse of the Gods', he made a remarkable discovery. At the point where the snow had come away, the surface sagged precariously, leaving a scooped-out defile of virgin-white. Below this, huddled on a narrow ledge, sat the figure of a dead man. His legs and the lower portion of his anatomy had long ago disintegrated into bone, but the chest and head were totally preserved from long immersion under the ice. The corpse's skull was facing north, its shoulders turned to the west, hugging the rocky contours. The skin had darkened to a degree where the features were not easily discernible, but Binder noticed that the eyebrows were intact, the lips drawn tightly over a line of long even teeth. The man's expression was peaceful, his eyes lightly closed. He looked as though he belonged there, a forgotten human organism absorbed into the strata of centuries, ready at any moment to come alive.

Binder's first reaction was one of disbelief. To his knowledge, no climber had gone missing on the North Wall in recent years, and all previous assaults were already accounted for in the Grindelwald records. Then, as he leaned forward to study the corpse more closely, he made a second astonishing discovery. The dead man was wearing a windproof anorak, sage green in colour. It had a drawstring hood and two breast pockets. On one was embroidered a small flower encircled by twisted ropes, on the other the eagle emblem of Nazi Germany. On his head was a Gebirgsmütze, the distinctive forage cap unique to the German Alpine Corps, the Gebirgsjäger.

Binder knew the war had been over for almost forty years. Finding the preserved corpse of a Nazi soldier halfway up the most dangerous mountain face in Europe seemed beyond the bounds of credibility.

Something at the dead man's throat caught his eye. The head was inclined on the chest as if in sleep, but beneath the chin Binder could see a ribbon, discoloured with age, and a thin metal chain. He reached out, shrinking as his fingers touched the crinkled skin. The chain came away in his hand, its fastenings made brittle by years of burial. It was a small metal locket, rusting with age, and a military medal. The medal was the Knight's Cross with Oak Leaves. Binder turned it over, rubbing his thumb across the surface. Engraved on the back were the words: *Erich Spengler* and the date *October 1942*.

He examined the locket, prising it open with his fingernail. Inside was a picture of a young woman. She was strikingly beautiful, with dark hair, radiant eyes and a clear pale skin. The photograph was faded with age, but the loveliness of the woman was unmistakable. He slipped the picture out of its slot and turned it over. On the other side was scribbled a name: *Helene Rössner*.

Binder's hands were trembling as he belayed himself to the cliff and brought up Arbenz on the rope. The two men decided to leave the corpse where it was, push on to the top as quickly as possible and contact the police when they got down.

The weather remained good as they moved on to the treacherous 'Spider' icefield and scaled the narrow exit crack, reaching the summit in the late afternoon. They descended the mountain's west flank and made their way to the little complex of hotels on the Kleine Scheidegg plateau as darkness fell. Binder's first act was to telephone their news to the constabulary in Grindelwald then, having missed the last train to Wengen, they drank two steins of beer at one of the bars and set out to walk the few miles down the track to Binder's home.

When they reached the village, they found the narrow

streets flooded with light, and men swarming everywhere. There were uniformed policemen in neatly-pressed tunics, plainclothesmen in herringbone jackets, soldiers in jackboots and little képis, all hovering around the entrance to Binder's chalet.

Binder and Arbenz were taken by special train to police headquarters in Interlaken and for the rest of that night were interrogated by members of Swiss military intelligence. Again and again, they were compelled to go over the details of their story, describing the corpse, marking its location on enlargement photographs, drawing sketches of the position of the body and the precise way in which it had been lying. When morning came, worn and haggard after hours of questioning, Binder and Arbenz were released with instructions to tell no one about their discovery.

At noon, a helicopter from the Lauterbrunnen Valley deposited an army climbing team on the glacier between the Eiger and the Mönch. From there, they ascended the snowslope to the Eiger's summit, and using metal cables and winches recovered the body from the 'Traverse of the Gods'. It was flown back to Lauterbrunnen where it was transferred to a military ambulance, driven off to an unspecified destination, and never seen again. No explanation was given by the authorities for this behaviour and no mention of it appeared in the Swiss press.

There the story might have ended, except that ten days later, Laurence Hemsworth, a BBC research assistant looking for background material on the Eiger, heard rumours of the incident and decided to investigate. The information he received and the facts he later uncovered were so incredible that Hemsworth devoted the next months of his life to travelling over Europe, checking out evidence, conducting interviews and trying to unravel the fusion of fact and mystery which obscured the stories of Erich Spengler and Helene Rössner. What follows is an account of a series of astonishing events which took place in the summer of 1944. It has been fictionalised to bridge the many gaps which occur in the narrative, and also to give flesh and blood to the people involved. Much of it comes from ex-German soldiers tracked down in Munich, Koblenz and Mannheim, some from an aged Dane called Walter Lasser, and a very great deal from Hemsworth's own supposition. No attempt has been made to catch the various cadences of German phraseology. When authors do, it often seems stilted and unreal. The Germans in this book speak in colloquial English, as they would in the hands of a good translator. Nor has any assessment been made, moral or otherwise, of the political issues of the time. History itself will do that.

What it amounts to is one of the most remarkable stories of the war, a story which, for reasons that can only be guessed at, has been kept a closely-guarded secret for almost forty years.

PART ONE

The Warriors

One

On 17 June 1944, eleven days after the Allied landings in Normandy, Franz Heppeler, Special Assistant at the German Embassy in Berne, staggered out of the pine forest which cloaked the pastures above the little Swiss town of Grindelwald and collapsed face-down into the gravel of a dried-up riverbed. Against the blur of the night sky, the jagged outlines of the nearby mountains looked like crumpled carbon paper. Heppeler touched his side and his hand came away wet with blood. Just below the ribcage, a bullet had carved a deep funnel into Heppeler's insides, carrying fragments of bone splinters with it. He had taken off his undervest and strapped it around the wound as a makeshift dressing, but either the vest had slipped, or he was bleeding too copiously for the flow to be staunched. The bullet was still in there, of that he was certain. He could feel it lodged in his vitals. The effect was disorientating, as if something was pushing him out of alignment like a disjointed toy.

The lights of the little town spread like a starburst across the valley below. Heppeler shook his head to clear it. He knew he had no time for this. Got to keep moving, he thought. Must get to Willi's.

Painfully, he eased himself to his knees and then to his feet, struggling for balance as the earth reeled beneath him. He was a small man, lean and wiry, with long lank hair plastered damply over his forehead. Wiping the rain from his face, he began to stagger down the riverbed, grunting with pain as each laboured movement lanced into his insides.

Willi's house was on the outskirts. A light shone in one of the windows. Heppeler hung back as a car sped by, waiting until the street was empty before venturing over and hammering hard on Willi's front door.

The door swung open and Willi Fredier, tall, balding, thirty-eight years old, stood staring in astonishment at the

3

grotesque creature huddled on his threshold.

'Franz,' he gasped, 'for God's sake, what's happened?'

Heppeler collapsed into the entrance hall and Willi Fredier half dragged, half carried him into the drawing-room, stretching him out on the sofa. A log fire cast flickering shadows across the hearth. Fredier stripped away Heppeler's shirt, clucking deep in his throat as he examined the gaping blue-rimmed hole still pulsing out blood.

'How long have you been in this state?' he asked.

Heppeler shook his head weakly. His cheeks and forehead were glistening in the firelight. 'Forget the wound,' he whispered. 'My jacket pocket . . . right-hand side . . . quickly.'

Frowning, Willi Fredier picked up Heppeler's jacket and produced a little phial wrapped in silvery paper.

'What's this?' he asked.

Heppeler coughed, and more blood stained his shirtfront.

'It's a roll of film,' he said. 'You must take it to Berne immediately.'

Fredier hesitated, his face tight with concern.

'Later,' he promised. 'First, I have to get you to a hospital.'

'No.'

Heppeler's voice was barely a croak. His hand, smeared with dirt and blood, reached out and seized Fredier's wrist in a desperate grip. 'There isn't time,' he whispered. 'They're right behind me.'

'Who, Franz? Who did this to you?'

'You're wasting precious seconds, damn it. That film could be the answer to everything we've been waiting for. You must go at once. Now, do you understand?'

Fredier looked unhappy. He had known Franz Heppeler for almost four years, and though the two men had never been close, they had the common bond of having worked at the Tirpitz Ufer, headquarters of the Abwehr, German military intelligence in Berlin. He hated the thought of leaving Heppeler in such a desperate state.

'It is your duty,' Heppeler said swiftly, recognising the

4

hesitation. 'I shall be all right here. You can telephone for an ambulance when you reach Interlaken.'

Fredier sighed and nodded shortly. 'Very well,' he agreed.

Heppeler sank back in the sofa, staring at the ceiling. He felt weariness engulf him, a weariness that seemed to spread through his head and the back of his skull. He had done all he could. It was Willi's show now. He relaxed, breathing peacefully, and slept.

Willi Fredier went into the kitchen and washed the blood from his hands. Picking up the film, he studied it curiously. What did Franz mean: 'the answer to everything we've been waiting for?' What was contained on that little strip of celluloid that was worth the price of a man's life? He shrugged, took his anorak from the cupboard and slipped the film into the inside pocket. He glanced once into the drawing-room, peering anxiously at the motionless frame of Franz Heppeler, then he went outside and started his motorcycle.

Four hours later, the film was being developed in a hastily constructed darkroom below the staircase of the German Embassy in Berne. At nine o'clock, the negatives were conveyed in a diplomatic bag, first to Basle, then over the border to Freiburg in Germany. At six forty-three the following evening, they arrived at Gestapo headquarters on the Prinz Albrechtstrasse in Berlin.

Hauptquartier War Office, Berlin
To: Sturmbannführer Otto Skorzeny, Officer Commanding Special Troops 5, Friedenthal
Security: Category One
Copy to: Reichsführer Heinrich Himmler
  Identity of photographs now established beyond question. Outcome regarded as crucial to successful termination of war. Proceed with all possible speed.

Oberst L. R. Krassner,
LK 12, Staff Ops Branch

Italy, 2 July 1944

The farmhouse stood in a flat saucer of land, flanked on one side by a snatch of pine trees and on the other by a dusty paddock. Its walls were built of stone, painted white, the paint cracked and peeling in the midsummer heat. Beyond the farmhouse, the land fell into a small defile, cluttered with chestnuts and clumps of scrub oak. Vine terraces clung to the hillside. There was no movement, and no sound, except for the distant rumble of artillery.

Sergeant Erich Spengler of the German 14th Panzer Division, with no expression on his face, stopped the Schützenpanzerwagen he was driving and studied the farmhouse thoughtfully. Plenty of cover behind those thick stone walls, he thought, lovely spot for an ambush.

'What d'you think?' he asked.

Behind him in the vehicle, the four soldiers looked weary and dispirited. Their uniforms were grey with dust, their eyes dull and heavy.

'Maybe they've got food in there,' Zimmerman said, moistening his lips at the thought.

Their field rations had run out fifteen hours ago, and so far the only food they'd managed to scavenge had been some cheese and grapes at a farmhouse near Pisa, and a pan of fried potatoes from a mobile German kitchen.

'They could just as easily have a brace of machine-guns,' the sergeant grunted. 'Let's box clever and move in slowly. Zimmerman, see if you can circle around to the rear, using the chestnuts as cover. Stoltz, take Felix and follow the stream bed until you can approach from the opposite side. I'll try the front door. Max can give us cover from the car.'

Wearily, the four men spilled into the road and scattered through the undergrowth. They moved with neither energy nor enthusiasm, which was hardly surprising, Spengler thought, for they'd had a basinful these past few days, trying to stem the enemy advance in Tuscany. Bitter fighting had taken place between the rows of cypress trees and the ochre-washed villas. It had come as a relief when the Oberstleutnant had ordered them back down the line for a breather. Spengler, who had fought in France, Poland and Russia, did not believe the Allies could be held in Tuscany. In the heavily-wooded countryside, the German tiger tanks were forced to operate on the roads, making them vulnerable, not only to an enemy breakthrough, but to numerous bands of guerrillas who set up barriers of felled trees, or blew up bridges, then brought the helpless vehicles under merciless crossfire. He was grateful at least that the Allied landings in France had led to large elements of their air force being withdrawn to support the new offensive. It meant there was a blessed relief from the fighters which had plagued them ceaselessly throughout their withdrawal from Cassino.

He did not think of these things, however, as he squirmed through the dirt holding his rifle crosswise beneath his chin. He thought instead of the discomfort, the heat, and the sweat oozing down his face and throat, tracing patterns in the dust which had caked there during the day.

He kept his eyes fixed on the farmhouse door, watching for any movement, no matter how slight, which might indicate the presence of human life behind those blank walls. A patch of brambles blocked his way and Spengler detoured around them, hugging the ground. The sun turned his helmet into an oven. For a moment he lay still, panting hard, peering at the building standing silent as a grave. Between the spot where he lay and the door itself stretched a patch of sandy soil. There was no cover, nothing to give him protection in that blinding afternoon. He felt alarmingly vulnerable here in the paddock.

With a deep breath, Spengler rose in one movement and scuttled crablike across the dusty earth, flinging himself hard against the farmhouse wall. Sweat streamed into his eyes. The trees danced in the sun's glare. He could see the outline of Max's head watching him above the rim of the armoured car. He counted slowly under his breath; 'One . . . two . . . three . . .' then, gripping the rifle hard, he drove the door open with one thrust of his boot and hurtled inside.

Blessed coolness engulfed him. He stood blinking in the change of light, ready to blast apart anything that moved. The farmhouse seemed to be all one room, like a primeval cave. At one end, the ash of an ancient brush fire lay untouched in the grate. From the roof hung lumps of tallow, used for greasing boots. Pitchers of water lined the walls. In the far corner, huddled behind a cluster of beds, crouched the farmer and his wife. They were dressed in peasant clothes, the man in jacket, trousers and a collarless shirt, the woman in a flannel blouse and heavy grey skirt. Beside them cowered four children, their eyes bright with alarm.

Spengler stepped backwards through the door, keeping his gaze fixed on the people in the corner. 'Zimmerman, Stolz, it's okay.'

Whooping excitedly, the others ran across the paddock, crowding under the low roof, glad to be out of the sun at last. The people behind the beds had not moved. They watched Spengler with the air of cattle, their faces pale and apprehensive.

'Ask them if they have any food,' Spengler said to Stolz.

Stolz cleared his throat and spoke briefly in Italian. The farmer answered. He was about fifty, solidly built, moustached, olive-skinned. His voice had a wheezy sound, like that of an asthma sufferer.

'He says they've had no food for nearly three days now,' Stolz translated.

'Do you believe him?'

Stolz shrugged. 'Who knows? He looks pretty fat to me.'

'Search the building,' Spengler ordered. 'See if they've anything hidden away.'

They moved among the sparse furniture, brushing aside piles of sacking, opening cupboards, peering into corners.

Spengler propped his rifle against the wall, took off his helmet and ducked his face into a pitcher of water. Oh, for a bath, he thought, and a change of clothes. There were times he really believed he would never get clean again, as if some monstrous deity had ordained a punishment to fit the crimes of his past life by proclaiming that he would continue his existence in a state of sustained and progressive filth. He was a tall man, heavy-shouldered and slim-hipped. His face was hawklike and burned red by the sun. As he straightened, drying his cheeks against his sleeve, he spotted through the window a second building, this one timbered, its roof formed by corrugated metal sheets. 'What's in there?' he asked.

Stolz translated the question into Italian, and the farmer answered.

'It's the barn,' Stolz explained. 'At this time of year it should have been filled with maize cobs, but he says the German army commandeered his entire harvest.'

'Better check,' Spengler ordered, 'he could be lying.'

Zimmerman opened the door and crossed the paddock, his powerful body shambling in the heat.

Felix stared balefully at the farmer. 'He looks too well-fed for my liking,' he muttered.

'Why don't we eat the old goat,' Stolz suggested, 'let him die a hero's death. It's all these Eyeties are bloody good for.'

'He didn't ask for this war,' Spengler said.

'Watch it, Unterfeldwebel, they shoot men for that kind of talk.'

Felix was still studying the farmer, a tricky little smile playing around the corners of his mouth. 'Look at the old bugger,' he grunted. 'He'd like to murder us all. Wouldn't you, Eyetie? Like to put a bullet in our skulls and finish us off for breakfast?'

'Leave him alone,' Spengler ordered.

'Oh sure, you feel sorry for him now. They all look harmless when you've got them in your rifle sights. It's a different story when the boot's on the other foot however. Don't expect mercy from these bastards. In the mountains, the partisans are cutting off the heads of the men they shoot.'

'Where did you hear that?' Stolz asked.

'From a corporal in the Grenadiers.'

Spengler chuckled. 'Well, this boy's no headhunter. Look at him, all he cares about is keeping his family alive.'

He took out a packet of cigarettes and offered one to the farmer, who made no attempt to take it. Instead, he stood motionless, staring at Spengler with eyes like over-ripe cherries. Spengler placed a cigarette between the farmer's lips. The farmer watched him without expression. He seemed to be waiting for something.

At that precise moment, a scream echoed across the

paddock, loud and shrill, taking them by surprise. Spengler felt his wrists turn icy. The farmer's wife shouted and began to run for the door, but Felix stopped her with his rifle. 'It's Zimmerman up to his bloody tricks again,' he yelled.

Spengler swore angrily. He was through the door in an instant, running hard, feeling the sun hot against his shoulders, crosssing the paddock to the heavy wood barn. The building was empty except for an old horse-wagon parked against the far wall, and a number of dirty wine bottles. Strands of hay scattered the earthen floor. On the ground, writhing like a snake in Zimmerman's clutches, was a young girl, fourteen or fifteen years old. Her dark hair was tangled wildly across her pale cheeks, and a smear of blood smudged the skin around her nostrils. Her blouse had been ripped wide open, exposing small, scarcely-formed breasts. Her skirt was bunched around her waist, and her long legs thrashed helplessly as Zimmerman, poised above her, fought for balance. He tugged at his trouser band and as Spengler watched, his broad buttocks slipped into view, twisting from side to side as he struggled for position.

Spengler moved. With a clump, his boot drove into Zimmerman's ribs, hurling the big man hard against the wall. The girl stopped struggling, peering up at Spengler through terrified tear-stained eyes.

'Get out of here,' Spengler snapped, 'get back to the house.'

Gathering the torn remnants of her blouse together, she scuttled into the sunlight, running barefoot across the sandy earth.

Spengler glared down at Zimmerman, fury welling inside him. The fat man was groaning and clutching his ribcage.

'I told you what would happen if you tried that again,' said Spengler.

Zimmerman pulled a face. 'I was only going to tickle her a bit,' he moaned. 'She wouldn't have twittered once I'd got it in. They're all the same, these Eyeties. They like to make a noise at first for appearances' sake.'

Spengler stepped in again, kicking him with relentless

persistance, going to work on his chest and shoulders while Zimmerman, squealing, squirmed helplessly against the barn wall, his erection deflating like a punctured balloon. Spengler felt his muscles quiver as he slowly regained control. Zimmerman's face registered relief as he realised Spengler's madness had passed.

'You bastard,' Spengler growled. 'You're a bloody animal.'

'What are you going to do?' Zimmerman asked petulantly, 'Have me arrested? After what happened at Anzio, they'll give me the Knight's Cross.'

Spengler did not answer. Zimmerman was right. With men dying by the wagonload, no one would take the charge seriously.

'Pull up your pants,' he snapped. 'You look disgusting.'

Still blazing with anger, he turned and strode back to the farmhouse. Zimmerman was unreachable, he'd known that from the beginning. The man was nothing but a brute, callous and insensitive. Spengler would have to watch him more closely in future.

At the house, he found Stolz smiling. On the floor was a small heap of orange maize cobs. 'They were hidden under the bed,' Stolz said. 'The cunning old fox knew what we were after.'

The farmer muttered something in Italian and Stolz translated.

'He says it's all they have to keep them alive. The German army took their cattle and goats. They took their maize harvest. These cobs were all they managed to glean from the fields when the soldiers went away.'

Spengler looked at the children. They were sorry-looking specimens in torn trousers and shabby pullovers. They peered back at him with eyes that were hopeless and lost. 'He's telling the truth,' Spengler murmured. 'Leave the cobs where they are.'

Stolz protested. 'For Christ's sake, Erich, he's not the only one who's hungry. I can't feel my belly any more.'

'We'll find something up the road,' Spengler said. 'There's bound to be a village soon, or an army kitchen.'

Felix gave a hiss from the window. He was peering

intently through the dusty glass. 'Unterfeldwebel, come over here.'

Spengler crossed the room and looked over Felix's shoulder. An open staff car had drawn up alongside their own vehicle on the road outside, and a man in the uniform of an SS Sturmbannführer was questioning Max. Beside him sat a second man in a grey raincoat and floppy-brimmed hat. 'Gestapo,' Felix whispered. 'What the bloody hell do they want?'

Spengler said nothing, but something moved inside him, a stir of apprehension. The Gestapo and the SS were a law unto themselves. He felt uneasy.

Max clambered out of the Schützenpanzerwagen and came running towards the farmhouse. 'Erich,' he exclaimed, 'they're asking for you. They have an order from the High Command, signed by Himmler himself.'

Spengler grinned wryly. 'Pull the other one,' he said. 'What the hell would Himmler want with me?'

'Max's face was pale and disturbed. 'You'd better go talk to them,' he advised. 'You don't play games with those bastards.'

Spengler sighed. He replaced his helmet, picked up his rifle and strode out into the sunshine. The men in the staff car watched him approach, their faces neither friendly nor hostile. The SS Sturmbannführer carried an inscription on his arm: *Leibstandarte SS Adolf Hitler*, the Führer's bodyguard. He returned Spengler's salute haughtily. 'You are Sergeant Spengler of the 14th Panzer Division?'

Spengler nodded.

'You are to come with us,' the SS Sturmbannführer stated in a flat voice.

Spengler hesitated. 'Am I under arrest?'

It was the man in civilian clothes who answered. His voice was softer than his companion's. 'You will please get in the car,' he said. 'Do not ask questions. Simply obey orders.'

Spengler stared at him in silence. His uneasiness grew stronger. He glanced back and saw his men watching from the farmhouse window. Their faces carried the air of spectators at a slaughter house. Spengler shook himself. In such unsettled times, one did not defy an officer of the élite Leibstandarte, much less a member of the Gestapo. Without a word, he opened the car door and clambered in. The driver engaged the gear, did a swift U-turn, and started back the way they had come.

For almost an hour they drove without speaking. When Spengler attempted to draw the Sturmbannführer into conversation, the man disdainfully ignored him. Spengler folded his arms and watched the traffic rumbling by. There were armoured personnel carriers and Red Cross ambulances returning from the front, grey scout cars, Panzerjäger tanks with heavy artillery and convoys of Sturmgeschütz IIIs. Refugees choked the road for nearly eleven miles. Their driver kept one hand on the horn as he nudged his way through.

Spengler watched the throngs of tired, frightened people, the columns of vehicles with their hot, dirty and exhausted passengers, and felt the sickening sensation of defeat. This was no strategic manoeuvre he was witnessing. The men out there were as shattered as he was. They had been pushed to their limit, and then beyond. The German army was in full retreat. It seemed a far cry from the early days of the war, the Polish campaign for instance, when they had taken the field with fifty-three divisions and sliced through the enemy defences with a speed and assurance that had left the rest of Europe gasping. Spengler had seen Polish cavalry, wielding nothing more effective than swords and lances, hurl itself against the might of the German panzers. Nine dive-bomber units flying Junker JU 87 Stukas had launched crippling bombing attacks along the Polish reserve lines, opening up the route for the most incisive onslaught in military history. By the time the Poles had fallen and Germany had turned her attention to the tempting targets of Belgium, Holland, Norway and France, Spengler and his comrades had begun to believe no army in the world could stand against them.

Until they got to Russia.

Spengler settled back in his seat, his mind filled with despondency. He could still remember the stench of death which had hung over the dour little villages south of

Smolensk, and the hordes of tattered prisoners, hundreds of thousands of them, flowing back down the line in an endless river of humanity. He remembered the snow, and the incredible distances, and the marshes peppered with shell-holes. But most of all, he remembered the sheer unstoppable force of the Russian people, who had hurled themselves point-blank against howitzers and artillery, scattering the ground with their dead and dying and yet still coming on. Russian tanks, the notorious T–34s, had butted through the German armour with the imperviousness of battering rams. It was at Jelnja that Spengler had been awarded the Knight's Cross for wiping out three 30-tonners while they were still in motion, leaping on to the machines to hurl grenades down their canon throats.

Spengler fumbled in his pocket for his cigarettes. He would never forget Russia, he thought, for it was there that he had paid the price of his naïvety. He had lost his belief in German military might. Now, as he peered out at the remnants of his own retreating army, he was filled with a sense of futile disgust. The wheel had turned, he told himself sourly. The boot was on the other foot.

They came to a village where throngs of German soldiers flocked the streets. He spotted troops from the 14th Panzer Division and the 104th Rifle Regiment. Artillerymen in Waffenrock tunics clustered around a woman wearing a *Deutsche Wehrmacht* armband, who was handing out packets of cigarettes.

The driver pulled to a halt outside a villa with a majestic eagle above its door. A detachment of SS stormtroopers stood on guard. Their officer saluted, his death's-head cap badge glinting in the sunlight. Without a word, Spengler followed the Sturmbannführer and his Gestapo companion into the building. This was like some kind of bad dream, he thought. An hour ago he had been just another sergeant, doing his job as best he could. Now, for some reason he could not fathom, he had been singled out for this extraordinary attention. A mix-up no doubt, a case of mistaken identity, but realising that made him feel no better. In these madcap days, they made up the rules as they went along. How he hated the Nazis.

The lower part of the house had been turned into an

office of sorts, the furniture thrust back to accommodate the QMC-issue desks and stools. The Gestapo man sat down and studied Spengler with a cold professional air while the SS Sturmbannführer strode up and down, slamming his heels on the bare wood floor.

'Take off your clothes,' he ordered.

Spengler stared at him in surprise. 'My clothes?'

'Quickly. We're short of time.'

Spengler shook his head in bewilderment. The situation was growing more farcical by the minute. Without a word, he began to undress. When he reached his underthings, he stopped.

'Those too,' the SS Sturmbannführer snapped.

Spengler disrobed entirely. Naked, he felt exposed and helpless. Was this how it started, the scrutiny, the cross-examination? But the Sturmbannführer scarcely glanced at him.

'This way,' he said.

Still naked, Spengler followed him into the next room where two men in white coats were busy filling an old tin bath.

'You will cleanse yourself,' the Sturmbannführer ordered.

Again, Spengler was shaken by a sense of unreality. He stared at the bath in bewilderment. It was nearly a fortnight since he had enjoyed the luxury of soap and hot water. Now he was being ordered to indulge himself by an officer of the Leibstandarte, no less.

Spengler stepped into the tub and sank back, letting the warmth lap around his aching limbs. One of the white-coated men lathered his throat and chin and carefully shaved his beard stubble. The other shampooed his hair, then neatly trimmed it with a pair of scissors.

Spengler let himself relax. Whatever they had in store for him, he could at least enjoy this. He scrubbed his skin, putting all thoughts of the future from his mind. When he had finished, he dried himself and strolled back into the other room, the towel around his waist. The Sturmbannführer handed him some underclothes and an immaculate dress uniform.

'You are no longer Sergeant Spengler of the 14th

Panzer Corps,' he announced. 'You are now Unterraturmführer Spengler of the 5th Gebirgsjäger.'

Spengler stared at him in astonishment. 'Second Lieutenant?' he echoed.

'You will be issued with a more appropriate uniform later, but for the moment this one will have to do. It belonged to an officer killed at Salerno, so he no longer has any use for it. The size is roughly correct.'

Spengler shook his head in disbelief. 'Listen,' he said, 'there must be some mistake.'

The Sturmbannführer went on as if he hadn't spoken. 'When you finish dressing you will join us outside. Please hurry, we are already late.'

Spengler climbed into his new clothes then, bathed, shaved, but still baffled, stepped again into the sunlight.

Through roads choked with northbound vehicles he was driven two miles to a small airstrip, where a tiny spotter aircraft stood ready for take-off. The Sturmbannführer shook his hand and saluted smartly.

'Where am I going?' Spengler asked.

'That will be explained later. For the moment, you will obey without question.'

Spengler clambered in behind the pilot, fastened his seat-strap and sat back as the plane taxied off. He could see water meadows ahead, scattered with wild flowers. The wheels lifted as they soared skywards, and the staff car shrank dizzily below. Spengler stared down at parched fields and scattered villages. He felt remote and secure in his lofty perch.

The roar of the propeller drowned any attempt to question the pilot, so he settled back philosophically to enjoy the flight. A man in his position had to learn to accept small mercies in the spirit they were given, he thought. To have risen so dramatically from NCO to officer took a bit of swallowing, but who was he to question the wisdom of the High Command?

The coastline of Italy swept by below, and Spengler stared down in wonderment at vast columns of German vehicles choking the narrow roads. The entire army appeared to be on the move, giving the impression of the land skinning itself.

For some time, the scene changed little, stretching below them like an endless tabletop. Once, they put down to refuel at a tiny airstrip, but the pilot clambered out of the cockpit and Spengler had no opportunity to engage him in conversation. Soon they were in the air again, climbing above high craggy foothills. Spengler saw the snowcapped Alps ahead, and the glimpse of their summits etched against the sky sent his pulse racing.

They zoomed on steadily, sailing over small villages, mountain pastures, shepherds' huts, wheatfields and gaunt grey castles. At last, the pilot motioned downwards with his thumb, indicating they were coming in to land. There were deep chasms below, high-altitude pastures and sheer granite cliffs. Rivers flashed like darting fish in the sunlight.

They dipped earthward, picking a delicate route through a steep-sided valley where pine forests cluttered the narrow screes like hair on a human skin. Skimming over a line of hayricks, they touched down expertly in a field where cows stampeded from their path in panic. The pilot grinned and brought the Stork to a halt, switching off the engine and pushing up his goggles to mop his sweating face.

Spengler undid his seat-strap, opened the door and leapt to the ground. A man in major's uniform came strolling towards him, smiling affably. Spengler clicked his heels and was about to salute, but the man thrust out his hand.

'Major Otto Skorzeny,' he said. 'I'm delighted to see you, Spengler. We were half afraid you might have been bumped off in that unpleasantness at Cassino.'

Hesitantly, Spengler took the proffered hand. He had heard of the great 'Scarface' Skorzeny, commander of Germany's commando troops, the most celebrated soldier in the Reich army, the man who, in 1943, had led the spectacular raid on the Italian Gran Sasso, plucking Mussolini from his 'impregnable' mountaintop prison and whisking him back to Germany under the noses of his captors. Skorzeny was tall and strongly built, with piercing eyes and a ragged scar which ran from his left temple to the corner of his mouth, and then continued to the tip of his chin. His hair was neatly combed and cropped close to his skull.

'Have you eaten yet?' he wondered. 'I hope not. I was planning a little celebration tonight, a sort of welcoming feast. We must make the most of creature comforts while we can in this topsy-turvy world, and you'll have precious little chance to indulge yourself where you're going.'

'May I ask where that will be, Sturmbannführer?' Spengler murmured.

'Later,' said the major, 'and please call me Otto. If you've no objection, I'll call you Erich. As a member of our special Alpenkommando unit, you carry the same privileges as the SS, which means you are entitled to use the second person singular when addressing fellow officers, regardless of rank.'

They began to stroll across the field. Spengler could see a wooden gate, and a car parked on the road beyond. 'Where are we?' he asked.

'In the Alpi Lepontine, close to the Swiss border. Sorry we couldn't give you any warning, but speed was essential, and we took longer than we'd hoped in running you to earth. Our army's in a state of some confusion.'

They reached the gate and stepped into the road. Geese hissed at them from a nearby pond. Somewhere, a donkey was braying. It was a beautiful evening. Spengler peered at the hills, green and inviting in the stillness. It was hard to equate such peace with the turmoil he had left behind.

'It's strange,' he said, 'I feel disorientated.'

'War does that. It's always a madhouse of one kind or another.'

'It's as if I'm dreaming. Are you sure you've got the right man?'

Skorzeny smiled. 'You *are* Erich Spengler, the climber?'

Spengler looked at him. 'That was a long time ago,' he said, 'before the war.'

'Nevertheless, like cycling or swimming, climbing is something you never forget. At least, I hope not. We need your skills rather desperately.'

Skorzeny opened the car door and they clambered inside.

'We have a comprehensive dossier on your track record at SS headquarters,' Skorzeny said. 'Very impressive. You put up new routes on the Grosse Negita, the Aiguille du Magali and the north buttress of the Admonter Reichenstein. You took part in the 1932 Nanga Parbat expedition in the Himalayas, and scaled the ice-face of Ushba in the Caucasus. Isn't it typical of the army to stick you in a panzer division?'

'The panzer division was my personal choice,' said Spengler. 'I volunteered. You must understand I haven't climbed anything higher than the bedroom stairs for several years.'

'Don't worry,' the major smiled, 'I promise you within three weeks you'll be climbing better than ever. But this time, you'll be doing it for the Fatherland.'

They drove off, following a narrow road that sliced deep into the mountains. The hills tumbled into a steep grassy pass where a river gouged a route from the earth's flank. Flies hung in soft clouds above the scarcely rippling water. The air was heavy with a breathless humidity.

'Where are we going?' Spengler demanded.

'Well, first to the nearby village,' Skorzeny said. 'There's something I'd like you to see. It'll only take a moment.'

It was almost dusk as Skorzeny entered the cluster of houses by a girdered bridge, and drove down the deserted main street. He slithered to a halt outside a rambling warehouse half hidden in a copse of trees. Guards with swastikas on their caps saluted him briskly as he pushed back the sliding door so Spengler could step inside. The warehouse smelled faintly of turpentine. In the shadows stood line after line of dark barrels arranged in uniform order, like troops awaiting inspection. One of the barrels was open. Inside was a bright yellow powder.

'What is it?' Spengler asked.

'It's called uranium, mined in Czechoslovakia. To-morrow morning, we're shipping it back to Germany. It would be a disaster if it fell into enemy hands. You see, this innocent-looking powder is the military secret that is going to win us the war.'

Spengler stared at him in silence for a moment. 'Every

week they tell us about some new weapon for driving the Allies back into the sea,' he said bluntly. 'I've stopped believing all that.'

Skorzeny gave him a cigarette and lit one himself. 'This time,' he said, 'the claim is justified.'

'You seem pretty damned sure.'

Skorzeny's face was calm. 'I know it to be true,' he said. 'The uranium is to be used in the manufacture of an entirely new kind of bomb, a bomb more powerful than anything the world has ever dreamed of. We have the raw materials, we have the men to build it – there is only one thing missing, and you, my dear Erich, are going to get that for us.'

Spengler said nothing. He stood watching Skorzeny intently, smoke drifting from his nostrils. Skorzeny slapped him on the shoulder.

'I'm forgetting my manners,' he said. 'You look half starved. Let's go up to the house and eat.'

Two

A warm wind blew through Paris. It rippled among the trees which lined the centre of the Boulevard de Clichy, it lifted the canopies of the little cafés, making them flap and billow like schooner sails, it whipped at the hair of Helene Rössner as she turned out of the Rue des Martyrs and crossed the street towards the Place Pigalle, tall, tanned, innately sure of herself and of her beauty. She wore a light cotton dress through which the sun outlined her figure from the waist down, and a party of German infantrymen paused in their tracks to stare after her, smiling admiringly.

Helene paid no attention to the yearning glances of the Germans. She looked at her watch. Lambert had said four-thirteen. He liked to choose odd timings in the belief that it made detection difficult, and if at times he seemed over-cautious, she had to admit he had managed to survive four years of German occupation without a hint of suspicion. Never mock the professionals, she thought. They were the only ones who made any sense of this war. She had seen men transformed; quiet men, loving husbands, who, in peacetime, would have opted for security and stability, had assumed a new stature amid the rigours of occupied Paris. Lambert was like that. She knew she could never have survived without him. They had trained her in every aspect of espionage except one – the ability to remain sane in a hostile and frightening environment. Lambert had been her only contact, a laconic and oddly sullen young man about whom she knew practically nothing, beyond the fact that he was married to a girl from the Basque country who had been suffering for the past two years from tuberculosis. Perhaps it was that which made him sullen, or perhaps it was the permit he carried in his pocket, an exemption-from-labour document provided by the Gestapo as a reward for acts of collaboration. What the Germans didn't know was that the information Lambert supplied was a deliberate cover to ensure the safety of more vital operations. This fact neither improved Lambert's conscience, nor his disposition.

A German convoy rumbled up the street, and Helene glared at the vehicles balefully. She hated the German presence. When she had first come to this city from her comfortable life in middle-class Zurich, Paris had gone to her head like Beaujolais wine; the elegance of its boulevards, the symmetry of its buildings, the lyricism of its language.

Now the people seemed apathetic and dull. Their faces showed despair, wretchedness, defeat. Shops had closed down, houses were without gas, water or electricity, children looked pale and undernourished.

The rationing was punitive – 90 grammes of butter per week for a single person, one pound of meat for a whole month.

The old Paris had gone; this was a strange and frightening place where she lived like a fox, surviving on her wits and cunning. Day after day at the hospital, she watched for signs – a casual remark, a letter left carelessly on a bedside locker – and always she lived with fear, with the dread of discovery, with the terror of the pain it would bring. But she did it, and she knew she would go on doing it until either they caught her or the last German soldier had gone from Paris.

She spotted Lambert waiting on the café terrace, looking at nothing in particular. A copy of the morning paper lay across his knee. When he saw her coming, he picked it up and started to read, the signal that all was clear. She chose the table next to his. A party of German officers sat drinking at the far end, but they were too distant to eavesdrop. She called the waiter and ordered kirsch with *guignolet*, and a cup of black coffee. The coffee was not coffee at all, but a wartime substitute made from malt extract. The kirsch, however, was real. She opened her handbag and lit a cigarette.

'You're late,' Lambert said, using the newspaper to mask his lips.

She watched the German officers, holding the cigarette in front of her face. 'You said four-thirteen.'

'It's quarter past.'

'For God's sake, Lambert, what difference does a minute or two make?'

'It's the little things that count. You're forgetting your most important lesson.'

'All right, I'm sorry.'

She felt angry with herself. She knew Lambert's meticulous attention to detail. Check and double check, that was Lambert's way. He was right to chastise her.

'What have you to tell me?' Lambert asked.

She crossed her legs, pausing as one of the Germans glanced in her direction. 'The German 65th Infantry Division is being transferred to Northern Italy.'

'We already know. News came through from Le Mans yesterday.'

'Well, now it's confirmed.'

'Who told you?'

'We have a major undergoing a hernia operation. His orders arrived this morning. All documents relating to patients have to pass through the hospital personnel office. I managed to sneak in and sift through the intake tray on my way off-duty.'

'Risky.'

'War's risky.'

'Did you spot anything else?'

'The German navy is experimenting with a new type of helicopter to replace the Hummingbird. They've ordered thirty prototypes and fifteen production machines. It's much bigger than the Kolibri, and far more effective. It will have twin contra-rotating rotors built on outriggers, and a powerful radial engine buried in its fuselage.'

'What's its range?'

'Two hundred miles.'

'How many men can it carry?'

'Six.'

She paused as one of the Germans turned to signal to the waiter. 'That's not all,' she added. 'There was also an operational training directive from the Oberkommando der Luftwaffe on the Messerschmitt BF 109D. I scribbled a few notes.'

'Coded?'

'Of course.'

'Pick up your bill, crumple the two together and drop them on the ground beside my left foot.'

Helene put down her cigarette and did as Lambert ordered. Surreptitiously, he kicked the paper ball beneath his seat. She cast a glance at the Germans' table. They were talking animatedly.

It seemed madness to expose themselves like this, under the very noses of the enemy, but that was Lambert. He hated the furtive, the secret, the clandestine. Keep it open, he always said. Much safer. People never spotted the obvious. It was stealth and subterfuge that made them take notice.

'How are things at the hospital?' Lambert asked.

'Busy, as you'd expect. The casualties from Normandy now outnumber our civilian patients. I've had to leave most of the diabetic cases to Dr Frise.'

His eyes glittered angrily. 'To help the Boche?'

'They're wounded men, and I'm still a doctor, Lambert. I wish you'd try to understand that.'

'That's good, that's very good. On the one hand, you supply information to saboteurs and partisans, on the other you work your guts out to save the very people we're trying to destroy.'

'I took an oath,' she said. 'The war has no bearing on that.'

Lambert was silent for a moment as he turned the page of his newspaper.

'You look tired, Helene,' he said, 'You've lines around your eyes.'

'We've only eight fully-qualified physicians left,' she explained. 'The rest are at the front.'

'Nevertheless, tiredness leads to clumsiness.'

'For God's sake, Lambert, I've already apologised for being late. What do you take me for, a complete amateur?'

'Then perhaps you can identify your friend over there?'

'Friend?' She looked puzzled.

'Didn't you know you were being followed?'

Something cold turned inside Helene's stomach, and her hand holding the cigarette began to tremble. 'What?' she whispered.

'Don't look. He's watching you from the island, under the trees. Grey raincoat, dark trilby. Gestapo. You get to recognise them after a while. They're on to you for something.'

He seemed aloof and impersonal, as if years of unspeakable acts, unthinkable treacheries, had wrought in him an imperviousness to human fear. Helene held on to her calmness with an effort. In the training school, they had put her through a series of mock interrogations, complete with glaring lights, snarled commands and even, on occasions, actual physical blows, but she'd known in her heart she could never stand up to the real thing. She felt her mouth twist in a spasm of fear, and sucked hard at the cigarette, blowing smoke from her nostrils.

'What shall I do?' she whispered, her voice quavering.

'Don't go back to the hospital, not yet.'

'I'm on duty at seven.'

'Phone in. Is there anyone you can trust?'

'Dr le Gras. We're friendly in a professional sort of way. I'm sure he'd warn me if anyone had been asking questions.'

'Tell him you're sick. Ask him to cover for you. If the situation looks bad, call 220925 and ask for Luc. When he answers, say, "Congratulations on your new appointment, it's a big improvement on the fruit market." Have you got that?'

'Yes,' she whispered.

'In the meantime, try not to worry. It may be nothing more than a routine surveillance. They do that occasionally with professional people.'

'But if it isn't?' she said.

'If it isn't, call Luc.'

'Supposing I can't? Supposing they pick me up before I get to a telephone?'

He was silent for a moment. 'You have your L pill?' he asked.

She swallowed hard. 'Yes.'

'Well, then?'

He did not enumerate further.

Helene felt herself trembling. Fear swept her like a sickness, and unexpectedly she began to weep. Tears issued from her eyes and rolled down her cheeks.

'What is the *matter* with you?' he hissed angrily.

She sobbed.

'You damned idiot, you're drawing attention to yourself.'

She sobbed.

'Pull yourself together. You're endangering us both.'

'I'm frightened,' she whispered, choking back her tears. She took out a handkerchief and quickly mopped her face.

'They haven't got you yet,' he snapped. 'See if you can shake off our inquisitive friend over there. I'll contact Luc and tell him to expect your call. Good luck, and whatever you do, keep your head.'

Helene paid the waiter in a daze, and began to walk quickly in the direction of the Place de Clichy. She crossed the street, entering the ancient cemetery of Montmartre. Hovering in the shadow of the massive vaults, she watched the gate. No one followed. She felt a timorous surge of hope. Even Lambert wasn't infallible. He could have been mistaken.

She cut through the side entrance to the taxi rank on the Rue des Dames. A line of bicycle-drawn handcarts stood waiting for business. The petrol shortage had forced Parisian cabdrivers to resort to rickshaws. The drivers looked at her questioningly as she hurried by, but she shook her head. Too slow, she thought. At the end of the line stood a vehicle with a metal boiler strapped to its roof. It was a steam-car, propelled by coal gas. She clambered into the rear seat.

'Take me to the Palais des Congres,' she ordered.

Through the window, the city looked beautiful in the flush of early summer. Only the sight of German uniforms, German cars and personnel carriers spoiled the carefree June air. But not for long, she thought grimly. Every day, the Allied armies were drawing closer.

Paris was on the brink of liberation, and the people knew it.

Suddenly, she felt the taxi slowing down. Alarmed, she sat up, peering outside. A grey Citroën had slithered in front of their vehicle and a man in a trilby hat was signalling her driver to stop. Helene felt terror sweep through her limbs. There was not the slightest doubt in her mind that this was the man she was trying to escape. She watched him climb into the roadway, pausing briefly to flash his identification card at the driver before sauntering back to open the rear door. He was young and sallow faced, no more than twenty-eight or twenty-nine. His cheeks looked strangely gaunt for his age, his eyes cold and lifeless. 'Dr Rössner?'

She nodded, wanting to scream out loud. The young man's gaze seemed to bore through her skull. He reached inside his jacket and took out a photograph. It was a picture of herself taken in Switzerland before the war. She was wearing mountaineering garb. A rope hung coiled over one shoulder, and she was laughing in a careless unaffected sort of way, her hair streaming in the wind.

'Where did you get it?' she whispered.

He ignored her question.

'You are a climber, Frau Doktor?'

'I was, many years ago.'

'And you specialise also in diabetes?'

She stared at him, frowning. 'Yes,' she answered. What was the purpose of these idiotic questions?

The young man took off his hat and carefully straightened the brim. His movements were deft and sure.

'Frau Doktor,' he said, 'I must ask you to accompany me to the Avenue Foch.'

She felt panic force its way into her throat. 'Gestapo Headquarters?' she murmured. 'I'm afraid . . . it's inconvenient at the moment . . . I'm . . . expected at the hospital.'

He stared at her coldly, his eyes grim and penetrating.

'The hospital can wait,' he said. 'We must talk to you on a matter of the gravest urgency.'

From SOE Files:

MOST SECRET

Special Operations Executive, Baker Street, London
Subject: Helene Rössner, Codename: Sunflower

Subject born Switzerland 1908. Studied medicine in
Zurich, later specialised in diabetes in Berne, Geneva
and Paris, France. In March 1934 married German
solicitor Karl Ludwig Klempf and moved to Mainz in
the Rhineland. Two years later, became naturalised
German citizen and member of the Nazi Party. In
1938, husband imprisoned for broadcasting anti-Nazi
propaganda. Subject attempted to use her Party
position to secure his release, but Klempf died in
Telsfeld concentration camp. Official cause of death
bronchial pneumonia. January 1939, subject travelled
to Paris by train, offered her services to the French
military. Transferred to Britain on 4 February and
interviewed by BSC Officer Richard Hassel. Trained
in undercover work at Wansbeck and Bletchley,
and parachuted into France on 'blind drop' (night
jump from low flying aircraft) October 1941. Secured
job as diabetes specialist at Hospital of Sainte
Ambroise in Paris. Now attached to Paris section of
the PROSPER network. Quote from interviewing officer
Hassel:

'Subject is shrewd, ingenious and physically alluring. She has the added advantages of being a qualified
physician with genuine German papers, a Nazi Party
membership and a French residency permit. In this
officer's view, ideal material for covert action
operations.'

Unquote

The villa was built high on the mountainside, surrounded
on three sides by sharp rocky ridges, and on the fourth by
a series of vine terraces which descended into the valley
like a giant staircase. The dining-room was opulent to a
degree that Spengler found stifling. Huge wall mirrors
reached from floor to ceiling. Crystal chandeliers dangled
overhead. The chairs were fashioned in the style of

Venetian thrones. There was an air of decaying elegance, a hint of a society past but not quite forgotten.

The food itself was excellent: fresh trout, saddle of venison, potatoes, mushrooms and artichokes, served by waiters in spotless white tunics. After the hardship of the past few weeks, Spengler found such luxury almost unbelievable.

At table, they were joined by three pretty Italian girls in expensive evening gowns. They ate frugally, saying little, and when Spengler tried to draw them into conversation they answered in German with brief non-committal sentences. They appeared to be there for decorative purposes only.

Major Skorzeny was both gracious and charming. He talked endlessly, telling Spengler of his student days, his life among Vienna's comfortable bourgeoisie, his early war experiences in France, Holland, Yugoslavia and Russia, his assessment of the Russian character and his own first-hand account of his Mussolini adventure on the Gran Sasso. When the meal was over, he sat back and offered Spengler a thin cigar. 'You eat like a horse,' he chuckled. 'Combat must be good for the appetite.'

Spengler shook his head. 'It's not that. We ran out of field rations yesterday.'

'Sounds bad. When an army can't feed its own troops, it generally means it's running scared. How's morale at the front?'

Spengler hesitated. 'As you'd expect,' he answered cautiously.

Skorzeny laughed, tapping ash from his cigar. 'My dear Erich, I am not going to accuse you of defeatism. We are merely soldiers comparing assessments, that's all. If it's any consolation, I personally believe that had the Allies landed in Sardinia and Corsica instead of Salerno, the battle for Italy would already be lost.'

He poured himself another glass of wine and touched his cheek, smiling. 'You're looking at my scar,' he said. 'Not pretty, is it? I acquired it during my student days. I fought fifteen duels, you know, before the Party banned the practice.'

He shook his head reflectively. 'I've always regretted

the death of duelling,' he muttered. 'I regarded it then –
and still do – as a perfect instrument for instilling the
virtues of honour and fortitude into the minds and hearts
of young men. Even today, I can still smell the
disinfectant into which we dipped the sabre blades before
each encounter.'

'It always seemed crazy to me.'

'Crazy?'

'Trying to cut each other to bits. For what? An
imagined insult.'

'What about climbing? Isn't that crazy too?'

'Climbing's different. You don't have to hurt anybody
to get your thrill, only yourself.'

'I do hope your benevolence isn't too deeply en-
trenched, Lieutenant. Benevolence may be admirable in
peacetime, but at the moment I need qualities of a more
aggressive nature.'

'To do what, Sturmbannführer?'

'Patience, my friend. For a short time at least, the war is
over for you. Tomorrow you'll be moving higher into the
mountains. You've just become part of an élite all-officer
ranger unit attached to the 5th Gebirgsjäger. It contains
the finest climbers Germany has produced. I had the
pleasure of entertainig your future comrades yesterday
afternoon. Like you, they come from the battlefields of
Europe. Like you, they are about to enjoy a brief respite
from the rigours of war. At the SS mountain training school
above Assaro, you will be put through a mountaineering
refresher course. Mind you, it won't be easy. If you thought
life was tough at the front, there'll be times you'll wish to
God you were back there. But you'll be free, Erich, you'll
be able to forget the heat and the dust and the dying, you'll
be out in the good clean air doing what you were born for.'

'And then?'

Skorzeny winked. 'Let's just say that your training is
vital to the future of the Reich. Concentrate on getting
into trim again, polishing off those rough edges, working
yourself into peak condition. Try to think of it as a reward
for the hardships of the past, a little holiday at the army's
expense.'

Spengler said nothing for a moment. He peered at the

empty dishes littering the mahogany table. 'I think there's something you ought to know, Sturmbannführer.'

'When will I persuade you to call me Otto?' Skorzeny smiled.

Spengler ignored him. 'I've given up climbing,' he declared shortly. 'For good.'

'What?'

'I . . . I don't climb any more. It's nothing to do with the war, it's a personal decision, that's all.'

Skorzeny studied him thoughtfully. 'For what reason?' he demanded.

'Private reasons.'

'I see.'

Skorzeny sat back in his chair. His face became slightly less friendly. 'None of us has the right to make a separate peace, lieutenant. You have a talent, a very real talent, one which has suddenly become vital to the Reich. As a German soldier you must be prepared to make sacrifices. That includes the luxury of personal choice.'

Spengler felt as if the room had become an airless cavern in which he could not breathe. His throat seemed to constrict as old memories, ancient guilts rose inside him like an unstoppable flood. He had imagined there came a point where the body rejected guilt as it rejected pain, seeing in both a natural obstacle to survival, but now he realised the past had always been lurking just below the surface, waiting its chance to strip him of dignity and self-respect.

'You don't understand,' he whispered.

'You're quite wrong,' Skorzeny said bluntly. 'We didn't select you for this mission without going extensively into your background. We are well aware of what happened on the Eiger Wall.'

Spengler stared at his empty plate. It was like the exposure of a dark and shameful secret.

'That's all in the past, Erich,' Skorzeny said crisply. 'It was years ago. You can't go on blaming yourself for ever.'

'It feels like yesterday to me.'

'You were a hero, everyone said so.'

'That's good,' Spengler muttered bitterly, 'a bloody hero.'

'You did all a man could do,' Skorzeny said mildly.

'I could have died.'

'What would that have achieved? Good God, man, do you imagine you can absolve your guilt simply by dying? That's absurd. What's more, it's also irrelevant, since you're not in a position to decide one way or another. You've been selected for this mission by the Führer himself. Past guilts, real or imagined, are of no consequence whatsoever. From tomorrow, you climb for the Fatherland.'

Skorzeny looked angry, as though Spengler had let him down in some unthinkable way. He seemed suddenly anxious to bring their meeting to a close and looked at his watch.

'It pains me to break up an agreeable evening,' he said, 'but you must be ready to leave at dawn.'

Spengler nodded, understanding, and rose to his feet. 'In which case,' he said, 'If you will forgive me, I shall retire at once.'

He shook hands with Skorzeny. 'Goodnight, Sturmbannführer, I'm sorry if I've disappointed you.'

'Not "disappointed" Erich. Disturbed. I'd imagined your problems were under control. I see now I was wrong. You have a gruelling time ahead. Not only will there be physical dangers to contend with, but you'll have your own private piece of hell to endure into the bargain. I hope to God you survive.'

Spengler stared at him in silence for a moment, then he nodded to the three Italian girls and wandered upstairs to his room. He unbuttoned his tunic and stepped on to the balcony, staring into the darkness.

His private piece of hell, he thought, that was good, painfully good. Skorzeny was no fool. He knew his men all right, had learned to read the little tell-tale nuances of expression, the almost imperceptible signals of instability. And of course he would have read the record sheets, although what would they offer apart from an ocean of gobbledygook? Psychiatrists' jargon, that was all, as meaningless as hieroglyphics. Skorzeny could never really know, because Spengler's predicament was as removed from Skorzeny's world as a distant planet.

Did you think it was over, he asked himself? You poor naïve fool. He *had* thought it over, over and done with, lost in the dim recesses of his mind. Now it was returning like the haunting remnant of a painful love affair. Damn Skorzeny, and damn the Führer. Two years, that was how long it had taken to regain his sanity. Two years in a blind alley with no way out. His guilt, if not erased, had been thrust into a more palatable resting place, and would have remained there if Major Otto Skorzeny and the German army hadn't decided to dig it out and hit him over the head with it.

He heard the bedroom door open and turning, saw one of the girls who had sat with them at dinner. She was dark-haired and olive-skinned, and her figure, in the misty glow from outside looked strong and beautiful. Spengler frowned. 'Can I help you?'

She did not answer. Instead, she closed the door and stood in darkness, her face almost obscured. He could see the stars reflected in her glossy evening gown. Without a word, she reached behind, undid her dress and let it fall to the floor. Spengler stared at her in silence. Scooping up her hair from the nape of her neck, she shook it vigorously, then, without looking at him, unclipped her brassiere and dropped it at her feet. Spengler felt his mouth go dry. For several weeks, he had been removed from the company or proximity of women. The demands of battle, the problems of survival had been all-consuming. Now, faced with the sight of bared flesh, his past obsessions were forgotten as he felt his body respond with an unexpected urgency. 'Are you part of the service too?' he whispered.

She moved towards him, her eyes shining with a strange, faintly hostile gleam. 'Isn't this what conquerors customarily take?' she hissed.

'Conquerors?' He almost laughed.

'Of course. Spoils of war and all that.'

'You're not here willingly?'

'Being willing doesn't come into it. It was an order, an imperial command.'

He stared at her. Close, she was an oddly ugly girl, but

33

there was a compelling vitality in her too-long too-bony face.

'Am I some kind of animal,' he whispered, 'to be fed and watered, then serviced like a stud horse?'

'I don't care what you are, Lieutenant, or who you are, or why you're here. I get my orders, and they're all I'm interested in.'

'That's a whore's privilege.'

She smiled as if the idea amused her. 'If that means indulging in carnality in order to survive, I plead guilty,' she said.

'What d'you mean?'

'You think we always eat as we did tonight? You think the people who live in these hills enjoy such luxuries? My father was arrested ten weeks ago for stealing food. They threatened to send him to a concentration camp unless . . .' Her voice trailed away. 'He is old,' she added, 'he is no longer strong.'

Spengler thought of the easy informality of dinner, the tranquillity of the hills outside. They were all a façade. Underneath, the harsh brutality of war remained.

On an impulse he put out his hand and laid it on the girl's arm. There was a wiry strength in there, a warm suppleness.

'Put on your clothes,' he said gently. 'Get out of here.'

She looked alarmed. 'If you send me away, I'll be punished.'

Spengler was surprised. 'For what?'

'They will think I failed to please you.'

He sighed. 'Then stay,' he said, 'you may sleep on the bed, I'll use the sofa. Don't be afraid, I shan't touch you.'

He went out again to the balcony, his brain in a turmoil. He could see the lights across the valley in Switzerland. He stood for a very long time, waiting for the peace fatigue would bring.

But peace never came.

Something woke Spengler in the early hours. He opened his eyes and lay quite still, breathing deeply. The room was bathed with a strange greenish light which seeped through the window and gave him the sensation of being underwater. He rolled on to his side and almost toppled to the floor, stopping just in time as he realised he was lying on the sofa. He turned to look at the girl. She was fast asleep on the bed, her soft hair spread across the pillow. Spengler felt hollowed-out, the sour pall of the wine at dinner lying in his belly like a leaden weight. Suddenly he caught his breath and felt his body break out in sweat. Someone else was in the room, he could sense it.

He rolled over and reached for his watch, but as his fingers closed on the leather strap, a man moved out of the shadows and stood beside the sofa. His face was obscured in the dim light, but Spengler, peering up, knew there was something familiar about the shape of his shoulders, the outline of his head.

'What . . .?' Spengler began, but the figure raised one hand and a soft voice said, 'Sssssssh.'

It moved to the French windows, motioning him to follow. He flung back the blanket and reached for his pants. Half-naked and bare-footed, he padded across the floor and on to the balcony. Oddly, the mountains had disappeared. Great fields lay before him in a checker-board of green and gold. From somewhere near at hand he heard the sea. That's strange, he thought.

They moved down the iron staircase, then northward along narrow lanes and gravel footpaths. The strange figure shuffled ahead, pushing on into the wind. The night was warm, the breeze strong. Hard to breathe, Spengler thought, in this whirling whippeting worrisome whoosh. Bare to the waist, bare-footed, he padded in slow motion behind the shuffling stranger.

The road dipped down over a bridge, up between tall stately pines. Trees rustled, their branches brushing low over the path like distorted claws. Spengler saw the light fade, saw darkness appear in the sky like cancer spots. The blotches spread out, merged, swam together, became a great pulsing jelly which hovered menacingly above their heads. He gasped for breath, watching the silent figure with envious hatred. How did he do it? How could he keep going through this lot, that shuffling demented outline?

The sky became a swirling cloud, and as he paused, breathless, screwing up his eyes, there came a sudden burst of light which lit up the path zig-zagging off into nowhere. Sea over there. Breakers crashing in with a pounding roar.

They were on a beach. Pools of water reflected stars where there were none. Moss-covered boulders, a homely touch. Beaches of childhood, beaches of memory, beaches of forgetfulness. The sand lifted around his ankles like drifting snow.

Suddenly the figure stopped. It turned, pointing upwards. Spengler stared. What is it, you fool? Why don't you speak?

Then he saw it. High up on the forbidding cliff, a man was hanging. He swayed gently in the wind like a human pendulum. Oh God.

Suddenly the figure was at his side. The face that had been obscured in shadow was glowing next to his, pale and bright. It was not a living face but a death mask of white plaster, a player's mask with crimson cheeks and snow-white nose. The lips curled in an obscene grin, the eyes hung open humourlessly. Dead eyes, plaster eyes.

Then all at once he was in a city and it was broad daylight. There were swallows flying. A dark cloud of swallows whirling and swirling above the rooftops. A city of squares and oblongs and angles. Streets that criss-crossed up and downhill. White buildings that scorched in the sun. Drums throbbed in the flat sun-drenched air.

There were people. Arabs, Berbers, Rifs. In djellebas and sandals. Veiled women with eyes like black grapes thronged the lines of little shops; cobblers, barbers, dressmakers, grocers. Flies flocked the tray of sickly sugary candy in a sweet-seller's doorway. They hovered like locusts over the carcass of a kitten rotting in the sun. Children sat watching spellbound. Death weaved its fascination like the snake-charmer's flute.

And now it was night and he was running. This city was a prison, holding him in, a fragment from the deep recesses of memory, silent, menacing. The buildings were burnt-out shells, their walls peppered with shrapnel. The sky was lit by searchlight beams which swayed and dipped in a macabre ballet. In the distance, he could hear artillery. He thought: if I were not such an obstinate

36

fellow I might have given up back there and mingled forever on the wharves of Moroccan fantasy, but here in this Dr Caligari world I am thinking with amazing commonsense, which must prove something.

He stopped, clutching at a fire hydrant while he choked for breath. And then he saw Skorzeny. The major was strolling by a row of bombed-out shops, his body tall and straight. Spengler called his name but Skorzeny did not hear. Spengler's hands felt slippery and wet. He looked down. There was blood on his wrists, on his pants, his arms and naked chest.

A shadow fell across the pavement. Spengler looked up. The death mask came drifting in towards him, glistening in the streetlamps' light. The cheeks and chin shone like wet glass, the lips laughed silently. Without hesitation, he drove his fist between the plaster eyes. There was a distinct crack and he swung again. The mask crumbled, falling away, and underneath was another face, his own face.

As he stared unbelievingly, it began to chuckle. The chuckle started low down, drifting gently like an incoming tide, strengthening, bubbling up into a mighty roar that swelled and swelled, uncontrollable, unbearable, echoing through the dim deserted streets, mingling with the far-off rumble of wind and artillery fire, deadening Spengler's senses, filling his ears and head and brain till he writhed against the hydrant and screamed and screamed for it to stop.

Then warm arms encircled his shoulders, soft flesh cushioned his head. A voice murmured urgently in his ear: 'Wake up, wake up for God's sake.'

He started. He was on the sofa. The girl was crouching on the floor beside him, her face bright with alarm. 'What's happening?' he whispered hoarsely.

'You were screaming like a maniac,' she hissed. 'It's a wonder you haven't roused the entire household.'

'What time is it?'

'Four-thirty.'

'Jesus.'

Spengler let his head drop back, the sweat glistening on his cheeks and throat, his chest rising as he gasped for air.

He stared fiercely at the ceiling as if half-afraid the real world would fade, plunging him back into the torment of his mind. The girl studied him anxiously. She had pulled on her evening gown, but had neglected to do up the zip, so that it hung from her frame like a shapeless sack. 'What's wrong?' she whispered.

He shrugged. 'A nightmare, that's all.'

'That was no ordinary nightmare. How often do they happen like that?'

'From time to time.'

She stared at him in silence for a moment and then, with a knowledge born of past misery, said: 'It's the bloody war.'

Spengler shook his head. 'No, it's nothing to do with the war. It's something else, something personal I have to live with, that's all.'

Her fingers were cool on his forehead. 'You're still sweating.'

'I think . . . I'm going to be sick.'

'Hold on,' she ordered. And rising to her feet, she went to the washbasin, filled a glass with water, and coming back, raised it to his lips. 'Drink,' she commanded.

'I'll cough it up.'

'Go on, do you good.'

The liquid was cold and tasteless, but it brought back a semblance of reality. The dark world in which he had been wandering faded into the night. He looked at her with gratitude.

'Better?' she asked.

He nodded.

'Think you can sleep now?'

'I can try.'

She stood up, staring down at him with a gentle expression on her face. 'You're not like the others,' she said. 'You don't belong here, you don't belong in this war at all.'

'Nobody belongs in this war.'

'Some do. They like it.'

'Not any more. We're too bloody tired, all of us.'

'How long have you been fighting?'

'Half my life, feels like.'

'You look done in.'

'I'll be all right.'

He moistened his lips with his tongue. 'Would you do something for me?' he whispered.

'If I can.'

'Will you lie beside me? Just for a while. I'll settle down in a minute or two.'

She hesitated, studying him seriously. Her eyes were soft, almost tender. She placed one hand on his forehead. 'My poor lieutenant,' she said soothingly, 'you're not so tough after all.'

'Christ, no,' he murmured, 'I'm not tough at all.'

He eased back and she stretched out beside him on the sofa, smiling secretively, tugging the blanket over them both. He could feel the warmth of her body against his. It felt oddly familiar, reassuring.

'How's that?' she asked.

'Better.'

He could see her teeth gleaming.

'When I was a little girl,' she said, 'I used to get nightmares too. We had a tree which grew in our garden. When the wind blew, the branches would scrape against my bedroom window. I'd dream the spirits of the dead were coming to carry me off.'

'It's worse when the dreams are always the same,' he said. 'You reach a point where you know what's coming next.'

'Like being able to foretell the future?'

'Sort of. That's the frightening bit.'

She was quiet for a while. Somewhere far to the west, an owl hooted twice, shrill and lonely like the whistle of a distant train. 'Have you thought of seeing a doctor?' she asked suddenly.

'I've seen dozens.'

'Didn't they help?'

'They did for a while. The nightmares stopped, at any rate. I thought I was cured. Now I realise it was only an illusion. There's no cure for what I've got. I'll carry it inside me till the day I die.'

He was aware of her eyes upon him, and stared fiercely at the ceiling like a small boy caught in a shameful act. It disturbed him to confide in strangers, and yet the need for confession was strong within him, as if only by acknowledging his guilt could he find any hope of salvation.

The girl's eyes shone in the soft light from the window.

'Do you want to kiss me?' she asked.

He stared at her quietly in the darkness.

'You can, if you like,' she said.

Somewhere outside, the owl hooted again, and a dog answered mournfully. Its sound was like the crying of young children drifting through the night. Her fingers touched his neck as he leaned over and pressed his lips to her. Her mouth opened and he felt her first insistent surge of passion. His hands moved among her clothing, finding her breasts. There was a flurry of rustling cloth, a gasp as the night air touched naked skin, and then her body was locked against his, her mouth on his ear, warm and moist. She began to speak, but he stopped her. 'Don't talk,' he said.

He did not want to talk, nor to hear her talk. He could see the curve of her throat, feel her cool palms upon his spine, her breasts plump and soft against his chest. He made love with an almost desperate passion. She had ceased in that moment to be any single person. She was simply female. A transcendental embodiment of all women. And he buried himself inside her, thrusting, desiring, escaping, as though in some primitive and immensely timeworn ceremony, he could return to the comfort and security of the womb.

Three

The truck lurched along the unpaved road to the north, its wheels wafting dust clouds across the jagged landscape. Mountains leaned dourly into a swirling sky. The fine weather of the previous day had deteriorated, and the clouds looked menacing, hanging over the summits like soggy grey blankets. Rivers rippled among the bracken, hissing and gurgling through limestone and granite gorges, but Spengler thought there was no pleasure in their melody; they seemed dark and dismal, as they brought down grit from the higher peaks and distributed it among the glistening boulders of the valley below.

He felt wretched, as if there dwelt within him the seeds of a deep and overwhelming malaise. The doctors at Koblenz had promised the worst was over, that he had worked the demons out of his system; his dream last night had convinced him beyond any shadow of doubt that they'd been wrong. Even the girl had been nothing but a diversion. There could be no escape for him. The mountains were like the bars of some incredible prison. A refresher course, Skorzeny had said. Back to the peaks, to the strain and stretch of muscle and sinew, to the inevitable and inescapable collision with his past. When he thought of what lay ahead he felt a chill on his heart, as if someone had touched just for a moment the most precious and fragile possession of his life, threatening its existence with idle curiosity before passing on.

He trailed his arm through the open window, feeling the air cool against his fingers. 'How far now?' he asked.

'Almost there, Lieutenant,' the sergeant driving said. 'Another mile, that's all.'

'Is it always this cheerless?'

The sergeant grinned. 'We don't see the sun much,' he admitted. 'Sometimes we're wrapped in fog for days on end. You get to feel the world outside doesn't exist any more.'

'How do you stand it?'

'Like toothache, you just learn.'

Spengler fumbled in his pocket and offered the sergeant a cigarette. The man shook his head. He wore the normal service dress of the Gebirgsjäger, but carried the insignia of the Waffen SS. 'You'll have to leave those in the school office when we arrive,' he warned. 'Smoking's against the rules.'

Spengler pulled a face. 'What are you running up there, a concentration camp?'

'It's no rest home, Lieutenant.'

'Have the others arrived yet?'

'They came yesterday.'

'How many?'

'Eight. We never train more than a handful at a time. School policy. Last month we lost three trainees.'

'Lost?'

'Yeah. Sometimes men crack under the strain.'

Something cold moved inside Spengler. He remembered Skorzeny's words: 'You'll wish to God you were back at the front.' What kind of lunacy was he about to embark on?

They chugged along in steamy silence, the engine buzzing inside his skull. Though the truck was rusty and mud-spattered, it took the bumps like a game little terrier, nosing unerringly up the twisting mountain track past fractured cliffs, wind-torn trees and ragged scrub-cluttered gullies. In the gloomy humidity the terrain looked so desolate it chilled his blood.

They topped a small rise and Spengler saw rearing out of the fog a massive grey stone building. Tall and forbidding, its walls gave it the appearance of a prison block rather than a training school. Camouflaged defence bunkers lined its forecourt, and squads of MPs patrolled the assault guns which bordered its barbed-wire perimeter fence. An SS Unterscharführer saluted as they drove through the compound gate and came to a halt in front of the main door.

The driver led Spengler into a bleak reception office.

'You'll have to see the doctor,' she said. 'She'll be through directly.'

'She?' Spengler echoed.

'Yes, Lieutenant,' the sergeant grinned, giving him a conspiratorial wink. 'We have all the creature comforts here.'

He turned and sauntered out, and Spengler peered around the room. Its walls were plastered with a shiny substance that gave it the air of a hospital mortuary. Chairs had been arranged around its perimeter in an attempt at some minimal comfort, but the floor was carpetless and Spengler's boots rang against the concrete. He stood at the window and peered at the peaks twisting into the fog like breakers in a frozen ocean. The sheer uncompromising austerity of the place seemed overwhelming.

'Lieutenant Spengler?' The voice was crisp and business-like.

He turned. The doctor was in her middle thirties, tall and straight with brown hair, long slender legs and that self-conscious look of composure women adopt when trying to appear sexless.

'I'm Dr Rössner,' she said. 'Will you come this way, please.'

He followed her along a stone-flagged corridor into a brightly-lit surgery. Rows of coloured bottles lined both walls. Dr Rössner closed the door and began to scribble something into a large book. Spengler studied her with interest. She was lovely, he decided. Not in the obvious sense. Her face was quite plain really, but it was an exciting plainness, a feminine plainness. Her skin was shining where the sun had caught it the previous day, and there was a smattering of freckles across her cheeks and the bridge of her nose. Her hair was tied loosely at the neck with a ribbon, and she had clearly tried to make herself schoolmistressy, a ploy that hadn't altogether worked.

She spoke without looking up: 'I thought we'd lost you. The others arrived yesterday.'

'Sorry. Things are a bit confused in Tuscany. We're on the retreat.'

'Is it really that bad?'

'It's bad enough.'

43

She glanced up at him. 'You're Erich Spengler, aren't you? I used to read about you before the war. You were quite a celebrity in our house. My husband was a mountaineering fanatic.'

'You're married?' he said, feeling, absurdly, a sense of disappointment.

'Widowed,' she corrected. 'Karl was killed before the war began. But we used to climb together in the early days. Strictly in an amateur sense by your standards, of course.'

He examined her approvingly. He couldn't help feeling her calmness was just a façade, created for reasons only she was aware of.

'What are you doing in the army?' he asked. 'It doesn't look like your sort of thing at all.'

'I'm not in the army,' she said. 'I'm a civilian.'

'Then why . . .?'

'I was invited to volunteer. By the Gestapo.'

He was surprised. 'You mean you're a trainee, like me?'

'That's right.'

'But you're running the surgery.'

She smiled. 'They like to get their money's worth, that's all.'

He thought for a moment. Trainee or not, she had official status, which meant she might know more than she was saying. 'Any idea why they've brought us here?' he asked.

'None whatsoever.'

'They must have told you something.'

'Nothing.'

'You mean you volunteered without knowing what for?'

'It was my duty as a German citizen,' she said mildly. 'The men of the High Command don't tell me their secrets.'

He tried to get a clue from the expression in her eyes, but she was peering downwards, frowning slightly as she concentrated on her writing.

'I'm not a workhorse,' he said. 'I don't like being treated like one.'

'You'll get used to that,' she murmured without looking up.

'I wouldn't count on it.'

She smiled thinly. 'Such arrogance, Lieutenant. There are no individuals here, only different cogs in the same machine. If a cog snaps, they pluck it out and toss it on the scrap heap. They're good at that sort of thing.'

She's cool, he thought. Composed. Knows her position and likes to keep it intact. But something bothered him, a sense of intangibility, a feeling that everything wasn't quite as it seemed.

'Was your husband a doctor too?' he asked.

'No, he was a lawyer.'

'What happened to him?'

'He made his living with the use of words. He used them very persuasively, often brilliantly, only sometimes they were the wrong words and he was too naïve to see it. They cost him his life in the end. He made the mistake of denouncing the Nazis. Hardly a wise thing to do in 1938.'

She stopped suddenly, as if she had said too much. Her skin looked pale above the sharply-etched cheekbones. She was angry with herself. They had touched on matters too painful to refer to. Now, her reserve stood between them like a barrier.

'What are you doing here?' he demanded. 'You must hate the Party and everything it stands for.'

She stared at him coolly. 'I took an oath,' she answered. 'To preserve life, relieve suffering. All you need to know is that I'm a qualified physician, and I'm on this course to learn, like you. Now, please remove your clothes.'

He stared at her blankly. 'What?'

'Just lay them on the chair.'

'Why?'

'I have to examine you. That's my job.'

She was looking at him with an air of detached professionalism but he had the idea she was less sure of herself than she seemed. He felt gauche and inhibited. It wasn't easy to maintain one's dignity without clothes on.

'Lieutenant Spengler,' she said irritably, 'I've had a tiring day and you are wasting my time. Will you kindly undress and allow me to proceed with your examination?'

Spengler unbuttoned his tunic. He felt de-humanised. He had been bathed, clothed, fed and serviced with the unfeeling impartiality afforded an animal being prepared for the meat market.

A slow dull anger pulsed inside him as for the next half-hour Dr Rössner tested his blood pressure, his heart and pulse rate, his muscle reflexes, and his eyes, ears, nose and throat. When it was over, she again opened the book and began to scribble inside.

'Do I pass?' he asked.

'You're in excellent shape.'

'I'll need to be, stuck up here at the end of the world.'

'I'm sure it will have its moments,' she said in her cool schoolteacher's voice.

Something snapped inside him. Damn it, he was a human being, not a laboratory specimen. He felt an urge to break down her mask of professional control, to say or do something that would shock her into recognising his presence as an individual.

'What sort of moments are you talking about?' he asked.

'I beg your pardon?'

'You mean the physicals?'

She looked blank. 'I don't understand.'

'Are they what you use for recreation, Frau Doktor? Is that how you stay sane in this frozen mausoleum?'

She stared at him in silence for a moment, then without warning she moved so fast that her hand was a blur. Spengler tried to dodge back, but she caught him in her grasp. They peered into each other's eyes, Dr Rössner's calm and controlled, Spengler's bright with alarm.

'Gently,' Spengler whispered in a hoarse voice, 'gently.'

'Cough,' she ordered.

Spengler coughed.

'Again.'

He coughed again.

His examination over, Spengler was taken upstairs to the barrack room, a room as cheerless as anything he'd seen in his army career. Its bare walls and high ceiling gave it the appearance of an elongated prison cell. Seven men sat watching curiously as Spengler chose a bunk near the door and began to unbutton his tunic. Two of them he recognised. One was Rolf Notz, who had made the first winter ascent of the Dango Pillar, the other Hans Gotsch, the rock maestro from Singen with whom Spengler had once passed a stormy bivouac high on the snowclad Weisserhorn. Though they were old friends, they greeted each other cautiously, for five years of war had distorted the world they had left behind, making it distant in their memories.

A tall raw-boned man with a bloodless face came over to shake hands. Lines of weariness showed around his eyes, and Spengler recognised the look. Like himself, this man had come straight from the front.

'I'm Kurt Hüsser,' the man said. 'Where did they pick you up?'

'Italy,' Spengler told him. 'We were on the run through Tuscany.'

Hüsser pulled a face. 'They grabbed me in France,' he said. 'Things look bloody grim there too.'

'I'm Arno Richner,' said the man on the next bed. 'Didn't you climb the Drejesknollen with Ludwig Gurtner?'

'That's right.'

Richner was short and plumpish, with a round boyish face that would probably retain its youthfulness well into middle age.

'They dragged me out of Norway for this fiasco,' he complained. 'God knows what they expect. I mean, I'm not like you lot. I'm a fake, a phoney. I never wanted to be a climber in the first place. I'm even afraid of heights.'

'Then what are you doing here?'

'I grew up in Bavaria. Have you ever been in Bavaria? For some Godalmighty reason, it's considered an important part of the social graces to be a good mountaineer. My brother used to take me on his little jaunts. I hated it, but I didn't dare refuse. I just happened to be there when he put up a new route on the Gross Strahlerhorn, and by a fluke my name got into the record books.'

Spengler grinned. He had to admit Richner hardly

looked the outdoor type. His skin had the texture of pink blancmange.

'I had a nice little number going in Norway,' Richner moaned, his face assuming an air of bitterness. 'I worked for the Quartermaster in Alesund. Nothing dangerous, just a simple storekeeper's job. Now they drag me over here and stick me in this madhouse.'

'He makes a fuss out of everything,' Hüsser growled. 'You'd think he had the angel of doom sitting on his shoulders.'

'Maybe I have,' said Richner. 'Maybe we all have. A sort of deathwish. Some people have it, you know, without even knowing. Like cancer. They think they're normal like everyone else, and all the time they're running around with this insane desire to break their own necks. Besides, I don't like the dreams I've been having lately.'

Spengler stopped smiling. The mention of dreams made him uneasy.

'What kind of dreams?' Hüsser demanded.

'I've been having bad dreams. I keep seeing myself dead on top of some mountain. It's always the same dream over and over. I'm always dead in it. And it's raining. I see the rain washing down my dead face.'

'Dreams don't mean a thing,' Hüsser snorted.

Richner shrugged. 'My mother kept getting those dreams too. Before she died, she kept seeing herself laid out in bed with all the family standing around. She had the same dream every night for two weeks. And then she died.'

Spengler shifted uncomfortably. The memory of his own nightmare came back with startling force. He saw again the glistening death-mask, heard the sound of his screams and the voice of the girl comforting him as he lurched into consciousness. To change the subject, he asked as casually as he could: 'How did it go today?'

Hüsser shrugged. 'We only arrived last night,' he said. 'We've been sitting around the barracks waiting for you.'

'Have you met our Dr Rössner yet?' Richner whispered. His face had lost its woeful look. Now he seemed wistful, dreamy.

'I've met her,' Spengler said.

'Isn't she an eyeful? Imagine finding a bit of stuff like that in a place like this? Mind you, she's a cold fish. Like ice. I doubt if there's an ounce of softness in that gorgeous frame. What a waste.'

'Did they take your cigarettes?' Hüsser asked.

Spengler picked up his tunic from the bed, fumbled in the pocket and tossed the packet to Hüsser who caught it eagerly.

'Keep them if you like,' Spengler offered, 'I've got some more.'

Hüsser looked grateful. 'Thanks. When they took our fags, I thought the world was coming to an end. What are they running here, a bloody torture chamber?'

'Anybody got any idea what happens when our training's over?' Spengler asked.

'Christ knows,' said Notz. 'We're going to win the bloody war, apparently. A new secret weapon, they said. Did they show you the uranium?'

'Looked like washing powder to me,' Spengler grunted.

'Well,' said Hans Gotsch from the other side of the room, 'anything's better than slogging it out in Russia. Climbing mountains is the only thing I was ever good at, anyhow.'

He smiled, turning his left hand slowly in the light. 'See those scars? I got those on the Schladderspitze. That was when Horst Eckstein and Wolfe Sonnenhuber were so exhausted I left them belayed on a ledge and went the last thousand feet alone. Neither would believe I'd done it till Rainer and Wödl climbed it in the following week and found my name scratched on the summit. At Nuptse in the Himalayas, I was laid up for nearly a month with altitude sickness, but it's still the only thing I ever cared about. They can do what the hell they like when the course is over. I'll still take my chances here.'

'I see we're all the same rank,' said Arno Richner, stretching back on his pillow with his head resting on both hands. 'Fastest promotion I ever had. Storekeeper to Second Lieutenant in one day. Think they'll let us keep the title when this thing's over?'

Hüsser grinned down at him. 'Not a chance,' he

said. 'When it's over, it'll be off to the mass graves for you.'

Richner peered at Spengler. 'He's such a reassuring bastard,' he murmured.

It was late afternoon when they first met Henke. A hush fell across the room as he stepped inside the door, a tall man, heavy-boned but built like an athlete. He looked handsome in an arrogant sort of way, and his eyes held a brightness that was difficult to identify – was it pleasure or malevolence? An enamel Edelweiss badge clung to the breast pocket of his tunic, proclaiming him to be a Bergführer, or mountain guide. As he stood surveying them, legs apart, hands resting loosely on his hips, he seemed to emanate a strange air of evil. 'I'm Henke,' he announced, 'your instructor. Over the next few days you'll get to know my face as well as your own. I have no doubt you'll also get to hate it. Well, I thrive on hate. I've been hated all my life. Just don't make the mistake of trying to be friendly or I'll snap off your head like a mad dog.'

He began to stroll down the aisle between the beds, studying them each in turn with an amused, disdainful expression on his face. He moved gracefully, his spine erect, his chin held high. Spengler watched him in silence. He knew Henke's type. A swaggerer. A bully. A member of the Führer's new super-race.

'So you're the little band of legendary heroes who opened up our great ascent routes,' Henke said. 'Well, don't imagine your past achievements hold any sway around here. In my opinion you were lucky, every last one of you. There was no competition. All you had to do was break a little new ground, then lie back and wallow in the applause of the ignorant masses. Today, a new breed of climber is emerging in Germany, a climber capable of feats none of you have ever dreamed of. Most of us were too young to make our mark before the war, but I give you my word, gentlemen, once it's over we'll push your pretty exploits into the category they really deserve.'

He turned, still smiling thinly, and began to stroll back towards the door, his eyes startlingly blue against his suntanned skin. 'You're here to relearn the art of survival in high places,' he said. 'It can't be done easily and it can't be done safely. The course we run has already claimed three victims this year. Your training will be tougher than theirs because you are being prepared for a specific project. Over the next few days, you will relearn how to handle a variety of emergencies. Most of them will be physical emergencies, which call for strength and courage, but by learning to meet the physical challenges you will also prepare yourself mentally for any kind of situation, physical, emotional or whatever, which may threaten you in the mission ahead. Where you'll be going is not a safe secure place, and this is not a safe secure course.

'As experienced mountaineers, some of the things we'll cover will seem elementary to you in the beginning. This is because the war has interrupted your activities, making it necessary to go over some of the fundamentals. Be patient. I promise you'll soon be climbing better than ever.

'Though this is a Gebirgsjäger unit, it is also part of the Waffen SS, and since we are all the same rank we will address each other by name only. That also applies to me. We are brother officers united in a glorious tradition. However, I would remind you that as instructor I carry a special authority and expect to be treated with respect. Anyone who fails to show this respect will suffer the consequences.'

He paused to see if anyone was prepared to challenge this remark. No one was.

'We eat in the mess on the ground floor, three times a day,' he said. 'Breakfast – 05.30 hours. Order of dress number 4. Lunch – noon. Dinner – 20.00. Lights-out is at 22.00 hours. No one is permitted to leave the dormitory after nine. I don't give a damn who you are, or what mountaineering miracles you claim to have performed before you came here, either you'll obey orders or I'll break you into little pieces. Is that clear?'

They lay on their bunks staring at him in silence.

'Any questions?'

'When do we begin?' Rolf Notz asked.

'In the morning,' said Henke. 'I'd advise you to get all the rest you can. I will not tolerate slackers.'

'What's this mission we're being prepared for?' Hüsser murmured.

'You'll be informed of that when necessary.'

'Will you be coming too, Lieutenant?'

The reply was like a pistol shot. 'Henke. Address me by name only, understand?'

Henke flexed his shoulders. 'The mission will be led by Sturmbannführer Otto Skorzeny. I shall be second-in-command.'

He turned to go, then paused as a sudden thought struck him. Looking back, he said: 'Occasionally, a man takes it into his head to make a run for it. Let me warn you, it's a long way to freedom and the hills below are swarming with partisans. If they don't finish you off, our stormtroopers will. They have a special technique for hanging deserters. They do it slowly to give you lots of time to reflect on the error of your ways. Take my word, it's not a pleasant end.'

And with the threat hanging in the air, he went outside and closed the door behind him.

'Richner, you're like a pregnant cow. Get that rope higher, hold it there, for Christ's sake, hold it there.'

Henke's face was twisted with exasperation as he stood bellowing at the unwieldy shape of Arno Richner struggling to abseil down the mountain crag. It was a pleasant day; the storm that had raged since early morning had lifted towards noon, and though the sky was heavy, patches of dappled sunlight rippled across the snowcapped peaks, giving a sense of emerging life. On the higher slopes, traces of white glowed among the rocks where fresh snow had fallen and was melting now as the barometer rose, sending streams of pearly grey water hurtling through the gullies.

Spengler stood with the others, chewing on a grass stem as he studied the pitiful motions of Arno Richner, who had confided from the beginning that he was terrified of heights, and who was now caught in his private nightmare, suspended eighty feet up with nothing but the precipice and a gaping void below.

They were four days into the course, and Spengler felt he was at last beginning to find his feet. They had re-learned the skills of the past, practising the basic principles of high-altitude survival: the use of twelve-point crampons (or 'Lobster Claws' as Henke called them); the art of bivouacking in driving blizzards; negotiating arêtes and hanging cornices; and, most significant of all, traversing glaciers with ski-sleds (this latter covered in such detail that Spengler felt convinced it must hold a special importance in their mission ahead). Most of the techniques were familiar to Spengler and, so far at least, he had managed to hold on to his sanity. As long as they stayed on the lower slopes, he thought, then he would be all right. Glacier-work in particular was simple plodding, really. All it required was a trained eye, a little expertise and a chestful of wind. If things stayed like this, he might yet come through intact. It was only if they progressed to the demands and hazards of a major ascent that he ran the risk of disintegration. Nevertheless, he was finding it increasingly difficult to swallow the insults which dropped daily and liberally from Henke's tongue. Henke seemed to delight in humiliating others, and as Spengler stood watching Arno Richner's pathetic attempts to drop down the mountain face, he saw in Henke's eyes a gleam that was half fury, half demented pleasure.

Somehow, sliding downwards in dribs and drabs, Arno Richner managed to reach the cliff bottom and, visibly trembling, shook loose the rope from its anchor. Henke strode over to him, stepping across the boulders and loose moraine which littered the ground.

'Richner,' he growled, 'that was the worst descent I've ever seen. You are a disgrace to the name of mountaineering. My God, if only the war hadn't come along, I'd have shown you what climbing's really about. Look at this man, all of you. Now do you realise how easy you had it in the old days? Even rubbish like this managed to find its way into the record books.'

Richner looked sulky. 'You know bloody well I hate abseiling.'

'Then what the hell are you doing here?'

'I don't know,' Richner yelled. 'I've never liked climbing, never. I don't belong with the others, and you know it, Henke.'

Henke spat on the ground. 'You gutless bastard,' he breathed. 'You're not going to wriggle out of this operation by malingering. Get back up there and let's see you do it properly this time.'

Richner stared at him, licking his lips. 'No,' he whispered, 'My God, I can't.'

'That's an order, Richner.'

'Do what you like, Henke, I'm not making that descent again. You're not bloody God, you know.'

'You know the penalty for insubordination?'

'Think again, you Nazi bastard. You're the same rank as the rest of us, so go stuff yourself.'

For a moment, Henke stood quite still, his eyes glittering. The wind caught his scarf, fluttering it into his face. He brushed it away, a muscle in his cheek beginning to quiver.

'What did you say, Richner?' he breathed softly.

'I'm not going up that bloody rock again, Henke. I don't give a tuppeny damn about you or your threats.'

'Richner, will you repeat what you just called me.'

There was a long silence. A terrible hush settled over the little group of spectators. They stood waiting, dry-mouthed.

With his voice quivering, Richner gasped: 'You're a Nazi bastard, Henke.'

Henke moved. The punch came from low down and seemed to sink into Richner's belly, taking the flesh with it so that the bulges spread outward as Richner doubled over. They heard his hiss of exhaled breath, saw him stagger back against the cliff wall, tears of pain and disbelief shining in his eyes. Henke stepped in with the grace and precision of a trained fighter, two blows this time, the first driving into Richner's ribs, the second clipping his jaw just below the ear. Henke's fists were a blur, landing almost simultaneously. Spengler felt his stomach lurch with each individual crack. Blood came out of Richner's mouth, trickling in a thin stream over the beefy underlip. His body burrowed backwards against the rock, as if the cliff face offered the only protection he could hope for.

'You bullying swine,' he hissed. 'You miserable sadistic pig.'

Henke went to work on Richner's stomach, choosing his targets with skill and dexterity. Richner, half-crazed with pain, tumbled to his knees and covered his head with his arms. Spengler felt his hands turn cold. Why are we standing here watching this, he wondered? If that bastard doesn't pack it in, then court-martial or not, I'll tear his bloody head off. But Henke stepped back, his eyes gleaming like a man in a moment of deep fulfilment.

'Richner,' he breathed.

'You bullying sod,' Richner sobbed from the ground.

'Get up that rock, damn you.'

'You know I'm afraid of heights.'

'Then get unafraid, damned quick.'

Richner stumbled to his feet. Tears traced uneven patterns through the dirt on his cheeks. His eyes were wild with pain as, sobbing soundlessly, he coiled the rope and began to climb. The route was easy enough and they had all done it a dozen times, but there was something pathetic in the way Richner twisted and swayed, holding himself tight to the cliff as if only the solidity of the granite could give him strength and hope.

At the cliff bottom, the little knot of spectators waited in silence. Only Henke was smiling. He watched Richner's movements with a delight that seemed to Spengler almost pathological.

'Come on, you fat blubber-barrel,' he kept shouting, 'get that leg up. Lift it, Richner, lift it.'

Trembling like a jelly, Arno Richner reached the summit of the crag, clutching at the rock with an agonised expression.

'Okay,' Henke grinned. 'Anchor the rope and let's see you come down.'

Richner uncoiled the rope and looped it over the granite spur, taking his time, putting off the dreadful moment of descent as long as possible. Even at that distance, they could see the fear in his tear-stained eyes. Mist swirled around Richner's head, teasing his shape so that it swayed and twisted like an image in a fairground mirror.

At least he isn't badly hurt, Spengler thought. Henke had worked him over like a true professional, invoking the maximum pain with the minimum injury, a skill he'd probably learned beating up innocent Jews in the streets of Hamburg or Berlin. Spengler had seen Henke's type before. He was a tank, devoid of sympathy or emotion.

'Come on, Richner,' Henke yelled. 'Get your backside down here.'

With the rope curled around his body, Richner eased himself out from the summit, walking backwards down the vertical wall, letting the rope slide through his hand in classic abseil style. He moved hesitantly, dropping a few feet then pausing until his nerve returned.

'Get a move on, Richner,' Henke bellowed. 'If I have to come up there and get you, you'll wish to God you'd never been born.'

Bit by bit, slowly, shakily, Arno Richner made his descent. When at last his feet touched the grass, Spengler breathed a sigh of relief. He glanced across at Helene Rössner. She had discarded her customary white tunic for climbing breeches and anorak, neither of which had succeeded, even in the slightest way, in toning down the lines of her explicit body. Her face looked ghastly.

Richner's legs seemed to crumple at the cliff base, and he collapsed like a drunken man among the stones and moraine. Henke stared at him with disgust. 'You miserable toad,' he growled. 'It makes me sick just having you in my company.'

'Leave me alone, Henke.'

'I'll leave you alone when you do the job you've been brought to do. I warned you at the beginning that I hate malingerers. If you look like endangering the lives of the men on this mission, I'll put a bullet in your carcass and leave you to freeze on the ice, that's a sacred promise.'

Without waiting for Richner's reaction, Henke turned and strode off across the hillslope, nodding to the others to follow. Spengler stepped over and helped Richner to rise. The bruised face was white as milk, and there was blood on his cheeks and jaw. His eyes shone with a wretched helplessness.

'Jesus,' he whispered.

'Easy now.'

'I think I'm going to cough up.'

'Don't. Henke would like that.'

Spengler took out his handkerchief, dipped it into a rocky pool and carefully wiped the blood from Richner's face. It was nothing more than a gesture, he realised, for Richner was not badly hurt in spite of his beating, but Spengler felt he had to do something. And perhaps, he thought, there was just a trace of guilt that they had stood there, all eight of them, and watched Richner's humiliation without even an offer of help.

Suddenly, someone took the handkerchief from Spengler's hand and began to dab delicately at Richner's cut lip. It was Helene Rössner. 'Your nose is beginning to swell,' she said. 'Come to the surgery as soon as class is finished and we'll see if we can patch you up there.'

Richner peered at Spengler. 'Erich, he can't do this, can he? I mean, even up here, there are still rules.'

Spengler sighed. 'Henke's deliberately riding you, so try and stay calm, understand? Don't lose your temper. You can always hit him with a rock or something when the course is over.'

He hooked one hand under Richner's armpit, pulling him away from the cliff-face. 'How d'you feel now?' he asked.

'Wobbly.'

'Think you can pull yourself together till we get back to barracks?'

'I'll be okay.'

'Come on then. We're keeping the class waiting, and there's no sense antagonising the bastard.'

'I'm dying,' Richner moaned, 'dying.'

It was ten o'clock, and they were sprawled on their bunks in attitudes of helpless exhaustion. Outside, a storm was brewing.

'That bastard Henke,' Tauer growled. 'Somebody should stick an iceaxe in his gullet.'

'I wouldn't care to try,' Gotsch admitted, 'he certainly knows how to handle himself.'

'He had no right to treat Arno like that,' Rolf Notz murmured, 'no right at all.'

'Why don't you file a complaint?' Tauer suggested. 'Redress of grievance.'

'What good would that do?' Richner asked.

'Damn all,' chuckled Gotsch. 'By the time it got through the admin office we'll all be dead, the way he's driving us.'

'Why won't they tell us what it's all about?' Hüsser wondered. 'They'll have to, sooner or later.'

'Maybe they're afraid we'll desert.'

'Think it'll be that bad?'

'Anything to do with Henke's bound to be bad.'

'Go to sleep, for Christ's sake,' Höflehner complained. 'Let's have some bloody quiet in here.'

'How can I sleep when I'm under sentence of death?' Richner demanded.

'Try,' said Höflehner, rolling on one side and tugging the bedclothes over his head.

Outside, the storm raged steadily on, but inside the dormitory there was only the ticking of the clock, and the muffled breathing of exhausted men.

Helene Rössner lay awake in her room, listening to the storm outside. She could hear the slow rhythmic stride of the sentries in the corridor, and the faint murmur of a radio drifting down from the MPs' quarters on the floor above. Her body ached with fatigue. She'd never known weariness like it, not even after she and Karl had made their ascent of the Grandes Jorasses. She was beginning to wonder if she'd last the course. Not if it went on like this, she thought. Bad enough for the others perhaps, but with her there was the added discomfort of knowing she didn't belong. She was alien. She was the enemy.

Life had never been easy in Paris, the rationing, the isolation, the danger (which she'd recognised and accepted, finding in it a strange regeneration after the

58

suffering of her past). She'd thought things bad in Paris, but at least in Paris she'd still had Lambert. Lambert, her contact, had been no uncle figure, God knew; compassion and understanding had been as alien to him as fear, but he'd been a link with the outside world. Here, she was utterly alone.

She realised, of course, that it had been a miracle they'd come to her at all, one of those incredible twists of fate which sometimes transform the affairs of men and of nations.

'We need a diabetes specialist,' they'd told her at Gestapo headquarters on the Avenue Foch, 'a diabetes specialist who is also a high Alpine mountaineer. There is, regrettably, no physician in the German army with those dual qualifications.'

So they'd chosen her. A thousand to one shot. A doctor who, incredibly, was also an undercover link between the French Resistance and the British forces in Europe. The chance of a lifetime, she thought. She knew what she had to do. No arguments. No excuses. Find out what this was all about, and get the word back as quickly as possible. That was her job.

She had considered already various possibilities. There was Henke, for example. She had noticed Henke peering at her covertly from time to time, and she had no doubt that a woman with her wits about her could soon wheedle her way into Henke's confidence (he was hardly over-burdened with the gift of intelligence) but there was a strong possibility that, instructor or not, Henke knew no more than she did. And besides – she shuddered at the thought – she found the man utterly repulsive. He was handsome enough in a cold sort of way – his face was chiselled in the style of the old Greek gods, but all the good looks in the world didn't make up for the sheer unpleasantness of his personality. And the way he baited Richner was ugly to watch. Henke, she realised, was a little boy who had never grown up, except that he'd retained, not the endearing qualities of boyhood but the less engaging traits, like selfishness and spite. He was a man who lived to take stands, draw up sides, mark and acknowledge the presence of new enemies, finding in that a strange satisfaction. Anyone who stepped in his way, he crushed as swiftly and as ruthlessly as he could. No, Henke was out of the question, so there was only one alternative that she could see. The offices on the second floor. If she could manage to break in upstairs, she might find some kind of document, some clue to why the Germans had assembled their finest mountaineers in this desolate retreat deep in the Italian mountains.

She slipped out of bed, pulled on her clothes and, shivering in the damp chill air, padded to the door and listened hard. She heard the sound of a heel scraping against stone. One of the sentries was hovering, probably loth to leave the comparative warmth of the corridor for the storm outside. Damn the man. What if he decided to hang about all night? Can't risk the passageway, she thought. That leaves only the window. She slid it up with a soft screechy sound and the wind drove into her face with a force that took her breath away. She stared out across the valley, the river winding far beneath her, the hills curling south, pale and grey in the darkness. She leaned forward, sticking out her head. The ground was twenty feet below, but there was a tiny ledge, no more than an inch and a half wide, running from below the sill to the outermost corner of the house. It offered only a toe-tip stance, but it would take her as far as the next window. It was worth a try.

Helene hoisted herself on to the window sill, her heart hammering rapidly. For a moment she crouched there, gathering her strength, then slowly, carefully, making each move as deliberate as possible, she turned and eased out on to the ledge. The wind caught her clothes, threatening for a second to drag her off altogether, but somehow she managed to hold on, driving her fingertips into the narrow cracks between the rough blocks of stone. Standing there, numbed by the gale, she almost changed her mind, but some inner streak of stubbornness would not let go.

Gingerly, she began to inch along. She reached the other window, groped down with a tentative hand and tugged at its rim. The window remained firm as rock. The damned thing was locked.

Helene felt panic surge through her. Another minute and her strength would give out. Bending slightly, she felt a surge of hope as she realised the fastener was one of the old-fashioned kind, a metal lever on the upper section which slid into a groove on the lower. She groped in her pocket with her free hand and brought out her nail file. Reaching down, she slid the thin blade through the crack between the upper and lower panes. She touched the metal fastener, got the blade to it, and carefully, cannily nudged it along. It slipped a fraction, then again, and suddenly, with a distinct 'plop' it jumped free of its groove and she felt the pane shudder against her knee. She let the nail file drop into the darkness, and swinging the window open, slid her feet into the room and collapsed on the floor with a sense of relief.

For more than a minute she lay quietly fighting for breath, trying to pull her senses together. No more risks, she promised herself as she clambered to her feet and slid the window shut. She would just have to pray the sentry had disappeared when the time came to return.

She peered about her in the shadows. She was in the men's shower room. She could see the dark outline of the cubicles, and the small gunmetal nozzles protruding from the ceiling. She tried the door. It was locked. Her heart sank. She was no better off than when she'd started.

She moved around, squinting hard through the curtain of muggy grey. In front of the cubicles was a large wire grill which appeared to lead into some kind of ventilation tunnel. She crouched in the darkness tracing the grill rim with her fingertips. She could feel no screws or fastenings, and when she gripped the wire and tugged it came away with a soft metallic clunk. She held her breath and listened. No sound came from the corridor – only the whining of the wind outside.

Carefully she laid the grill in the dust, and tucking her head low, edged into the tunnel. Inky blackness wrapped around her like a shroud. She could smell the odour of soot, urine and ancient brick dust. She peered to her left. There was nothing to see but a wall of unrelieved black. She looked to her right, and there, just ahead, was a patch of grey, a shift in density. Reaching behind her, she picked up the grill and carefully fitted it back in its place, then without a second's pause she began to shuffle forward on her knees, feeling the sides of the shaft rub against her shoulders, closing around her like a suffocating coffin. How easy it would be to smother in here, she thought. She watched the patch of grey float nearer and then, gratefully, she was upon it. It was a second grill, this one peering in over some kind of storeroom. Helene put her hands against the wire and gave a sharp push. With a 'plop' the grill came away, and she lowered it carefully to the floor. Kicking out her feet, she slid quietly into the room. The only light came from a tiny slit of a window which cast ripples of silvery grey across a cluster of haversacks, sleeping bags, iceaxes and coiled climbing ropes. Helene replaced the grill and padded softly to the door. She opened it and peered outside. There was no sign of the sentry. She slipped into the passageway, listening for any sound, however slight, which might signal the chance of discovery. There was nothing but the roar of the wind, and the almost imperceptible drone of the radio on the floor above.

She slid along the corridor as quickly as she dared, looking for a staircase, pausing only once to check a room on her left-hand side. It was empty. Like most of the rooms in the building, its walls were whitewashed, its floor uncarpeted. There was not even the investment of furniture to give it a fragmentary illusion of comfort. She continued on, expecting to find a turn-off to the floor above, but the corridor came to a halt at a heavy metal-studded door. She tried the handle. It was unlocked, and she stepped into what was evidently a lecture room. Rows of chairs faced towards a central dais on which stood a table and a large lantern screen. Something on the table caught her attention. It was a model of sorts, a structure unlike anything Helene had seen before. Roughly three feet high, flattish and circular, it was comprised of two rings, one inside the other. The inner ring was criss-crossed by a complex frame, rather like the frame of a crossword puzzle, while the outer was packed with what appeared to be a series of tiny bricks.

Helene stared at it in bewilderment. It represented

nothing at all she could put a name to. Shaking her head helplessly, she stepped back into the corridor and quickly retraced her steps.

The passage ahead took a sharp twist to the right, and she was edging towards it when, without warning, a hand fastened across her mouth and she felt herself being tugged bodily into one of the darkened doorways. She struggled hard, but the wiry strength of the limbs encircling hers seemed unbreakable. She felt her senses reeling with shock. Then her mouth was released and she turned to see a face, half-obscured by shadow, peering down at her. It was the man Spengler, a cigarette dangling from his lips.

'Shhhh,' he whispered, 'don't make a sound.'

'What are you doing here?' she hissed back, trying to cloak her fright with a show of aggression.

'Same as you,' he said.

'What d'you mean?'

'Those damned goons can smell a smoke a mile off. Safer not to do it in the barrack room. I slipped out for a quick one.'

She stood for a moment, gasping heavily, her heart fluttering inside her chest. 'You know smoking's against the rules,' she accused.

He grinned. 'So's wandering the corridors after lights-out. If you'd stepped around the corner, you'd have run straight into the arms of the sentry. Listen.'

She held her breath. Footsteps rang in the passageway outside. She heard them scrape as the man turned the corner and paused outside their doorway to blow his nose. Then he continued on, the sound of his boots fading in the opposite direction.

She felt dizzy with tension. Another second and he would have caught her, and what then? She had no cigarettes, like Spengler, to offer as an alibi. How would she have explained her nocturnal wandering?

She heard Spengler chuckling deep in his throat. He seemed to find the situation oddly amusing. He dropped his cigarette on the floor, grinding it beneath his toe, then without warning, he seized her suddenly in his arms and kissed her hard on the mouth. My God, she thought wildly, and tried to pull back, but his grip was like a vice. Damn fool. He would get them both caught.

But something else disturbed her far more than the fear of discovery. Ever since the death of her husband, Helene had lived a life of total celibacy. Now, unexpectedly, infuriatingly she was filled with a fierce sexual awareness. The tension of the night, Spengler's sudden appearance, the closeness of his body seemed to melt one into the other, transmuting into a cataclysm of longing and desire. She felt his hand groping beneath her jacket for her left breast. What on earth am I doing, she thought? Pulling herself together, she ground her heel hard on the top of Spengler's instep.

'Ouch!' he exclaimed, jumping back.

Without hesitation, she ducked into the passageway and, forgetting all sense of caution, scuttled back to her room without encountering another sentry. Slamming the door behind her, she stood for a moment with her eyes closed, breathing deeply. Close, she thought. Closer than she had realised. Spengler had touched something inside she'd thought already dead. She walked over and lay on the bed, staring at the ceiling. She was tired, she realised, very very tired, and the strain of pretending lay heavily on her shoulders.

But the memory of Spengler's closeness hung about her like an inescapable odour. She could still feel the pressure of his mouth, the hard persistence of his thighs against hers. It had been a long time, she thought, a very long time since any man had held her like that.

'Oh Karl,' she murmured, and breathing her husband's name brought him back to her, as real and as tangible as if he had just entered the room. Her fingers clutched the locket at her throat. It was a simple thing, a cheap little trinket which carried her own photograph inside, but it was the locket Karl had worn around his neck and she wore it now reverently, as a priest might display a sacred crucifix.

Dear Karl. Dear, beautiful, sensitive, utterly irresponsible Karl. His irresponsibility had bubbled out of him like cosmic fluid, and if she were truthful about it, it had been that irresponsible streak she'd loved most of all. If there was any one thing she regretted, it was that he'd had a mind of his own, he'd been a separate entity with thoughts, feelings, desires she could not understand, perhaps not even satisfy.

She realised now that Karl had been too artless ever to survive. He had hated Hitler with an all-consuming passion. He had frightened her sometimes when his friends had come to visit, sitting on the floor drinking schnapps while Karl, wild-eyed, wild-haired, suntanned and reckless, talked in an incessant stream, pouring out his fury with the simple intensity of a man who loved the feeling and the meaning of words. He said things other men would never dream of saying. It was madness of a type, of course, she realised that. Eventually, he even looked mad. She watched his transition over the months with mounting alarm. His skin grew tight as stretched rubber, as though it could scarcely wait to plunge from his cheekbones into the hollows on each side of his mouth. Sometimes when she looked at him, all she could see was his eyes, dazed and hungry, devouring her with their hunger. They darted like moths when he talked, and he talked endlessly, speaking about his beliefs as if they were living flesh and blood and he their lover, sometimes fond, sometimes jealous, always passionate. She began herself to think of them like that, as rivals, hating them with the unreasoning hatred she would normally have reserved for another woman. Only in the sweaty heat of sex was his obsession forgotten. That was her moment of triumph, when the hard lean body was clasped in her thighs, when the mouth on her ear whispered the meaningless things which belonged to an older and more vital passion than politics could ever inspire. But once it was over, as they lay breathless with hearts pounding, he would start again. Even the thrill of orgasm was merely a diversion.

'I need you,' he told her one night. 'You are my only grip on sanity.'

'You need me, but sometimes I wonder if you love me,' she answered sadly.

'Need *is* love,' he said. 'You love according to the intensity of your need. It transcends everything. It is deeper, purer and more lasting.'

In the end, she had joined the Nazi Party in a futile attempt to conceal Karl's activities from the eyes of the authorities. She immersed herself in every aspect of Party life with a zeal and passion that impressed even the most fanatical leaders. Seeing her as a valuable disciple, they tried in the beginning to warn her about her husband's indiscretions. She insisted his outbursts had nothing to do with politics at all, and were merely symptoms of a long-standing marital dispute. He was trying, she said, to hurt her, by attacking the thing he knew she deemed most important, the Party. It gained Karl a brief respite, but eventually his outbursts became too extreme to ignore, and she knew in her heart that even her reputation with the Nazis could not save him. She didn't cry when they took him away. She tried instead to concentrate her energies on the simple process of survival.

And now, a decade later, here she was still fighting Karl's fight, still risking her all for the cause he had died for. For Karl, she wondered? Was it really for Karl, or was it simply to anaesthetise herself? It was a dirty underhand trick, this love bit. It wasn't at all like the songs said it should be. She tried not to dwell upon the future. And to put from her mind any thought of that day she knew must eventually come, when the war would be over, and she would have to go back, inevitably, to pick up the shattered pieces of her life again.

Miserable and discouraged, she took off her clothes, switched off the light and climbed into bed in the dark.

Four

'Always remember when traversing on snow, keep your iceaxe on the slope above. If the snow is soft, hold the axe across the front of the body, one hand on its head ready to go into the "braking" position in the event of a fall.'

They stood in silence on the steep snow-slope, watching Henke's demonstration. Below, the snow dropped almost vertically to the lip of a sheer precipice, three or four hundred feet high. Over west, storm clouds hung like dark fluff above the distant valley, but here the sun was high and bright. It glinted on vast scree-slopes, great sweeps of rock and shale which curved from the very tips of the snowcapped peaks like immense bridal veils. Here and there, straggling strips of pine found their way up the folds like the outriders of some advancing army.

It was two days since Henke's pummelling of Richner, and neither Henke nor Richner had referred to it since. Richner's bruises had all but disappeared, and some of his old spirit was drifting back, helped no doubt by the fact that for forty-eight hours, Henke had left him largely alone.

Spengler stood with the others and watched as Henke carefully chopped a small platform out of the snow. 'Belaying on soft surfaces can sometimes be tricky,' he said, 'but if you use the indirect method, you'll find it the safest. First, cut out a small ledge to stand on, then drive your axe-shaft into the snow at waist level. Make sure it's slightly to one side of your stance where the surface hasn't been weakened by the cutting. Drive the shaft in at about 90 degrees. That way you'll be able to insert it as deeply as possible. Once you're satisfied it's secure, loop the climbing rope around the wood at snow level, and fasten yourself on.'

Spengler eased himself back against the snow. The sun was warm on his face, and he felt his concentration slipping. It seemed so pleasant to stand here on this steep slope peering down at the valley far below, at the friendly nearby peaks, at the foothills to the west, their brown flanks scarred by a hundred sparkling streams. He had dreaded his return to the mountains, seeing in it a nameless terror promising darkness and ultimate death. Yet it hadn't been like that at all. Not yet, at any rate. He was still untouched. Still whole. No qualmy feelings in the pit of the belly. No panic just around the corner. If only they stayed away from the higher summits, from the serious rock-and-ice work, he knew he would be all right. The glaciers, he could handle. The lower slopes instilled in him a strange solace. They were home, the only home he had ever known, the only peace he had ever known. It was here, in this indescribable land, where colours changed almost minute by minute, where the sunlight lingered lovingly over every contour, that he had found his only true identity. The war, and everything connected with it, seemed a million miles away. Except for Henke.

'In the event of a fall,' said Henke, 'extend the left leg, keeping the right bent and pressed against the slope. Grip the axe-head with the right fist, driving the blade into the ice as a brake and pressing down on the adze with the lower part of the chest so that maximum pressure can be brought to bear on the pick. With luck, this should bring you to a halt before any serious damage has been done. If you're left-handed of course, simply reverse the procedure. Now let's see if you've been paying attention.'

He straightened, smiling thinly. 'You, Richner,' he snapped.

Before anyone realised what was happening, Henke suddenly swung his iceaxe in a rapid arc, driving Richner's legs from under him. Richner, knocked clean off his stance, hit the slope with a squeal of alarm and began to skid dizzily earthwards in a great spray of churned-up snow and ice. Spengler felt his insides freeze. My God, he'll go over the edge, he thought. Richner was hurtling down the steep incline, clawing frenziedly at the crisp surface, his face grey with shock and terror. Below, the cliff loomed menacingly.

Henke was laughing out of sheer enjoyment. 'Get over

on your side, you fool. You're waddling down there like a bloated porpoise.'

Spengler felt himself gasping as he watched Richner's downward flight swiftly gather speed. He'll never make it, he thought, he'll never pull up in time. The empty void loomed fearfully below. Richner's feet kicked at the air and his arms flailed helplessly as a cascade of ice granules followed his frantic descent.

'Richner, stop clowning about,' Henke bellowed. 'Get that axe-blade in. Bend your leg, dammit, push your chest down on the adze.'

Somehow, Richner managed to roll on to his side. They saw him clutch his axe-shaft, bringing it across his body and driving its tip hard into the icy slope. He was fighting desperately as he slithered downwards, churning up the snow in wild billowing waves.

'Harder, you bloody idiot,' Henke yelled, 'harder.'

Spengler couldn't seem to think any more. He knew it was only a matter of seconds before Richner went over the rim. He was holding on to his iceaxe like a drowning man, the loosened snow swashing against his legs and hips. Spengler knew his arms must be aching in their sockets, his muscles screaming with strain, but somehow, bit by bit, his acceleration slowed, and as Spengler stood holding his breath, Richner slithered to a halt and lay peering up at them, eight feet from the brink, no more.

Henke laughed heartily. 'I thought we'd lost you there,' he called. 'A few more feet, Richner, and you'd have taken the quick route down.'

He turned, still chuckling. 'I always find there's nothing like a handy precipice to give a man the will to learn,' he said.

They stared at him in silence, their faces pale, their eyes expressionless. Spengler knew what they were thinking. It was like being in the company of a mad beast.

'I've got to get out of here, Erich,' Richner whispered that night in the dormitory. 'If I stay any longer, that bastard'll kill me.'

'Forget it Arno,' Spengler advised. 'You'd never make it to the village. And even if you did, where would you go?

If the partisans didn't get you, Henke would stretch your neck like a chicken.'

'Makes you wonder, doesn't it,' said Rolf Notz, 'about what happened to those other men, the ones who got killed? I'll bet Henke finished them off.'

'Beats me how he's managed to get away with it for so long,' Hüsser murmured.

'No one lives to tell the tale, that's how.'

'He'll kill me too if I don't get out of here,' Richner wailed.

'You could always get him first,' Notz suggested.

'How?'

'Wait till next Thursday when we do the Calania Tower. A nice little accident, no witnesses. Who'd know the difference?'

Spengler sat up sharply, leaning forward so he could see Rolf Notz's face. 'What did you say?' he demanded.

'Just a joke, Erich. Don't do something unpleasant in your underpants.'

'Not that. The bit about the Calania Tower.'

'We're going out to climb it if the weather holds.'

'Who says?'

'Henke. They've decided we've spent enough time on glaciers. Now they want to try us out on one of the classics.'

Spengler lay back on the bed, his heart beating quickly. Christ, he thought. He should have realised this was coming. It had to, sooner or later, any fool could have seen that. He'd been over-confident; a few scrambles around the lower peaks and he'd thought he could take it all in his stride. But the prospect of a major ascent – an ascent like the Eigerwand – not so terrifying, but an ascent nevertheless, brought back his guilt with an astonishing force.

Henke's bullying of Richner was forgotten. Fear rose through Spengler's body like an impending sickness. He could hear wild geese on the lake outside, their wings beating the water like the put-put-put-put of a high-powered speedboat, and he listened as a condemned man might listen on his last fatal night, hungrily, for any sound, sweet or discordant, which might give a sense of reality or hope. The fear inside him was not the familiar fear he felt in the mountains, which he understood and knew how to handle, but a slow insidious fear like that which in childhood comes in the night, strange, distorted, oddly shapeless, taunting him with terrifying imagery: Toni's vomit-stained lips, Toni's eyes in their snow-white mask, the frayed rope dancing mockingly in the wind. Oh God, he thought. He had lost his soul on those sombre walls, and he knew he could never be the same again.

Helene Rössner woke to the sound of someone pounding on her door. The room was in darkness, and for a moment she struggled to grasp the meaning of this strange intrusion, then the door swung open and Rolf Notz stood outlined against the corridor light. 'The dormitory, quickly,' he hissed, and turning, vanished along the passageway.

Helene Rössner shook her head to clear it. Flinging back the bedclothes, she tugged on her robe and began to run. When she reached the men's quarters, she saw a crowd grouped around one of the beds. They had the slightly cantankerous look of sleepers aroused unwillingly from rest. 'Who is it?' she demanded.

'It's Spengler, Frau Doktor,' Kurt Hüsser said. 'He's gone crazy.'

The men drew aside to let her through. Spengler lay stretched on his bunk, his body glistening with sweat. He looked dreadful. His pyjamas clung to his limbs like soggy blotting paper, and his eyes, staring at her from the haggard expanse of his face, seemed demented with fear.

'What happened?'

'He was shouting and fighting,' Hüsser said. 'We had to hold him down for his own good. He looks calm enough now, but he's burning up like an oven.'

She touched Spengler's cheek with her fingertips. She could feel his heat radiating through her nerve-ends. 'Bring him to the surgery, quickly,' she said.

They seized Spengler and hauled him from his bed, carrying him down the aisle with the air of men who had neither time nor patience for the niceties of life. At the surgery, Helene guided them through the narrow doorway. 'Sit him over here, away from the window,' she ordered. 'That's fine. Now, leave us alone please.'

Closing the door behind them, she opened the drug cabinet, and rummaging among the bottles, took out a box containing a hypodermic syringe. Swiftly, deftly, she began to assemble the various pieces, slipping the needle out of its sealed wrapper and fitting it to the narrow glass phial. Spengler watched her in silence. His eyes seemed suddenly sensible. 'What are you doing?' he demanded.

'Sssssssh, just relax,' she said.

'What is that stuff?'

'Something to help you sleep.'

'I'm not crazy,' he growled moodily.

'Who said you were? Overwrought, that's all. Roll up your sleeve.'

Spengler pushed her away. Despite his pallor, he looked grim and determined. She stared down at him, recalling how he had caught her in the corridor, pressed himself against her, kissed her lips. He'd looked cocky then, full of self-assurance. He looked far from cocky now.

'Look,' he said, 'I had a nightmare, that's all. I used to get them all the time before the war.'

'As bad as that?'

'Sometimes.'

He peered at her with a faint smile on his lips. It wasn't a humorous smile. His face, still glistening with sweat, looked haunted and sick. 'I spent two months in the army hospital at Koblenz,' he told her. 'Psychiatric ward.'

He said it almost triumphantly, as if it was a secret he could no longer bear to keep. She knew he was watching for her reaction. She forced herself to remain impassive. 'Is that on your file?' she asked.

He smiled grimly. 'You mean will I crack up when the pressure starts? Forget it, Frau Doktor. I've been through four campaigns and I haven't cracked yet.'

Helene dismantled the syringe, then cleaned the parts at the surgery sink and placed them back in their cardboard box.

'What causes them, these nightmares?' she asked.

'Cheese and pickles,' he said, 'last thing at night.'

'Don't joke.'

'Don't stick your nose into my business then.'

'That's my job. I *am* the doctor here. Didn't you talk to the doctors at Koblenz?'

Spengler twisted his lips wryly. 'Talk?' he echoed. 'Christ, yes.'

'Did it do any good?'

He stared at her. Some of the colour had returned to his cheeks, and he looked puzzled, as if he didn't understand her concern. Well, what did this man mean to her, she thought? He wasn't even a patient in the strictest sense. He was a German soldier, the enemy she had sworn to destroy. You're slipping, girl, she told herself. It's nothing more than the old biology bit ticking over. Don't lose your wits along with your head.

'The nightmares stopped, at any rate,' he admitted grudgingly.

'So it's not as stupid as it sounds.'

'It's just . . . I get sick of talking, that's all.'

'Think like that and you'll never be well,' she said. 'Psychiatry's not my strong point, but I often find talking can be a therapy in itself.'

He looked at her. 'But it's nearly one o'clock in the morning.'

'Sleep is often a luxury in my profession, Lieutenant.'

She took a brandy bottle from the cabinet, filled two glasses and pushed one into Spengler's hand.

'This is one of the privileges of being a physician,' she said. 'I keep it strictly for emergencies, of course.'

She finished her drink in a single gulp. Spengler looked impressed. 'You must have a cast-iron stomach, Frau Doktor.'

'Some people say I'm cast-iron all over,' she smiled, rinsing her glass at the sink.

Spengler sipped his brandy. He was coming round, she could see that. Slowly. Reluctantly. He seemed to be steeling himself, as if the prospect of exposure would be a sign of weakness. And yet, she knew he wanted to. He wanted to talk, to divulge, to confess. She waited. It was as if some inner force had instilled in her a new sense of awareness. When he began, he spoke haltingly at first, unsure of himself, uncertain of her reaction and even of his own willingness to continue, but as his words gathered momentum she felt his confidence grow, and soon it was pouring out of him like poison from an inner putrescence. As she listened, a languor seemed to settle over her limbs, as if his torment had become hers too, altering thought processes, changing behaviour patterns of a lifetime.

Spengler's story was a strange one. He had been just fourteen when his father died, the result of a lingering illness caused by injuries sustained at the Battle of the Marne in the First World War. Spengler senior had always dreamed of sending his only son to university, in the hope that an education would give young Erich the kind of start in life that would not be hamstrung by industrial unrest or physical disability, but with the old man's death, Spengler had had no alternative but to go to work in the Hamburg shipyards, a job he hated with an unfailing passion whilst recognising that in such un-settled times, any job at all was a godsend.

For escape, he turned to mountaineering, an activity to which he was introduced by a workmate who could have been a mountaineer of some distinction had he not found it necessary, like Spengler, to maintain a widowed mother and two young sisters. He taught Spengler the rudiments of the game, and Spengler took to it with the inherent grace of a natural climber. Never had he experienced such pleasure, or such a sense of permanent and peaceful aloneness, as that which climbing gave him. It was a complete contrast to the harrowing, scavenging, boot-in-the-groin world in which he made his living. Each weekend, and every holiday, he took the train to the mountains and devoted himself to the only pursuit he had ever been good at. Within three years he was an acknowledged expert on rock and ice, and by the time he was twenty-five his name was appearing with gratifying frequency in the Austrian mountaineering magazines, and even the city sports writers had begun to recognise in the young man from the Hamburg shipyards, a climber of exceptional quality.

When Spengler was twenty-seven, he joined the army, the 100th Mountain Ranger Regiment stationed in Bad Reichenhall. In those early days of Hitler's Chancellory, young men from all over the country were taking to the peaks in a wave of patriotic fervour, attempting new and hazardous ascents for the glory of the Fatherland. The most coveted prize of all was the North Face of the Eiger, six thousand feet of concave ice and limestone, a cliff swept continually by rockfalls and avalanches and considered by some of the greatest experts in the field to be naturally unclimbable.

Spengler had seen it for the first time in the summer of 1934. He had been standing on the summit of the Tschuggen just as day was fading. Across the valley, the Eiger had reared like a primeval beast, stark and bare, its buttresses split and fractured in a million years of wind and weather. Sunlight had played along its east and west ridges, tinting the snow a pastel pink, but over the great concave cliff had hung a menacing curtain of shadow. It had perched like a sentinel above the alpine pastures, and Spengler knew that every storm which swept across Europe hurled itself against that mountain like the hammer of God. Looking at the Face, Spengler had felt his genitals move in an involuntary spasm, and had known deep in his heart that more than anything else in the world he wanted to climb it. It was a need to transcend the ordinary, to strive for something beyond attainment, to reach what seemed to his impressionable brain the peak of fulfilment.

In the spring of 1936, on leave from Bad Reichenhall, he again went to Switzerland, and though it was too early in the year for serious high altitude work, he sat for hours on the Alpiglen pastures, studying the Eiger's Face at close hand. The great raw wall looked ominous. There was plenty of fresh snow high up, and the walls were streaming with moisture. It would be a tough one, he calculated, as with pencil and paper he drew a rough outline of the mountain, and with infinite care marked in the main features, the probable difficulties and a possible ascent route. When he returned to barracks, he showed his sketches to his two closest friends, both of

75

them devoted mountaineers, Toni Kurz and Anderl Hinterstoisser. For days on end, he held them spellbound with stories of the Eiger's Wall until he had instilled in each the same unreasoning passion for conquering the unconquerable which inspired himself.

When July came and the regiment took its summer leave, the three young men decided to tackle the Eigerwand once and for all. Since Spengler had promised to visit his mother in Hamburg, it was arranged that Kurz and Hinterstoisser would make their way to Switzerland and set up camp in the high meadows above Alpiglen where they could study the route for a few days until Spengler was able to join them for the actual assault.

Spengler arrived at Interlaken on 16 July, but by then something had happened, something he could not easily explain, not even to himself. Later, he was to reflect on that fateful moment of his life a thousand times, wondering vainly what mutinous seed of fate could have altered his psyche, opening the door to misery and disaster. The truth was, he'd become afraid. The mountain that had filled him with fire and excitement, now filled him only with dread. He recalled old friends who had died on the peaks, lurid rumours of horrifying accidents. He remembered Max Schumann from the shipyards, the man who had taught Spengler everything he knew, all the tricks of the trade, and had then fallen on a miserable twenty-foot practice slab in the Dolomites and burst his skull open like an egg on the rocks below. Spengler had been in Bad Reichenhall when the news had come through and, not able to believe it, had travelled through the night and arrived at Cortina just in time for the funeral. There had been people in the crowd he'd recognised, and people he had not known but had read about: Helmut Wollen, Enrico Julian, Heini Riedl – men who lived to climb and climbed to live – and in their eyes he'd seen no look of regret, nor of sadness even. There'd been instead a kind of universal acceptance as a man might feel on a battlefield when friends are killed. In the little cemetery, the first snowflakes of winter had begun to fall, and Spengler had watched the pallbearers in their canvas anoraks, the snowflakes whirling sadly around them, and had gone off because he could stand it no longer, to spread his sleeping bag under the bridge in the keen snowfilled air.

When Spengler remembered Max his blood ran cold. The Eigerwand was madness, he thought. Only a lunatic would risk his neck on those icebound walls. Why not call it off? There was still time. He could take the train up to Alpiglen and tell Toni and Anderl he had changed his mind. He could tell them anything he liked, that he was scared even. He knew they wouldn't laugh. But he couldn't. He just couldn't.

For a few days he kicked his heels around the backstreets of the little Swiss town, and by the time he'd recovered his nerve sufficiently to take the train up to the plateau, Kurz and Hinterstoisser had joined forces with two young Austrians, Edi Rainer and Willi Angerer, and had begun the climb without him. The atmosphere at the little hotel complex was electric. There were people all over the place, huge throngs of tourists queueing like ghouls at the coin-operated telescopes. The day was Monday, 20 July, and the party had already been on the Face for three days and two nights. According to spectators Spengler spoke to, they had started magnificently, moving with precision and speed up the lower and middle sections and reaching a point closer to the summit than any party had managed before them, but for some reason – nobody quite understood why – they were now in full retreat, struggling desperately downwards over the complex jig-saw of fractured rock and hanging icefields. Spengler felt a sense of deep foreboding. It seemed to his irrational mind that the misgivings he had experienced had been an omen of sorts, an alarm bell that only he had chosen to acknowledge. The realisation saddled him with an awesome responsibility. At the very least he should have warned them, he should have tried to dissuade his friends from such obvious folly.

For hours, he followed their progress through his field glasses as they moved steadily downwards, picking a treacherous route from the Second Icefield to the First. Here, they prepared for their third night on the mountain. Spengler knew that each successive bivouac must be sapping the climbers' strength, and his sense of apprehension grew stronger. He waited until he was certain they were bedded down, then made his way to the steep alpine pastures and put up his tiny tent.

That night, he woke unaccountably. It was nothing to get concerned about, he told himself – a ripple in the wind, a snatch of cloud drifting in from the east, a sudden drop in temperature. But for some reason, he felt uneasy. The air smelled different.

He peered at his watch. Two o'clock. I'm getting to be an old woman, he thought, and went back to sleep.

At two-thirty, he woke again. The cloud was coming in fast and the breeze lifting noticeably. A pitiless sky to be under. He knew the signs, he had seen them often enough before, in happier places. The weather could change, but it would not, he knew that. There was a pattern to such things, as in life, and you accepted it without question otherwise you became a maiden aunt looking under the beds in fear and hope. The weather had been perfect all month. Why should it change now? Once more, he went back to sleep.

At three forty-five he woke again. The sky was blotted out completely. Flurries of snowflakes filled the air. Mist swirled around his face. A freak squall, he told himself, it will pass. Nevertheless, he did not sleep again.

The wind whipped up with the speed of an express train, and by four-fifteen it was lashing the rock above with hurricane force. There would be an explanation of course; high pressure areas, low pressure areas, polar air streams. It would be double dutch to him anyhow. It was no freak squall, he knew that now. The weather had changed. His friends' luck had run out.

By the time he reached the plateau on the morning of Tuesday, 21 July, the entire Face was wreathed in a blanket of mist. There was nothing to see, nothing to do but wait, wait and pray, while the wind rose, and the rain churned the Kleine Scheidegg plateau into a quagmire of slippery mud and clay. The spectators left the telescopes and crowded into the shelter of the hotel bars. Here, they listened to the roar of avalanches drifting through the fog like distant thunder. Perhaps they were dead already,

Spengler told himself. But he could not bear to think about that. His legs went rubbery when he thought about that, or when he thought about them being up there, actually up there on that miserable mountain. Once, during a gap in the cloud, he spotted the climbers through his field glasses as they attempted to traverse a slab of smooth rock leading from the First Icefield. They'd clearly negotiated it on the way up, but had made the mistake of retrieving their rope, and now the slab had iced over, shutting off their solitary escape route. Spengler felt his mouth turn dry. It was pitiful to watch Anderl struggling to get across. He chipped at the glistening verglas with his ice-hammer, but again and again was forced to retreat. At last, overcome by exhaustion, the party began sorting out the ropes for an apparent abseil. Spengler realised what was in their minds. Seven hundred feet below, the Jungfrau railway burrowed for four-and-a-half miles behind the Eiger Wall to the summit of the adjacent Jungfraujoch. During the railway's construction, the engineers had drilled out on to the cliff itself to dispose of rubble and dust. Spengler knew that if the climbers could reach the gallery window, they would be able to escape into the safety of the tunnel.

He was scarcely able to contain himself. Everything he'd said in the past few weeks, all the blandishments, persuasions and sly subtle references seemed suddenly luminous in his memory, and he knew that if he wanted to preserve his own peace of mind, then whatever happened, they had to survive that abseil. The mist drifted back, blotting out the Face entirely, and Spengler stood fuming on the storm-tossed plateau, his mind in an uproar. An hour passed. Another. There was no word, no news, nothing to give him hope in the dowsing drowsing downpour. It was impossible to see the mountain in the fog and rain – only last year's bracken which glistened and crackled underfoot, shiny dead stalks to taunt him through the drip-dreary afternoon. Restless and ill-at-ease, he sat in one of the bars drinking beer, peering through the window at the nearby river which looked fat and bloated from its forced feeding, like a great pale slug.

Even the trees seemed to drip mournfully like lost souls in an expressionist nightmare.

At three o'clock, the telephone rang. A few minutes later, the hotel manager entered the bar and called for attention. His face was pale. The tourists stared at him expectantly.

'There's been an accident,' he announced, and a gasp went around the crowded room.

'The news isn't clear yet, but they've almost certainly fallen.'

Spengler felt his stomach contract. He braced himself against his chair, caught in a moment of calm that seemed distorted and terrifyingly fragile. The story was fragmented but bloodchilling. Anderl Hinterstoisser was dead. He'd dropped all the way to the screes below. Edi Rainer had been pulled up against a snaplink and had frozen to death. Willi Angerer had been strangled by the rope. Only Toni Kurz remained alive. The section guard at the gallery window had heard him shouting. He was dangling helplessly from the mountain face, trapped.

The next few hours remained confused in Spengler's memory. He remembered making his way to Eigergletscher Station, where the tiny platform was milling with people. Policemen and railway officials struggled to prevent the crowds swarming over the rails. They had laid on a special train to carry a rescue team as far as the gallery window. Three guides from the village of Wengen had volunteered to venture on to the storm-bound North Face. Spengler managed to elbow his way through the throng, and by luck one of the guides remembered him from a climb they'd done together some years earlier. Spengler persuaded them to take him along. Against the imminence of his friend's death, he forgot his fear of the Eigerwand as the train carried them up the steep mountain tunnel and stopped at the gallery entrance. As they ventured out on to the sheer rock wall, the wind hit them like an artillery barrage. Spengler had never experienced a gale of such coldness and ferocity. There was mist everywhere, swirling into their faces, curling around their legs. They could scarcely see each other in the fading light. A flash of lightning split the air, then another. They heard the thunder almost simultaneously. It seemed to rip the sky apart above their heads. They watched streaks of electricity ripping into the cliff above and below where they stood. Fierce contours of rock were thrown into violent relief, scarlet, black and yellow.

Weakly, they began to climb, using the flashes to pick their way. They caught glimpses of the valley below, and of the line of hills far to their right. But the mist, and the few square feet on which they moved, seemed their entire world for an immeasurable time.

Hail filled the air, shooting down the cliff in a frenzied deluge, spattering their skulls like machine-gun fire. They were stopped in their tracks by the sheer incredible force of it. It ripped into their faces, cascaded from their shoulders in wild abandon. For some time they hung motionless, hammered to a standstill by the storm's fury, but then, slowly and stubbornly, they began to move doggedly upwards.

Spengler never understood how they managed to make that ascent, but somehow, whether by luck or judgement, they reached a point about three hundred feet below where Toni was hanging. They could hear his voice quite clearly, even above the howl of the wind. Spengler cupped his hands to his mouth and shouted his name. He thought if Toni knew there were friends below it might give him hope, some added shred of strength. But by then the light was fading and each of them knew that if they remained where they were they stood a good chance of dying.

'There's not a damn thing we can do for him today,' one of the guides said. 'He'll just have to stick it out for one more night.'

Spengler knew he would never forget the sound of Toni's voice calling through the blizzard as they left him hanging there and headed back for the safety of the tunnel. They had to fight every inch of the way, fight for breath, fight for balance, until, when they reached the opening and finally eased their stunned and punished bodies to a halt, it was with a sense of both surprise and wonder that they realised they were still alive.

That night, the sky seemed to come down and wrap itself around the earth. The temperature dropped to sub-zero levels, and the wind pounded the Eiger's Face with the relentless implacability of a battering ram. Spengler slept little. For hour after hour, he sat smoking cigarettes, listening to the storm outside and thinking about Toni. He had to be dead by now, Spengler felt. No human being could have endured such conditions. He'd been practically dead when they'd left him. It was beyond credibility that he could have survived the night.

At dawn, they set off again, Spengler having resigned himself to the fact that they were on their way to recover a corpse. This time they managed to get within a hundred and thirty feet before being halted by an ice-glazed bulge. Spengler shouted up, and incredibly Toni answered. Against all odds, he'd managed to hang on to the flimsy tatters of existence. His left arm had frozen into a useless stump, and icicles dangled from all parts of his body, but by some miracle he was both alive and conscious. They tried sending up a rock attached to rockets. With a rope, they hoped he could let himself down to their position. But the rockets fell short, and finally they could think of only one alternative.

They called to Toni to cut himself loose with his iceaxe, then to ease down to Willi Angerer's body and cut him loose too. Then, by uncoiling the frozen strands of hemp and tying them all together, he could lower a line to which they could attach a fresh rope and equipment. It seemed a chance in a million. Even for a man with his strength intact, what they were suggesting was unthinkable. Toni had just spent four nights on the Face in the most appalling conditions, and his left arm was virtually useless. Nevertheless, somehow he did it. It took him five long painful hours, but slowly and systematically he managed to cut the rope and unwind the strands with his one good hand and his teeth. By the time he had finished, they knew he was close to the limits of his endurance. He let down the line and they tied on pitons, a hammer and a new rope. Realising one rope wouldn't be long enough for the descent, they tied on another. He hauled them up, and with the storm still raging, anchored the rope to the cliff

82

and began to inch his way down. They watched his progress, shouting encouragement. Spengler felt a paralysing fatigue drift through his limbs, a mindless misery that made no sense and followed no rational pattern. He could see Toni's legs just above the bulge. Another few feet and they'd have him. By reaching up, Spengler could almost touch the icicles on Toni's crampons, and yet the sense of foreboding persisted, swelling inside him like a terrible longing that had to be assuaged.

Suddenly, Toni's descent stopped. The knot tying the two ropes together had jammed in the snaplink at his waist. Spengler swore. 'You've got to force it through,' he said. 'You're almost down, for Christ's sake. Try.'

Toni tried. His hands were useless. He tugged at the knot with his teeth. Spengler waited, holding his breath. To have come so far, to have suffered so much, and now, only inches from rescue, to be halted by such an idiotic thing seemed the cruellest of ironies.

There was no specific moment when he realised Toni wasn't going to make it; more, it was a realisation that had been with him from the beginning, a portent of disaster that had grown stronger and more compelling as time went on, so that now, facing the culmination of his friend's ordeal, Spengler seemed to be stumbling into wakefulness from a deep and troubled sleep. For a few minutes Toni struggled with the knot, then suddenly he tipped forward, swaying in the wind above their heads like some mad pendulum. After hours of unspeakable punishment, his poor heart had given out. Dangling only a few feet from safety, Toni Kurz was dead.

Something changed in Spengler when he returned to Bad Reichenhall. It was nothing he could put a name to, nothing physical like a twisted shoulder or a crippled hip, but deep down, something basic, something terribly essential was out of place. He was living in a distorted world, or at least, if the world was as sound and acceptable as he had every good reason to believe it must be, then he was looking at it from a distorted viewpoint. He had heard of experiments where the entire psychological make-up of human beings could be changed by passing an electric charge through the brain. What had happened on the Face seemed like that – a point in time and space where he had somehow got out of alignment like a warped penny which no longer fitted into its accepted slot. In the first place, he had wanted to die. He had wanted to die because it seemed illogical that he should still be alive when the others were dead, and because he did not like to think about the others being dead when he, Erich Spengler, who had talked them into actually doing the thing, was not. And in the second, he had the awful conviction that something *had* died up there, some integral and indefinable part of himself, leaving him not truly a man any more but a piece of organic matter which went through the processes of being alive with the unfeeling consistency of a well-oiled machine.

He went over the events of those four fateful days, but no matter how he tried to rationalise them away, somehow the responsibility settled firmly and unshakably upon his own shoulders. He began to suffer fits of depression. Sometimes they lasted for days without cause or reason. Often too, especially at night, he would be filled with a nameless brain-numbing fear. He could not say what it was he was afraid of, yet it was so real, so intense that he would lie for hours, rigid with terror, while sweat bathed his skin and his limbs shook convulsively.

The nightmares started some weeks later. They were only spasmodic at first, but they followed a similar theme, and that was what made them frightening. He would dream he was back on the Face, wrapped in a subaqua-like world of drifting mist. There was always someone else along; he never knew who it was, but in some odd way, the stranger and the nameless waking fear were bound together.

He asked for a transfer to a panzer division and swore never to climb again. During the day, he found himself living almost permanently in the past. His recollections of people, places and events were almost uncannily clear. He could remember the smallest details with unerring accuracy. The disturbing thing was, the past seemed much more real, much more lucid than the present. As time went on, he began to change. He lost interest in his appearance. He turned out on parade in uniforms which looked as if they had been slept in. He talked to himself in strange places. He began stealing things, nothing important, just small things – a teacup from the mess, a paperweight from the Quartermaster's office. But worst of all, he seemed to lose all conception of time. He would disappear for days on end and return to camp with no idea of where he had been. In the end, the army transferred him to the military hospital at Koblenz. In the weeks which followed, Spengler felt his discontent begin to fade, so that his sense of futility, the complete emptiness of the world around him lost its importance. He moped his way through life sustained by the one thing which remained truly constant during that odd fantasy-touched period, his memories of the Eiger. And at last, emotionally bruised and utterly bewildered, he emerged from the gloom into a kind of fragile normality.

Helene Rössner listened in silence. She had been standing in the same position for some considerable time before she realised Spengler had finished speaking. Now he was staring at the window, peering into the darkness beyond.

Waiting.

She took a deep breath. 'You were lucky to come out of it alive,' she whispered.

'Lucky, yes.'

'I meant the Eiger. In that weather, you could have finished up like Toni Kurz.'

'I know. Christ!'

Helene shook herself. Spengler's story had affected her more than she could say. He had told it so graphically, and with such an outpouring of emotion that merely by closing her eyes she could see the Eigerwand, wisps of mist curled about its rock like regal lace. It excited her to see it, no heavenly vision could have stirred her more. 'I used to dream about the Eiger,' she murmured. 'We all did, in the old days. To Karl, it was the ultimate, the peak of mountaineering achievement.'

Spengler did not answer. He was still sitting exactly as before.

Still waiting.

The expression on his face made her heart melt. She chose her words with care.

'The brain is a curious instrument, Lieutenant. I'm no psychologist, but even the so-called experts know very little about the way it works. They grope about in the dark, letting in a little light here, easing a little pressure there, but few of them delude themselves that they know what they're doing. You talked your friends into tackling a climb which you yourself shrank from. Result: the friends died, and you remained – at least physically – intact. Even the most insensitive man would feel some self-reproach after an experience like that. But if you believe that by giving up climbing you can somehow make amends, purge yourself of blame, then not only are you mistaken, but no amount of therapy in the world can help you. You've got to climb again, can't you see?'

She felt the Face was the crux of Spengler's problem, the crux, and therefore the solution. It seemed the most obvious answer of all as well as the simplest. If he could climb again, she reasoned, his life might go back to normal. If one mountain had scarred him, then another might just as easily make him whole.

'Don't you think I've already considered that?' he grunted. 'Christ, a thousand times.'

'Well, then?'

'I can't. Don't you understand? I just can't.'

'But you've been climbing all week.'

'Simple stuff. Strictly for beginners.'

She paused as the truth suddenly dawned on her.

'The Calania Tower,' she breathed. 'That's what's worrying you.'

He nodded.

'But a climb like that could give you a chance to find yourself again.'

'Or finish me off altogether.'

She thought for a moment. Words wouldn't do it, she realised. She had to give him a boost, something he could get a grip on. She had to give him something to hate.

'You must pull yourself together,' she said, 'it's not only your peace of mind that's at stake. There's Henke to consider.'

He looked puzzled. 'Henke?'

'You know he's a psychopath? Look at what he's doing to Richner.'

He frowned at her. 'What the hell has Henke to do with this?'

'Somebody's got to bring him into line. And you're the only one capable of it.'

'Me? You're the doctor. If it's your medical opinion that Henke's a psychopath, why don't you report the bastard?'

'I've already tried. They told me politely to keep my nose out of SS business. This mission is too important for last minute changes. Henke stays until it's completed. However, he may seem heartless and untouchable on the outside, but he does have one weakness. His vanity. Prick that, and you'd soon see him crumble.'

He stared at her, forgetting his anger for a moment, seeing only her brown eyes and full lips, and the way she wore her hair coiled on top of her head in a loose disorderly mass that threatened to come undone at any second.

'What are you talking about?' he whispered.

'If you want to beat Henke, you've got to humiliate him. It's the only thing he understands. At the moment, his conceit is beyond belief, but destroy the reasons for that conceit and indirectly you'll destroy Henke.'

Spengler frowned again. He had the feeling he was being manipulated. 'Go on,' he said.

'Do you think you're capable of beating Henke to the summit of the Calania Tower?'

'You mean . . . a race?'

'Why not? Nothing in the world would finish him more effectively. Think about it, Spengler. If you can overcome your idiotic sense of guilt, you have the power to put Henke in his place once and for all.'

Spengler didn't answer. He looked like a man who had just been faced with a blinding truth.

Watching him, Helene smiled to herself. It had been a piece of inspirational genius, she realised. Henke was the one thing strong enough to jolt Spengler out of his morbid guilt-ridden fear.

87

'I haven't attempted a serious climb in eight years,' he whispered.

'I didn't say it would be easy.'

'You're crazy. I couldn't do it.'

'You have no choice. There's nobody else good enough.'

'Hüsser.'

'Against Henke? He wouldn't stand a chance.'

'Gotsch.'

'Gotsch is too old.'

Silence. Spengler licked his lips. 'Frau Doktor, will you give me another glass of brandy?'

She studied him shrewdly. She hadn't convinced him yet, not quite. But she would. She'd stake her last penny on that. All it needed was a little gentle persuasion. She had to choose her words with care. Above all, she mustn't rush things.

Strange, almost forgotten emotions rose again inside her. She had never, by nature, been the flirtatious type. After Karl's death, she'd lost interest in her body's reactions. Now, for the second time that week, she felt the stirrings of returning life.

Keeping her face impassive, she walked to the medicine cabinet, opened it and took out the brandy.

'Lieutenant,' she said, giving him her most winning smile, 'why don't you just sit right there while we finish the whole damned bottle?'

Five

Spengler woke early, coming out of sleep like a man in a state of semi-coma. A soft breeze lifted the tent roof, making it flap and billow. For a moment, he could not remember where he was, then his brain cleared and his memory swivelled into focus. The Calania Tower. Today was the big day. Last night, they had driven through steep mountain passes to the shores of Lake Pavano, making camp on the pastures above a line of high river bluffs. If the weather held, they hoped to reach the summit by late afternoon and return to the training school that evening. Spengler was tense with excitement. This would be his first serious ascent in eight years. Did he still have the dexterity, the flair? More important, was he still good enough to lick Henke? He had set his heart on that. A duel. A personal vendetta. His phobias had been forgotten. The prospect of demeaning Henke in front of the entire class was so exhilarating it made Spengler's limbs feel weak. She'd done that. Dr Rössner. She'd achieved something the doctors at Koblenz had never been able to. She'd taken away his fear, given him something to live for.

Spengler's experiences with women in the past had been perfunctory and transient, caused largely by the demands of being a soldier in peace and war. He had whored with a passion which had never, he had to admit, transcended the level of the physical or pecuniary. Now, he was finding to his surprise that Helene Rössner was establishing a new extension of himself, an extension he had never dreamed existed.

He heard people moving about outside, the clanking of ironmongery. Struggling into his clothes, he crawled out of the tent, feeling the grass dew-wet on his hands and knees. Around the campsite, men were busily sorting out equipment. It was still dark and the trees looked grey and still. He took a deep breath, shivering in the cold. 'What time is it?' he asked Kurt Hüsser.

'Four o'clock, I think.'

'Jesus.'

A chill silence hung over the land. Spengler shook his head to clear it. 'Christ, it's freezing. What's our altitude at this point?'

'I don't know. Five or six thousand feet, I reckon. Stick around, this cold'll go through you like a dose of salts.'

'Look at Henke,' Rolf Notz growled, 'he's like a dog hauling at its chain.'

They peered across the glade to where Henke knelt packing his rucksack. His movements were swift and eager, as if he could scarcely constrain himself. Spengler felt a momentary surge of doubt. Henke looked so fit, so full of vitality that the thought of beating him seemed absurd. But what worried Spengler most was the realisation that just beating him might not even be enough. To make the lesson stick, Henke needed a proper antagonist, one who had suffered at his hands, one who'd be able to turn the tables dramatically and squash that haughty arrogance once and for all. It had to be Richner. Only Richner could produce the kind of debasement Henke deserved. Richner was an experienced climber, but could he ignore his inherent fear of heights?

Spengler picked his way over to where Richner sat coiling the ropes. 'How d'you feel?' he asked.

'Like a brass monkey,' said Richner.

'Scared?'

'Not so I can't manage. Henke gets me on edge, that's all. I can climb as well as any man, when I have to.'

'Want to team up with me?' Spengler asked. 'We'd make a good rope.'

Richner looked surprised. 'You mean you don't mind dragging a bundle of firewood?'

'That's just it, Arno, I do.'

Richner frowned, peering at him shrewdly. Something in Spengler's voice alerted his senses. 'What's on your mind, Erich?' he whispered.

'I want you to climb like you've never climbed before. Forget your nerves for just this one day.'

'Why?'

Spengler hesitated. 'I'm going to beat that bastard to a standstill,' he said.

Richner's eyes widened. 'Beat Henke?'

'Or die trying. But it's got to be the two of us, Arno. It's the one thing in the world that can make Henke squirm. Think you can do it?'

Richner considered quickly. In the darkness, doubt, apprehension, excitement flashed across his eyes. He wants to, Spengler thought. As long as he wants to, that's half the battle. Motive. Resolution. Guts come later.

Richner moistened his lips. 'Could you lead on the difficult bits?'

'I'll lead on the whole lot if you'll stick behind me.'

Richner gave a sigh. 'To beat Henke,' he whispered, 'I'd crawl all the way to hell.'

Spengler grinned. He knew Arno would be all right up there. There'd be no jitters, no heebie-jeebies. He'd go till he dropped.

'Then you're on,' he said.

Richner's face glowed like a pale turnip in the darkness.

'Let's get this stuff sorted out,' he whispered excitedly.

They went to work laying out their equipment, ropes, slings, crampons, pitons, iceaxes, down jackets and emergency bivvy sacks.

'I thought we'd carry the iron rations,' Spengler said. 'They'll be a lot lighter, and if we turn this into a race we'll need to keep the weight down as much as we can.'

'What about liquid?'

'We won't need it. There'll be plenty of water on the mountain, and we can always melt snow if we have to.'

The cold was an emasculating scalpel, it took away initiative. Spengler felt hollowed-out inside, like an athlete who, on the day of the big race, feels unaccountably stale.

When they had finished sorting out the gear, Richner produced a bottle of schnapps. 'Feel like a drink before we go? For luck?'

'Where the hell did you get that stuff?' Spengler asked with surprise.

'From one of the guards. I had to pay three times the

market price, but it was worth it. Got a packet of cigarettes too.'

They opened the bottle and drank surreptitiously. It tasted foul in the early morning.

'Here's to success,' said Spengler.

'To Henke's downfall.'

'I'll drink to that all right.'

Spengler heard a step on the ground behind him and turned to see Helene Rössner. She was dressed in climbing breeches and a heavy close-weave anorak. Her hair was tied tightly into a coil at the nape of her neck, and in the darkness her eyes glowed amid pools of shadow. 'Good luck, Erich,' she said.

Spengler looked at her. 'Thank you,' he answered softly. 'You too.'

Henke yelled at them across the campsite. 'Stop talking, and hurry up, for Christ's sake. We're wasting valuable climbing time.'

Spengler fastened his rucksack straps and stood up. Time to go. He felt very small, a small man in a huge land. This is it, he thought.

He watched the others unload the canoes from the trucks and glide off across the darkness of the lake. Turning, he looked back at the camp. A faint wind ruffled the tents, making the flaps flutter. For the first time since waking, he felt a shiver of excitement. His head was beginning to clear. He spat to get the bitter schnapps taste from his mouth, then he helped Richner load the last canoe with rucksacks, slings and ropes, and pushed off from the tiny beach, squinting into the darkness for the others.

A faint mist rose above the surface of the water. Everything was hushed and still. The sky was an enormous arched ceiling, studded with lights. Mountains huddled close like hunched giants. He watched Richner's outline in the darkness. Richner looked tense and restless, as if the excitement inside him was growing too strong to control. Spengler hoped he hadn't made a mistake in bringing Arno into this. It promised to be tough enough, without having to act as nursemaid. Stop worrying about Arno, he thought grimly, start worrying about yourself. Pray you've still got what it takes up there.

He heard the soft sploosh-sploosh of paddleblades and steered the canoe in their direction. He saw the twin outlines of Rolf Notz and Kurt Hüsser drifting through the mist, and steered expertly, flicking his paddle to keep the bow on an even keel. The clay bank loomed out of the night. They pulled up the canoes and began to unload the equipment. No one talked. In the chill pre-dawn air, there was only the clanking of snaplinks and the laboured breathing of the little band of mountaineers.

At last they were ready. 'Let's go,' said Henke.

They set off up the trail, moving Indian-like in single file, and Spengler listened with satisfaction to the chomp-chomp of their boots on the frozen earth. He was feeling better now, and warmer too, and as they climbed higher sweat broke out on his face and ran in tiny rivulets down his cheeks. The woods closed in, dark and sombre. Among the undergrowth there was a continual scurry of sound, of movement, of squeals and rustlings and branches crackling. He stopped once and looked back. The lake lay far below, a broad patch of mist among the trees. Over east, he could see the first streak of dawn above the mountain peaks.

The world was an ephemeral vision without contours or depth. There were only outlines, pink, black, grey, a mirage in which they climbed in silence with only the sound of their boots and their breathing to remind him it was really happening.

The land and its secrets, hiding its face like an April virgin. He was an intruder in the hushed realms of holiness, which he knew and understood and would not try to make better. Helen Rössner knew that. 'Good luck,' she'd said, because it was the conventional thing to say, but what she'd meant was 'go out and climb it', for it was a devil to be exorcised and she understood it probably as much as he did.

Helene Rössner, he thought. She was like a secret obsession, haunting him continually. Forget Helene Rössner. Concentrate on the job in hand. Henke. The mountain. Nothing else.

They went on up, climbing steadily, starting to talk now, and Spengler felt good, forgot his fears from the past, felt the sweat run between his shoulderblades in that icy pre-dawn morning and felt sunnily and gloriously happy. They crossed a stream where the water ran pearl-grey over white stones and climbed on, leaving the woods behind and skirting broad pastures strewn with boulders. Buttercups grew everywhere, yarrow and wild roses. Once, they stopped to rest at a wild strawberry patch. Arno knelt down, gathering the tiny berries into his palm and eating them by the mouthful. Spengler tried two or three, but their syrupy sweetness clashed with the metallic schnapps taste in his mouth and he spat them out.

'What I like about this country, Erich,' Richner said, 'is that you never see a soul on the tops. Not like Switzerland, which is really a kind of fairyland, with chalets every-where, and cowbells and peasants. You know, when we climbed the Wetterhorn, we could see the lights of Grindelwald at night, and hear people talking, actually hear their voices right up on the mountain. But up here you never see a damned soul.'

Spengler laughed. 'You were born about four thousand years too late, Arno. You belong in a cave.'

'Right. I've been in this war too long, I'm losing my sense of perspective. This is the only reality there is, Erich. Guns and uniforms, that's not reality, that's horseshit.'

He sucked hard at the air, catching his breath. 'Do you think this war will ever end?' he asked suddenly.

'Christ knows.'

'They say Hitler's dead.'

Spengler looked at him sharply. 'Who says?'

'The guard who sold me the cigarettes.'

Spengler twisted his face in derision. 'Rumours.'

'Sounds like the real thing, this time. Somebody blew him up at Rastenburg.'

Spengler wiped his sweaty cheeks. 'What difference will it make to us? They'll just stick somebody else in his place. Other faces, other people.'

Richner nodded grimly. 'People contaminate every-thing they touch,' he said. 'They never leave things alone. They have to build something up, knock something down. I mean, did you ever see the statue, or park, or painting that could beat this lot?'

Spengler looked around. 'I never saw anything that could beat this lot,' he said.

They went on talking in this way, climbing steadily, until in the first thin light of day, they reached the foot of the great cliff. Spengler's body tingled with excitement. 'Doesn't look too bad,' he said.

Arno Richner was silent. He was staring upwards, breathing heavily, no expression on his face. 'That's because we're at the bottom looking up,' he said. 'It's easy here, but another hundred feet can make all the difference.'

They stood in a group among the moraine, their breath leaving clouds of vapour on the chill mountain air. Henke called them together.

'This is it,' he said, 'the Calania Tower, the southern section of the Monte Calania massif, one of the great Alpine classics. The route is direct and clearly defined all the way to the top. It was put up by the British in 1902, and since then it's been used as a training climb by mountaineers from all over the world. The trickier sections have been well-pegged so they should offer little trouble. Once on the summit, it's an easy flog down the north flank to the river where the trucks will be waiting to transport us home. The summit stands at eight thousand feet, with about two thousand feet of actual climbing rock. There are two small icefields, both with an inclination of fifty-five degrees. Most of it's a scramble, with a few dodgy pitches higher up. However, make sure you keep to the right of those buttresses or you'll find yourselves meandering through a series of jutting roofs. We'll move two to a rope, Tauer and I leading. To avoid over-crowding, the ropes will set off at half-hourly intervals. We'll begin climbing now, the next team will follow in exactly thirty minutes. Watch out for new snow lying on old, and don't forget we're approaching midsummer, so if the weather stays fine, keep a sharp eye out for avalanches. Good luck, everybody.'

They stood watching as Henke led off, climbing free up the first easy stages.

'Who's next in line?' Kurt Hüsser asked, glancing at his watch.

'What's the hurry?' Notz shrugged, 'Nobody wants to climb behind Henke.'

'We will,' Spengler said, 'Arno and me.'

Hüsser glanced at the others, then back at Spengler.

'What are you up to, Erich?'

Spengler smiled at Arno and winked mysteriously. 'Wait and see,' he said.

They gobbled down a quick breakfast, which was not much, Spengler reflected, but enough for men about to start a strenuous climb: sardines, bread, and a little cold coffee (their last liquid that day bar water or melted snow, unless of course they got the chance later to boil up some cocoa on the mini-stove) and having finished, he and Arno roped up and started off, Spengler leading, Richner bringing up the rear.

The first part of the route followed the belly of a narrow couloir, ending eventually below several hundred feet of granite slabs. The grade wasn't steep, but the holds were all sloping and covered with loose stones and rubble which fell and clattered as they moved skyward. The rock was ice-cold in the chill dawn and Spengler had to massage his fingers to get the circulation going, but the sun was coming up fast and he knew that within an hour it would get too hot for comfort. His head had cleared completely, but he was climbing in fits and starts, stopping regularly to catch his breath and look out over the country which glowed with a pinkish sheen under the lifting sun. Have to do better than this if we're to lick that bastard, he thought. I'm a bit out of practice, but I'll get into my stride eventually.

There were streams below, cutting through the forest like silken thread, and as they climbed higher, more valleys came into view, some with lakes in them, and it was funny how different the country looked from up high. This was the same country they had driven through yesterday, and yet it looked different now in the early morning, and he kept stopping and looking back as if he was seeing it all, mountains, forest, lakes and rivers, for the very first time. He tried not to look up. There was a great immensity up there. The rock, the sky, where did it lead? A trail of ether, an Indian rope-trick into oblivion.

But there was always an enjoyment to be got from looking down, providing you did not do it with too much imagination. Imagination was the ever-ready enemy. Panic was just around the corner. The thrill was a precarious one, like riding a tiger, he supposed, lots of fun if it did not get away with you.

The couloir ended and they found themselves at the rocky slabs, but they kept moving upwards at a steady pace, picking their way with care up the steeper sections, and to Spengler's relief there were always plenty of good holds to choose from; it was, he reflected, a climber's dream, a virtual staircase really, completely safe, but with a good sense of exposure and superb country below to make it seem worthwhile. He thought jubilantly: if it stays as easy as this, we'll overtake Henke by lunchtime.

The sun grew hotter, warming his back, and he noted approvingly that Richner was climbing almost immediately behind. On these lower, easier levels, the angle was too elementary to waste time 'leapfrogging', climbing pitches individually; instead, they scrambled up together, sending stones scattering with a noise like distant thunder. There were snatches of pine below, and great waterfalls dropping sixty, seventy, sometimes a hundred feet, and in the distance, the snowcapped peaks of far mountains glowed like distorted lightbulbs.

Only once, when they paused to rest, did Spengler feel his old uncertainty returning. Peering up at the cliff, he remembered Toni Kurz and his whole body began to tremble. He looked at the rock and noticed the tips of a few rusty pitons tracing an uneven line towards the summit. It was like the exposure of a strange and shameful secret. He should be here alone, without Arno.

'Are you okay?' Richner asked suddenly.

'Sure.'

'You look ghastly.'

'Just a bit out of breath, that's all.'

Spengler shook himself. This was no time for memories. There was nothing to think of now but the job in hand, that awesome expanse up there which somehow must be scaled. It was his private battle, his intimate war, and if Arno must be there to witness it, then be there he must. But he owed it to Arno and to himself to blot out his brain, to think of nothing but that tiny point of ice and snow which was some unimaginable height above them, the summit.

They moved higher, working their way up a smooth buttress, ascending into a snatch of cloud which formed a swirling blanket around their legs, sometimes gliding below their feet like a wispy platform, sometimes opening up to afford generous views of the valley. Then soon the sky turned blue, and the cloud drifted from sight, and the peaks seemed lit by an unnatural light as if the entire range was about to burst into an unforgettable volcanic eruption.

As the route steepened, Spengler was conscious of an insane need to sprint as hard as he could, but he forced himself to climb the difficult pitches alone, bringing up Richner on a tight rope. He knew Henke couldn't be far ahead. We're coming, you bastard, he thought grimly, we're coming up behind you, and when we've finished rubbing your nose in the dirt, you'll never bully anyone again.

High on the cliff, Henke groped ahead for cracks and crannies, shifting his weight to straddle a groove or scale a buttress, scarcely pausing between one move and the next. Below, Tauer struggled breathlessly to keep up. They were roped together, but Henke did not stop to belay, for at this stage the route was a climb of no significance really, practically a scramble if you had the heart and lungs for it, with nothing to do except drag steadily on. Nevertheless, he was pleased it was no harder, or he had a hunch he might be doing it alone, without Tauer, the pace he was setting.

The morning sun grew pale, and clouds crept in almost imperceptibly from the west, but they were not storm clouds, and Henke was grateful to them for shutting off the sun, for muffling the hammer on the anvil on which they climbed.

He felt a sudden emptiness in his stomach. Time for breakfast, he thought, and lowered himself against a ledge. An eagle hung in the air, motionless, not far off but far enough to have lost its majesty, for it was below him and he watched it with the superiority of one who had been born for high places.

Tauer scrambled up to join him, his pale face shiny with sweat. 'Why are we stopping?' he asked.

'Food.'

'Thank God. I'm starving.'

His tongue snaked out, moistening his lips. He dug into his rucksack, took out some cheese and a chunk of rough bread, and began to munch thoughtfully. 'They're coming up that cliff at a rate of knots.'

Henke frowned. It had never occurred to him to look below. The possibility of being overtaken had seemed unthinkable.

'Who?' he demanded, feeling for the first time a pang of uneasiness.

'Spengler and Richner.'

'Richner?' he exploded. 'That's impossible.'

Tauer finished his cheese and licked his fingers. 'It's Richner all right,' he said archly, 'I'd recognise him anywhere.'

'That useless tub of lard?'

'He's not so useless today.'

'He couldn't . . .'

'Look for yourself.'

'Jesus Christ,' Henke breathed, as he saw Tauer was telling the truth.

'Think we can stay ahead?'

Henke glowered like a man who had been gravely insulted.

'Nothing in the world can alter that,' he said.

They moved on when they had finished breakfast, climbing more slowly as the grade steepened up, taking their time now, scaling pitches individually, fixing belays, bringing each other up on the rope until, just before ten o'clock, Henke spotted, to his surprise and consternation, the bright green anoraks of Spengler and Richner moving below them. My God, he thought, they must have come up that couloir like greased lightning.

He peered above. A series of long perpendicular grooves loomed as far as he could see.

'They're gaining, Henke,' Tauer called.

'Don't worry. They're still on the easy bit. They'll have to slow down when they reach here.'

'We'd better get a shove on though.'

'Take it easy. We're still ahead, remember.'

From time to time as they climbed, Henke saw silver flashes on distant mountainsides where the sun momentarily caught some isolated waterfall or cascading river. The sun moved steadily, or seemed to, for light and shade played tricks across the valley, and the shadows deepened until they lost their density and seemed to hang there, dark and flat and textureless.

After an hour, Henke paused to look down again, and the sight of the green anoraks below, roped together, climbing almost jauntily, brought a cold sweat to his throat and spine. They seemed tireless, moving without a break, even on stretches Henke would never have touched without a runner. A vague fear stirred inside his chest. What if they caught him up? He would never live it down.

'They're going to overtake us, Henke,' Tauer shouted.

Was the bastard deliberately trying to provoke him?

'Keep your mind on the pitch ahead,' Henke bellowed.

He scurried on, jamming his fingers into the crack inside the groove, bridging his legs across the gap and inching skywards as the sun grew hotter, threatening to pound him into submission. There was nothing to do but climb, not think, or feel, or hesitate, but move, move, move, shuffle, shuffle, shuffle, fight his way upwards in the stupefying sun. He used pegs sparingly because Tauer, coming second, had the job of retrieving them, and he knew it was always easier to hammer pegs in than to pull them out.

Another hour passed. Henke paused, sweating profusely, and looked earthwards. His heart sank. It wasn't possible, it just wasn't possible. No one could climb that fast. The green anoraks bobbed beneath him like a mocking challenge. Although they had been climbing nonstop for some time now, they seemed, Henke thought, incapable of fatigue, and in his heart he felt the first chilling possibility of defeat, the realisation that no matter how hard he tried, he could never match the performance of those supermen below.

He found a stance on a smooth ledge, selected a peg from the rack at his waist, tapped the sliver of metal into a handy fissure, then tied on and watched Tauer climb up to join him, eyes pale with strain and fatigue.

'Okay?' he asked.

Tauer managed a smile. 'Bit puffed,' he answered bravely.

He fastened himself to the piton. 'They're like a couple of mountain goats down there,' he said. 'Nothing slows them down.'

Henke rubbed his stubbled chin. His sense of helplessness deepened. 'I can understand Spengler,' he murmured. 'He was always a wizard on rock, but Richner . . . it just doesn't make sense.'

He looked at Tauer suddenly. 'Think you can manage without lunch?' he asked.

Tauer was surprised. 'Why?'

'Well, it would save us twenty minutes or so.'

Tauer thought for a moment, then nodded. 'Very well, Henke,' he said, 'if you think it's important, let's push on.'

One p.m. Henke's imagination was running haywire. They weren't human, he said to himself, they weren't real. Sooner or later, they *had* to stop, to slow down, to rest, to eat, to breathe. They *had* to.

He picked his way carefully up the steeply sloping icefield, cutting steps with his iceaxe, digging in the blade for support as he edged higher, feeling minute and unimportant, a flea-prick on the side of the earth. The sun beat down so fiercely it took Henke's breath away. He was thankful for the ice, which left a pool of blessed coolness six feet above its surface.

At the icefield's upper rim, he fixed a belay and brought Tauer slowly up on the rope. Tauer was ashen-faced and his eyes looked bleak and empty.

'I've got to stop,' he gasped, 'I can't keep this pace up.'

'Lean against the rock,' Henke ordered. 'I'll tie you on.'

He drove in a piton, looped a sling around it, and

clipped it into Tauer's carabineer. Tauer's lids were closed, his cheeks dull and lifeless.

'I've had it, Henke,' he whispered.

Henke felt a surge of panic. Tauer couldn't quit now, not now, with those bastards practically crawling at their heels.

'You'll be okay,' he said hastily.

Tauer shook his head. 'What's the use? They'll overtake us in an hour.'

Henke felt his reason snap. 'Shut up, you gutless bastard,' he yelled.

Tauer's lids opened. There was a strange triumph in his eyes. 'What's the matter, Henke?' he said. 'Have you finally realised you're just a human being like the rest of us, that you're not God Almighty, after all?'

Henke frowned, wanting to escape Tauer's disdain. Slipping off his rucksack, he unclipped the spirit flask from the side pocket and took off its top. 'Drink this,' he grunted. 'Take it slowly or your guts will bunch up.'

He couldn't stop his eyes from straying below. He could see them moving up the icefield with maddening ease, their anoraks glistening against the snow, the rope spun between them like a silken thread.

Tauer was watching him with a wry smile. 'You're going to lose, Henke,' he said goadingly. 'There's not a damn thing you can do. They're too fast, too good. You need a miracle.'

Henke watched the advancing figures with a dull throbbing hate, feeling desperation swell inside him, robbing him of logic, robbing him of control, and suddenly, in that instant, he knew what he had to do.

'I wouldn't say that,' he exclaimed hoarsely, 'I wouldn't say that at all.'

Untying himself from the rock he slithered downwards, using the seat of his breeches as an adhesive, testing with his crampons for a solid stance at the icefield summit. Tauer watched him, frowning, the gleam in his eyes replaced by a look of sudden concern. 'What are you up to, Henke?' he called.

'Sit still,' Henke bellowed. 'I'll be back in a minute.'

He found a ledge where a thin sliver of moraine zigzagged beneath the ice itself. He could see the climbers clearly now, Spengler and Richner, he could see the bright blobs of their canvas smocks, the grey bulges of their army-issue haversacks. He could see too their breath clouds on the thin frozen air, and hear, or imagined he could hear, the crump-crump of their crampons on the crusty ice surface.

He fumbled among the moraine and selected a stone the size of a small turnip. Balancing himself with his spine against the rock, Henke took careful aim.

'Henke,' Tauer screamed, 'what the hell are you doing?'

Henke let the rock go. It sailed through the air in a graceful arc, hit the ice and went whistling down through a feathery shower of spray. Spengler and Richner stopped dead, peering upwards in disbelief. He could see their mouths working, see their eyes bright with alarm. The rock zoomed towards them, swishing like the flight of a homing arrow. Spengler leaned out from the ice, his body swaying. The rock missed him by a fraction of an inch. He regained his balance and drove his iceaxe shaft into the snow for support. Henke laughed out loud and seized another stone.

'Henke,' Tauer shouted. 'For God's sake, do you want to kill them?'

'Stop worrying, I know what I'm doing.'

Spengler and Richner unslung their rucksacks and clutched them above their heads for protection. Henke hurled a second salvo, then a third and fourth. The boulders jumped and whistled and bounced. How do you like that, you bastards, he thought gleefully?

At last, inch by painful inch, Spengler and Richner began to withdraw. Henke picked up a final rock and sent it skimming downwards. He was filled with a curious peace, as if the exertion had brought with it a strange and satisfying tranquillity. He hugged the wall, feeling its harshness against his skin.

Tauer watched him with sickly disbelief. 'My God, you're crazy,' he whispered. 'That was the craziest thing I've ever seen.'

Henke lifted his right foot to a crack, let it take his

weight, searched with his right hand, found a jughold and inched upwards, his blood pounding. When he reached the point where Tauer lay belayed, he jammed his hand into a fissure and looked at him with a glare of irritation. 'Did you expect me to shake their hands as they passed us by?' he exclaimed. 'For Christ's sake, we're losing time. Get untied, let's move on.'

Spengler's body was shaking all over. That damned fool, Henke. He'd nearly finished the two of them. Those rocks had been perilously close. An inch either way and they'd have been plunging helplessly through thin air. He felt almost sick with the thought of it. Clearly, they couldn't carry on in Henke's wake any longer. For safety's sake, they would have to detour, and that meant leaving the acknowledged route and breaking fresh ground, picking their way through a series of jutting overhangs which looked from below almost unclimbable. Nevertheless, he was filled with a burning sense of determination. Now, more than anything else in the world, he knew he had to beat Henke.

Just before two o'clock, they reached their first major obstacle, a narrow crack topped by an ugly overhang.

'We'll need both ropes,' Richner said, screwing up his eyes.

'Possibly not,' Spengler murmured. 'Fix a belay, I'll go up and have a look.'

Richner stood at the base of the crack, playing out the rope as Spengler led off. Richner watched him climb with admiration. Look at the bastard go, he thought. Spengler moved cleanly and easily until he reached the overhang, then he stopped. He crouched under the bulge and felt around. A soft wind ruffled his hair.

'What's it like?' Arno called from below.

'Not bad. A bit strenuous.'

Spengler was groping around on the rock, his body twisting as he strove for balance. Richner wet his lips. 'Don't lean out too far,' he warned.

'It's okay. There's a good solid crack here. You can jam your fist in it.'

Spengler began to attack the roof, bending his spine,

thrusting his body away from the cliff as he edged tentatively outwards. Thrusting a hand inside the crack, he turned it sideways and clenched his fist, wedging it hard between the tight walls. Then Richner, watching below, felt his heart leap as Spengler swung himself into space, legs whirling in thin air, his entire body dangling from one wrist. Gasping with exertion, Spengler reached with his free hand up and over the lip.

'There's a jug above the rim,' he call

He groped upwards, the rope jerking and twitching inside the crack like an angry snake. Dust and small stones came clattering down the cliff. Richner saw the studded soles of Spengler's boots clogged with dirt, the padded seat of his climbing breeches swaying madly from side to side as he struggled for a hold, and then with a heave he was up, wriggling like a caterpillar over the hard smooth rock.

Richner took a deep breath. Now it was his turn. His shirt was soaked with sweat. Damn Henke.

'Come on,' Spengler yelled, 'It's a piece of cake.'

He took up the sacks on the rope, and Richner followed. He climbed slowly and with great care, shutting off emotion and imagination with an effort. Spengler played him like a fish on a line, keeping the rope not too taut, not too slack, taking care it did not catch in any fissures. Arno could sense Spengler's impatience through the pull on the line. Well, let him wait. He would not be hurried, Henke or no Henke.

He shuddered as he recalled how close those rocks had come. Only a lunatic would have pulled a stunt like that, he thought. The slightest error of judgement and he and Erich would have gone crashing to the valley floor. He made his mind go cold with an effort. He was on the rope now and could not fall if Erich was belayed well, but there was still his stubborn streak of pride. He filled his brain with thoughts to shut it up. Philosophy was the answer, the ever-ready antidote for fear. You could always get philosophical on a mountain. The peaks, the sky, the snow, they were a poetry in themselves, the most effective getaway kick Richner knew. What more consuming pastime could you pick than this – what it amounted to, when you came right down to it, was a kind of Russian roulette with fresh air.

He paused once to catch his breath. His heart was thumping. We're gaining altitude, he thought. He moved on, trying to recall from memory the route Erich had followed. He wished he could see his face. It was frighteningly lonely below the overhang.

He reached the bulge and crouched quite still, gathering his strength. He felt dangerously sick. Waves of nausea swept his body. He controlled himself with an effort. Biting his lip, he leaned up, thrust his hand into the crack and swung himself free as Spengler had done. Where the hell is that jughold? If I come off now I will look a complete and utter idiot, rope or no rope. He was filled with a sickening sensation of dangling dizzily in space. He saw the sky, piercingly blue, and the sun like a shimmering ball stinging his eyes. He swallowed wildly. Hold tight, he thought, fighting down a surge of blind panic. Now reach up. Almost had it. A few more inches. Ah.

Wriggling and scrabbling, he heaved himself up to the overhang roof. Sprawled on a narrow ledge smoking a cigarette, Richner felt blessed waters of relief flood through his veins. On a pitch like that, a man could live a hundred years in the space of a few seconds. But he felt good now, stretched out in the sun, relaxed, sucking the life-giving death-dealing nicotine into his lungs. 'How are we doing?' he asked.

'Not bad at all.'

'We can't keep it up, though. I mean, we can't beat Henke by this route. It's overhanging all the way.'

'Right,' said Spengler. 'We'll have to try and detour back. We should be able to traverse via the upper icefield. With luck, we'll come out above him.'

'Not much chance of that,' Richner murmured.

'Oh, I don't know,' Spengler said. 'Tauer was looking a bit drained. Henke's pushing him too hard.'

'Think he meant to kill us?'

'No,' said Spengler, 'but he damn well could have. He wanted to scare us, that was all.'

Arno Richner pulled a face. 'He succeeded in that all right.'

After a short rest, they set off up a gigantic wall caked with ice. Spengler picked his way cautiously up the glossy surface, stopping in places to chip away ice with his ice-hammer, and bit by bit, using piton after piton, he scaled the pitch and brought Arno up. At the top, breathless, sweaty, muscles wobbling from strain and effort, they strapped on crampons and began the traverse across the upper icefield. Strange noises like distant thunder echoed beyond the snow. Falling rocks, Spengler thought. He forced himself not to listen to their sound, to concentrate instead on the rough uneven contours of the ice-surface, which had looked from the valley as smooth as the frosting on a Christmas cake.

Crossing that icefield took a man's breath away, made him gasp for air like a salmon out of water. There was no talking now, it was too tough to talk in the gentle chill which hung like a vapour above the ice.

Within an hour, he spotted a line of rusty pitons on the rocks above, and realised they were back on the original ascent route. He could see no sign of Henke. He signalled to Richner, jerking upwards with his thumb, and Richner, seeing the pegs, waved to show that he understood.

All afternoon they climbed on steadily, moving like insects up the massive complex of cracks and buttresses, and as they got higher, their progress slowed. Once, Spengler came off while he was leading on a precarious groove, and Arno, scooping in as much slack as he could, watched the dark figure zoom over his head, hit the ice and go skidding downwards. Then the rope zipped taut across his shoulders, and twenty feet below Spengler came slithering to a halt in a great spray of snow and climbed back, swearing madly but completely unhurt.

In the late afternoon they found themselves at the foot of a sheer waterfall with no way around it but straight up, and had to climb the slippery rock while the icy water poured over their heads and into their clothes. When they stopped for breath they were soaked to the skin, but they realised with a sense of wild excitement that they had reached the ice-packed summit ridge. They could see the peak above them like the blunt nose of a torpedo warhead. A cry burst from Spengler's throat. 'We've done it,' he yelled. 'Come on, Arno.'

He began to move, swinging his iceaxe, chopping out steps in the crusty surface. His eyes fastened on the pinnacle with an almost demented joy. This time, nothing could stop them.

Clouds were running thick and strong towards the east, and Spengler eyed them shrewdly. Snow perhaps later, he thought, but not to worry; nothing to worry on now – the summit was nigh, and a friendly flank to come down on.

He screwed up his face and stared at the mountain peak hungrily, as if he needed to know every contour, every snowflake, every nuance of light and shade with the deepest intimacy. It was not a disappointment. Though wide as a dance-floor, it gave a surprising and satisfying sense of exposure.

They dropped their rucksacks and peered around. Far below, they could see the familiar half-moon shape of Lake Pavano and the steep river bluffs where they had pitched their tents, but on the moonlike world of the mountaintop there was nothing, only the snow, scoured by the wind, polished smooth by the sun, but untrodden for months by any human foot except their own. Spengler looked at its surface, scarcely able to believe their luck. He turned to Arno, smiling, filled with a sense of savage triumph.

'We've done it,' he whispered fiercely, 'we've beaten Henke.'

Fog swirled around the summit, turning the little pinnacle of ice and snow into a wavering spectre that danced and twisted beneath their feet. They changed out of their wet clothing, peeling off the soggy garments and tugging on dry breeches and heavy sweaters as a protection against the evening chill. Spengler stamped around, looking for a good way down; on the north flank, the ground dropped in a steep snowbank, falling almost vertically for a thousand feet or more to rough scree and the first patches of straggling pine forest – a perfect descent route. But neither of them intended to miss the sight of Henke's face when he came up the final section of the summit ridge and found them waiting. He'd know by now, of course, Spengler realised. He'd have seen their steps in the snow. But that wouldn't detract from their enjoyment at the moment of confrontation.

Arno Richner's face glistened with sweat in spite of the cold. 'I don't fancy going down much,' he admitted. 'I'm whacked.'

Spengler smiled. 'You look a bit done in,' he said, 'but you've climbed magnificently today. I never realised you could move so well.'

'Luck,' Richner murmured, 'and the thought of licking Henke. I still can't believe we've done it.'

'We must have overtaken him on the detour,' Spengler said. 'Tauer would slow him down. He looked pretty tired above the couloir.'

He opened his pack and thrust some food into Richner's hand.

'Chew this,' he ordered.

'What is it?'

'Cheese.'

'I'd be sick.'

'Get it down. Do you good.'

Richner fumbled in his anorak and tugged out his crumpled packet of cigarettes. 'Want a fag?' he asked. 'Only three left.'

Spengler shook his head. 'Better not let Henke see you with those.'

'Oh, he's miles back,' Richner said as he lit up, inhaling luxuriously. 'You know something?' he murmured. 'I can't feel my feet any more.'

'Stamp around in the snow,' Spengler ordered. 'Don't want frostbite at this late stage.'

'What I'd really like is a bowl of hot chilli,' said Arno. 'Have you ever been in Mexico, Erich?'

'No.'

'Now there's a country. I spent three years out there, for the firm I used to work for. You think of Mexico and you think of dusty little towns and peasants sleeping in the sun. But it's different in the cities, another world, you'd never believe it. Acapulco. There's a town makes Monte Carlo look like a rest home. And the food. It takes a bit of getting used to, but once you do it's something you never forget.'

Spengler heard the sound of boots on snow and gave Richner a warning glance. Richner quickly nipped the cigarette, slipping it away inside his anorak pocket.

It was Henke. He reared out of the mist like a strange beast. He had taken off the rope for the last haul up the summit ridge, leaving Tauer to follow on behind alone, and his eyes bulged with anger and disbelief. Spengler felt a sense of savage joy as he studied the emotions flitting across Henke's sweaty face, dismay, amazement, fury. Now you know what it's like, you bastard, he thought. It was the moment he had waited for, the confirmation of triumph and defeat, and he savoured Henke's distress with a fierce satisfaction.

Henke stood motionless in the fog, his gaze, glittering with hate, flitting from Spengler to Richner and back again. Then suddenly, another thought seemed to enter his mind. He frowned, sniffing the air. 'Who's been smoking?' he demanded.

Neither of them answered, but Richner, in an instinctive gesture for which Spengler could have choked him, placed one hand over the bulge in his anorak pocket. Henke's eyes narrowed.

'Richner, what are you hiding in there?'

'Nothing.'

'Get it out.'

Reluctantly, Richner produced the crumpled cigarette packet. Henke snatched it from his hand with a cry of triumph. 'Where'd this come from? You know smoking's against the rules.'

'What's the matter, Henke?' Richner snapped. 'Have we put your nose out of joint? Have you suddenly realised that when the others learn what's happened up here, you won't be able to strut and preen any more, you'll just have to resign yourself to being mortal like the rest of us. How does it feel, Henke?'

Henke's nostrils flared. Spengler, watching, realised he was in the throes of a fury too powerful to control.

Without a word, he hit Richner between the eyes. He did it so quickly that for a moment Spengler simply blinked. Arno slammed into the snow, blood streaming from his nose. He peered up through eyes glistening with surprise and pain. 'You bastard,' he hissed.

Henke was smiling now. 'I'm going to teach you a lesson you'll never forget, Richner,' he said, drawing back his foot to kick Arno in the mouth.

Afterwards, Spengler was never able to say with any certainty whether his action was impulsive or pre-meditated. More, it was the culmination of events which had grown too extreme to bear, the sudden breaking point after a period of intense tension. As Henke's leg lifted, Spengler hooked his boot over the instructor's instep and sent him sprawling face-down in the snow. Henke rolled over, his eyes bright with surprise. And then, as he peered up at Spengler, he began to smile. It was not a pleasant smile. He climbed to his feet, carefully dusting himself down.

'I wondered how long it would take, Spengler,' he said. 'I've been looking forward to this for a long time.'

His smile broadened, and the look in his eyes made Spengler's stomach crawl. His own anger had stopped. It was not gone, merely delayed, as if he had reached a point where time hung suspended and where, for a few memorable seconds, he could be ultimately and totally himself, with fibres and nerve-ends, passions and desires – the ugly, the secret, the sad, the contemptible – all exposed in one glorious moment.

Henke inched forward in a crouch, balancing his weight delicately on the balls of his feet, circling half to the right in a cautious catlike way as if trying to put Richner between them. His hands were raised, not defensively, but ready for the attack.

Spengler stood where he was, arms at his sides. He knew he was going to win, knew it instinctively and inexplicably. He hung back, cool and controlled, waiting for the moment he felt certain would come. The mist curled around Henke's pale cheeks, lighting the eyes so that their gleam seemed colder, more pronounced, tracing the thin line of his mouth and the evenly-spaced teeth. A tiny pulse in Spengler's throat had begun to throb. It was no fun to fight at this breathless altitude after a hard day's climbing, but if Henke wanted it, he was ready. He waited until Henke was almost within reaching distance, then, turning on his left foot, he thrust his free leg backwards with all his strength. He felt Henke's knee fold beneath his boot, and with a cry of agony the instructor staggered madly backwards over the snow, clutching the injured bone. Pain and fury blazed in his eyes. He rubbed his knee instinctively and, insane with anger, darted in fast, too fast, feinting to the left to try for a body blow. Spengler danced back and caught him with a tight jab in the stomach. The wide mouth flinched, the small eyes moistened with anguish. Henke was rattled, Spengler could see that. Spengler slipped forward, landed a sharp blow on the temple, and while the great head shook itself bewilderedly, he smashed his fist on the side of the jaw in a classic right hook. Miraculously, it seemed, Henke's body hit the ice with a resounding crash.

Without waiting for him to rise, Spengler leapt in and went to work with both feet, the memory of Henke's baiting of Arno imbuing him with a ruthlessness he had not realised he possessed. He lashed out like a demon, kicking and stomping as hard as he could, and from the corner of his vision he saw Arno watching, pale-faced and trembling, his clenched knuckles showing white through the skin.

Henke wriggled and twisted, but Spengler followed him ruthlessly, taking his time now, choosing his targets with the same cool deliberation Henke had displayed with Richner. He was just putting the finishing touches to his assault when Tauer appeared panting through the mist. For a moment, he stared at the scene in amazement, then stepping forward he grasped Spengler by the sleeve and pulled him gently away.

Arno knelt down and examined Henke carefully, raising the closed eyelids and feeling his pulse. He looked up and grinned, an expression of admiration and wonder on his face. 'I think we can safely claim,' he said, 'that we beat the bastard to a bloody standstill.'

PART TWO

The Mission

Six

On 19 July 1944, two travellers flew by special transport plane from Stockholm to Switzerland. One was tall and heavy-shouldered, the other medium-sized and slender, with hair receding above the temples. The names on their passports said 'Logan' and 'Dunninghan', Irish businessmen, but in reality they were Colonel Robert Simpson and Colonel Paul Olsen of the 'Alsos Mission', the US intelligence unit responsible for undercover work associated with atomic warfare.

After visiting the American Legation in Berne and talking for over an hour to Allen Dulles (officially Special Assistant to the Minister, unofficially head of the American Secret Service in Switzerland) the two men took a taxi across town and called on Ernst Wegmüller, head of Swiss Intelligence, at his home in Berne's Viktoriaplatz. Wegmüller lived in a pleasant penthouse apartment guarded by tough-looking plainclothesmen who studied Simpson and Olsen through a spyhole in the door before allowing them in. Wegmüller himself was a pale-skinned man of forty-eight with a pair of moist grey eyes which conveyed the impression that he was moody and introspective, and that he rarely listened to what was said. This impression was false however, for Wegmüller missed little of what went on around him, though for security reasons he cultivated the façade of the absent-minded intellectual. In reality he was a seasoned professional, sharp as chipped ice.

He had met the two Americans a number of times before, and knew they would not be here unless they carried news of a both urgent and significant nature. He invited them into his private office, waited until his bodyguard had withdrawn, then poured three generous measures of Scotch and sat back peering at his visitors expectantly.

'Bad news,' Colonel Simpson said, 'The shit has finally

hit the fan. Two weeks ago, one of our agents in France, a woman doctor operating under the codename "Sunflower" informed us she'd been recruited by the Gestapo for a military mission of the "highest strategic importance". Those were the exact words she used, coded of course. When she failed to contact us again, we assumed her situation was making regular broadcasts impractical, so we decided to see if, by using the data already on file we could work out what her mission might be. There was very little to go on. Then someone remembered a curious fact about "Sunflower". She's a diabetes specialist. Not only that, but before the war she was an experienced high-Alpine mountaineer. Put those together, Wegmüller, and like us you may reach a disturbing conclusion.'

Wegmüller stared at him in silence. Through the open window, the sound of traffic hung heavily on the warm summer air. House martins wheeled and dipped above the rooftops. Beyond the city rose a line of snowcapped peaks, and further off, more peaks, much higher, so far away Colonel Simpson could see no more than their ragged outline like the ramparts of some fantastic fortress.

'Is this definite?' Wegmüller asked.

'As definite as we can be at this stage. You have to admit it's a hell of a coincidence.'

'Then you must withdraw at once.'

Simpson sighed. 'I wish it was that simple, believe me. We can't withdraw at this crucial stage. There's too much at stake here.'

'If the Germans discover what you are doing, they could reverse the course of the whole war.'

'We know. Goddamnit, Wegmüller, believe me, we know, but we can't let panic cloud our judgement. Whatever happens, you must allow us to remain until we can finish what we've started. The alternative doesn't bear thinking about.'

Wegmüller turned his chair so he could look out of the window. The sky was blue and cloudless, tinged in the west with a soft pastel hue.

'We are a neutral country, Colonel Simpson. If the Germans attack, it would put us in a most difficult position. We could of course make a formal complaint to Berlin, but then we would have to explain our own involvement.'

'You could profess ignorance.'

'You think Hitler would believe it?'

'If you're worried about our paper-hanging friend in Berlin, I think you'll find he has his hands more than amply full at the moment. We intend to win this war, Wegmüller.'

'I have no doubt you will win,' Wegmüller said mildly, 'but you've missed my point. Above all else, the legend of Swiss neutrality must be preserved. We are not like the United States, gentlemen, we do not have unlimited natural resources. Our only strength lies in our stability. We sell it as other countries sell grain or engineering parts. We use it to bargain with. It is our one form of international currency.'

'Meaning what, sir?'

'Meaning that nations all over the world invest in our banks because they believe us to be immune from the kind of political upheaval which uproots other societies. We cannot allow that belief to be shaken, even in the most minor way. Our economy depends upon our neutrality.'

'Goddamnit, Wegmüller, you have a responsibility.'

Wegmüller lifted his eyebrows. 'To whom, Colonel?'

'The minute you agreed to let us in there, you automatically became responsible. For our welfare and protection.'

'Are you seriously suggesting the Swiss army should move in to protect an American military contingent?'

'No, sir. We aim to do that ourselves. All we ask is your okay.'

'I see.'

Wegmüller's face was calm, his eyes bland and inscrutable. Music reached them from the next room. Someone had turned on a radio. The noise sent vibrations along the carpeted floor.

'We're already playing a very dangerous game, Colonel Simpson.'

'It'll be a damned sight more dangerous – for

Switzerland, and the rest of the world – if you turn us out now.'

Wegmüller sat back, finishing his drink in one swift gulp. His face looked hard and assured, belying the uncertainty he felt inside. 'We might be prepared to authorise the entry of a US military force on one condition,' he said.

Simpson smiled grimly. 'I know. Swiss neutrality must be preserved.'

Wegmüller did not return the smile. He stared at Simpson for a long moment, as if trying to impress on him the seriousness of his request. 'For always, Colonel,' he said. 'You understand? Not just for the duration of the war, but for eternity. It may seem comical to you, but our livelihood depends on it.'

Simpson wiped the grin from his face. 'If that's the way you people want it,' he said, 'sounds okay to me. We'll make secrecy our top priority.'

Wegmüller sat back in his chair. In the next room, the radio switched to a ragtime tune. 'I will put this to my government,' Wegmüller said. 'You will please come back this evening, and I shall let you know their answer.'

Twelve hours later, on the mountainous island of Sicily, Major Lewis D. Shellburn of the Third US Army was summoned to the office of General Mark Gillman. Shellburn was a stocky man of less than average height, but powerfully built. His hands were large, his shoulders heavy. He looked at first glance like a farmer or lumberjack, but he had been in civilian life a civil engineer. Major Shellburn commanded a group of skilled mountain troops known as Unit D. They had been formed for special operations involving a high degree of mountaineering skill, and since the invasion of Sicily, Shellburn and his men had been training on the high granite cliffs and jagged peaks which towered above the shimmering Mediterranean. So far however, to their universal disgust, Unit D had been used solely as foot soldiers. Now, Major Shellburn stood in surprised silence as General Gillman outlined the orders which had just reached him. Fifty minutes later, supplies were loaded on to heavy US transport planes, and by nine o'clock that night, less than thirty hours after Simpson and Olsen's visit to Berne, Operation Sunflower was under way.

At the little railway station of Kleine Scheidegg in Switzerland's Bernese Oberland, Willi Fredier, German intelligence agent, watched curiously as a rack-and-pinion traction engine with four trailer cars was wheeled out of the workshop and left ready for departure on the line to the Jungfraujoch tunnel. Fredier was puzzled. There had been no trains to the Jungfraujoch for nearly three weeks now. According to official sources, services had been suspended owing to a roof-fall, and no statement had been issued regarding their reopening. Willi Fredier hated anything that did not fit into its accepted pattern. He had been given the job of watching developments around the tunnel mouth, and as he studied the train's preparation, he knew with chilling certainty that something unusual was up.

'Any chance of getting to the top?' he asked the man at the ticket office.

The official shook his head. 'Sorry, sir. Line's closed. It'll be another week at least before we can get things moving.'

'But there's a train at the platform now,' Fredier insisted.

'Ah, that's a special, sir,' the man said. 'We do manage to squeeze through the occasional freight to carry supplies to the summit, but only on the highest authority.'

The railway official winked. 'If you ask me, there's something funny going on up there at the moment.'

'Funny?'

'Well, you've seen the soldiers at the tunnel entrance?'

'I thought it was some kind of military exercise.'

'For three whole weeks? Now the rumour is that we're waiting for a detachment of American troops.'

'Surely not,' said Fredier, struggling to keep his face impassive. 'What would American troops be doing here?'

'I'm not saying it's true,' the official shrugged, 'but that's the rumour.'

Fredier was trembling with excitement. He had to get the message to Berne immediately. The telephone was out of the question. Lines got bugged, strangers listened in. He looked at his watch. Two o'clock. He would take the local train to Grindelwald, he decided, and hire a car in town.

Spengler woke to a flurry of noise outside the barrack-room window. Men were shouting, engines roaring. He heard the hiss of tyres on gravel, the clump of running feet, then an SS sergeant burst through the door and saluted smartly. 'The Brigadeführer's compliments,' he said. 'He wishes to see you at once.'

Puzzled, Spengler tumbled out of bed and reached for his clothes. Around him, the men stirred restlessly. What was this about, Spengler wondered? Why had he been selected and none of the others?

He followed the sergeant along the corridor, feeling uneasy. Could it be because of Henke? Henke had deserved his beating, and apart from cuts and bruises and a seriously damaged ego, was not badly hurt. Moreover, since they were both the same rank, no one could accuse Spengler of assaulting a superior officer. But these people seemed above the ordinary rules and regulations and he had the uncomfortable feeling that if they considered him an embarrassment, he would be quietly disposed of and left in some isolated crevasse high in the mountain glaciers.

Outside, a storm was raging. He could hear the wind howling, and the staccato rattle of hailstones on the window panes. The corridor ended at the lecture room, and Spengler stepped inside, hearing the sergeant close the door behind him. Empty chairs stood in orderly rows, facing towards a central dais. The walls were white, but not the stark whiteness of the dormitory; these textures had a gentle hue, and were lit from underneath by someone with an awareness of shade and tone. On a table in front of the lantern screen stood the curious structure Helene had discovered the week before. It was saucer-shaped, formed by two rings, one inside the other. A complex grill covered its hub, and the space between the inner and outer circles was padded with tiny bricks. Sitting behind it was a man in the full-dress uniform of an SS Brigadeführer. He had long slender fingers which dangled loosely, as if he had forgotten their existence, over the arm-rests of his chair. His face looked pale and haggard. As Spengler entered, he rose to his feet. 'Lieutenant Spengler?' he said.

Spengler clicked his heels. 'Yes, Brigadeführer.'

'My name's Krassner. I'm sorry to get you out of bed at this hour but, for reasons I can't explain, things are moving more rapidly than any of us had bargained for. Please sit down.'

Spengler sat warily.

'Would you care for a drink? I seldom touch alcohol myself, but I know how tired you must be after yesterday's climb.'

Spengler shook his head.

Krassner wore a pair of small pince-nez spectacles which gave his eyes a curious mesmeric effect. He smiled. 'You may be interested to hear that Henke's still in one piece,' he said. 'No bones broken, though that's no thanks to you. Some heavy bruising around the kidney area, but he absorbs punishment like blotting paper. Ten minutes after his examination, he went for a swim in the lake. The man's a marvel.'

A clap of thunder split the air outside, and the window rattled wildly. 'Filthy night,' the Brigadeführer remarked in a detached tone. He took off his glasses and nipped the bridge of his nose. Spengler noticed that his eyes were rimmed with dark circles and his hand was trembling. Again, he felt a surge of uneasiness.

'You must be wondering by now why I brought you here,' Krassner said. 'It was not to chastise you for Henke. Your private squabbles are no concern of mine. I sent for you because the time has come to explain the purpose of your training. You and your comrades are privileged to have been selected for one of the most audacious missions ever conceived, a mission which will change the course of world history.'

He paused for Spengler's reaction. Spengler kept his face impassive.

Krassner patted the object on the table. 'Know what this is, Lieutenant?'

Spengler shook his head.

'It's a model of an atomic reactor. It consists of cubes of uranium suspended in a moderator of heavy water and surrounded by a shield of graphite. It's being moved out of here tomorrow before our Allied friends come too close for comfort. Don't misunderstand me. The British and Americans have already progressed far beyond the reactor stage. What we're anxious to conceal is the primitive level of our research.'

Spengler stared at him in total bewilderment, and Krassner smiled. 'I'm sorry,' he said, 'I'm moving too fast for you. Let me explain from the beginning. At this moment, a team of British and American scientists is working on a new kind of bomb, a bomb more powerful than anything the world has ever seen before. It's based on the fission of the uranium atom. We too have been working on such a bomb, but sadly the Allies are far ahead of us in its development. If they manage to produce theirs before we can produce ours, then the war will be over for Germany in a matter of days.'

He walked to the window and stood peering out at the raging storm. His spine was straight, his carefully trimmed hair smoothed tight against his skull. From behind, Spengler thought, he looked every inch a Prussian officer. Only the absurd pince-nez destroyed the illusion, giving him the air of a bank clerk or insurance salesman.

'What I am about to tell you, Lieutenant, is for your ears alone. It's an idea which may seem on the face of it dangerous, ill-conceived, even foolhardy. Admittedly, it depends on a certain amount of luck, but then war itself depends on luck. "Is he lucky?" Napoleon once said when someone recommended a particular officer. Are you lucky, Spengler? I believe you are. I believe that with luck, and daring, you can draw our country back from the brink of disaster. Light, please.'

The sergeant standing by the door flicked the electric switch and plunged the room into darkness. Instantly, a picture flashed on to the lantern screen. It showed a train picking its way through high mountain scenery.

'I imagine you'll know what this is,' Krassner murmured.

'The Jungfrau railway in Switzerland,' said Spengler.

'Exactly. An engineering marvel. It was built at the turn of the century and climbs in stages into the highest mountains of Europe, the last stage tunnelling for four-and-a-half miles behind the North Face of the Eiger – your old stamping ground, Lieutenant – to the saddle of the Jungfraujoch, eleven-and-a-half thousand feet above sea level.'

Krassner snapped his fingers and the picture switched to an aerial photograph of the Jungfraujoch summit. Clearly discernible against the rock and snow were the oblong shapes of windows.

'At the top,' Krassner went on, 'stands a hotel complex, a restaurant, and a scientific research station with the most advanced laboratory of its kind in the world. At the moment, it is occupied by what the Swiss claim to be a party of Swedish professors, but one of our agents managed to photograph the Swedish group while they were waiting for a train to take them to the summit. Using a hidden camera, he produced these pictures.'

The image on the lantern screen changed again. Now the scene showed a group of men in civilian clothes. Most of them were young and athletic-looking. Only one was middle-aged. The slide switched to a close-up of the older man. He was small and wiry, with a craggy, aggressive face.

'That man is Dr Walter Lasser,' Krassner explained, 'the Copenhagen scientist who, with Neils Bohr, helped to split the uranium atom. The others are his bodyguards, American OSS agents. Lasser escaped to Switzerland just before our armies overran Denmark, and we know for the past two years he's been living in the United States, playing a vital role in their atom project.'

Krassner smiled thinly. 'However, the Americans have come up against an obstacle,' he explained. 'They've discovered their bomb will give off a form of deadly radiation which, unchecked, could easily wipe out their own side as well as the enemy's. We believe Lasser is using the Jungfraujoch laboratory to measure the short and long-term consequences of radiation in the atmosphere.'

Spengler frowned. 'Are the Swiss aware of this?'

'Of course.'

'Then they've violated their neutrality.'

Krassner gave a humourless laugh. He looked at Spengler like an indulgent father whose son fails to grasp the bitter ironies of life. 'We've known for some time,' he said, 'that the Swiss are more neutral to one side than to the other. Their intelligence services regularly pass information to the Allied forces.'

Spengler shook his head in bewilderment. 'But Switzerland isn't officially in this war. What makes the Jungfraujoch so important?'

'Its laboratory is unique. It was there that radiation was first measured back in 1927. Not only does it contain the most elaborate and up-to-date equipment, but it stands at such a height that a third of the atmosphere lies in the layers below, making it ideal for isolating and analysing radiation's effects.'

'But you've no real proof that the Swiss are involved.'

Krassner shrugged. 'The Jungfrau railway is Switzerland's biggest holiday attraction, yet the Swiss government has closed it down for two months. The hotel staff have been withdrawn, the restaurant has been closed, the trains have ceased running. Only the research station remains in operation. There can be no doubt they are working in collusion with the Allies.'

A flash of lightning lit the darkened room. Then another. The sky outside ripped open in a deafening explosion as thunder clattered across the hills. Krassner waited until it had died away before continuing.

'Only one thing stands in our favour,' he said, 'Though the British and Americans are leading the race, we do know that their uranium supplies are limited. Germany on the other hand has been stockpiling vast quantities of uranium from her mines in Czechoslovakia for almost four years. With our pool of raw materials, and Lasser's research knowledge, we could produce our bomb well ahead of the Allies and sweep to certain victory.'

So that's it, Spengler thought.

'You want him kidnapped,' he said.

'Simply borrowed for a while.'

'Out of Switzerland?'

'Why not? They destroyed their right to neutrality when they let Lasser in. Look at this.'

A second aerial photograph flashed on to the screen.

'Here's a detail of the area surrounding the laboratory,' said Krassner. 'As you can see, it's an area of mountain peaks and massive glaciers. The research station itself stands on the saddle between the summits of the Mönch and the Jungfrau. There's only one way in and one way out, via the railway tunnel. Naturally, any attempt to infiltrate the laboratory by this route would be extremely hazardous since Swiss troops are already guarding its entrance. However, on the opposite side of the massif, directly below the saddle, lies the longest glacier in the Alps, the Grosse Aletschglacier. Its lower reaches are only a matter of miles from the frontier. We believe that a small group of determined men could cross the line by glider, land on the saddle – where the snow will cushion their impact – occupy the research station and transport Dr Lasser by ski-sled back over the border to Baceno.'

Spengler listened in amazement. He had heard rumours of Otto Skorzeny's fabled commando force, but until now had never realised the extent of the risks they took.

'Have you any idea what that landing will be like, Brigadeführer?' he asked. 'The atmosphere at such an altitude will be rarefied, which means navigation will be difficult. And although the saddle may look smooth and inviting, from the air, there'll be rocky spurs under the snow. Hit one of those and we'll be buzzard meat.'

'Of course,' said Krassner. 'That's why your pilot will be Ernst Häutle. Before the war he specialised in mountain rescues, putting down aircraft where no one believed it possible. Major Skorzeny has the utmost confidence in him. He was one of the pilots on the Gran Sasso venture. That, I might tell you, was a far more hazardous descent. The Gran Sasso was a sloping shelf, more like a ski-jump than a landing field.'

Spengler said nothing for a moment. It was the sort of operation he detested. Harebrained and unpredictable. In spite of what Krassner said, they'd be working inside a neutral country. Not only would they have the physical dangers to contend with, but if things went wrong they'd have to explain the presence of a German combat unit on neutral soil.

'Where does Dr Rössner come into this?' he asked.

Krassner shrugged. 'Seizing Lasser is only part of the operation,' he said. 'Bringing him back alive is the other part. Lasser is a diabetic. We have no idea how he'll stand up to the rigours of extreme temperatures and high altitudes. It will be up to Dr Rössner to see that he comes to no harm during the long flight down the glacier.'

'She's a civilian.'

'She's also a devout Party member. What's more, she's the only diabetes expert we could trace who has the added advantage of being an experienced high-Alpine mountaineer.'

Krassner took out a packet of cigarettes, smiling. 'I think we can forget the rules for one night,' he said, offering them to Spengler.

Spengler put one between his lips and leaned forward so that the Brigadeführer could light it. His brain was spinning.

'A bold plan,' he murmured cautiously.

'Bold, yes, but the entire operation need take no more than a few hours.'

Spengler stared at him in wonder. It was all right for the Krassners of the world, he thought. They dreamed up their little fantasies, then left others to do the dying. Why don't you tell him, tell him the whole thing's crazy? But he knew what Krassner's reaction would be. Skorzeny had snatched Mussolini from the summit of the Gran Sasso. Why shouldn't Germany's top climbers achieve the same in the Swiss Alps?

'Brigadeführer, may I ask why you've selected me for this briefing and no one else?'

Krassner delicately flicked ash from his cigarette tip. 'Major Skorzeny has never asked his men to undertake any task which he himself would not undertake also,' he said. 'He has made a point of always leading his troops in person. However, yesterday at Rastenburg, a party of German traitors attempted to assassinate our Führer by placing a time-bomb under his conference table. They failed. The Führer is not dead. He is injured and badly shaken, but thank God still capable of fulfilling his destiny.'

The bastard bears a charmed life, Spengler thought.

'At the moment,' Krassner went on, 'the traitors responsible for the outrage are being weeded out. Major Skorzeny is in command of the War Office in Berlin. He has been ordered to maintain control of all German forces both at home and in the occupied countries of Europe, an unheard-of honour for such a junior officer. In his absence, the command and responsibility for this venture now pass to you.'

Spengler felt his pulses pounding. 'What?' he whispered.

'We've been studying your record, Lieutenant. You've done miraculously so far. And that little fracas yesterday . . .'

'Let me explain that, Brigadeführer.'

'No need. I don't disapprove of violence. Violence is our only guarantee that the strong will survive. Nevertheless, Henke is an accomplished brawler. You were lucky to subdue him so effectively.'

Krassner paused. 'You may wonder why we made everyone the same rank on this undertaking,' he said. 'We did so with good reason. We realised that mountaineers are, by nature, individualists. If things go wrong up there, any one of you may have to step into the leader's shoes. Henke is a good man. He's loyal and brave, but he lacks imagination and is therefore unsuited to the role of command. You, on the other hand, have fought through four major campaigns, you hold the Knight's Cross, your record as an NCO has been exemplary, and despite your confinement in Koblenz, you've never let personal problems interfere with either your judgement or your resolution. You will therefore assume command of this unit at once.'

Spengler sighed. There was no way out. He could see it in Krassner's face.

'Very well, Brigadeführer,' he murmured.

Krassner's pale cheeks had taken on a fresh colour, and behind the absurd spectacles, his eyes looked feverish and bright.

'Please return to the barrack room,' he said, 'and order your men to board the trucks for transportation to the airstrip. The final briefing will be given there.'

Spengler stared at him in astonishment. 'I . . . I don't understand,' he murmured.

'The Jungfraujoch operation is to commence immediately.'

Spengler felt a cold hand grasp his heart. 'Brigadeführer,' he whispered, 'Listen to the storm. It would be suicide to venture up there.'

He was uncomfortably aware of Krassner's gaze boring into his. There was no compromise in those blazing eyes, no indication that reason might prevail. But for his own sake, and the sake of the others, he had to try.

'Even if we managed to land the glider, which seems unlikely,' he said, 'our chances of surviving in such conditions would be minimal.'

For the first time, Krassner's eyes seemed to soften, displaying a look of génuine regret. 'I'm sorry Spengler,' he said, 'it's miserable luck this squall breaking like this, but my orders are explicit. For some undisclosed reason, zero hour has been moved forward. Whatever the weather, whatever the danger, I'm afraid you have to go tonight.'

Seven

The roar of the tow-plane jarred Spengler's senses. Wedged on his narrow pillion, he could do little but peer out at the broad sweep of the Grosse Aletschglacier skimming by in the flush of early dawn. In jump seats along the glider's plywood and canvas hull crouched the nine-man commando team. They were dressed in windproof anorak suits with draw-string hoods and Gebirgsmütze caps. Each man carried across his knee a Schmeisser submachine-gun. They stared moodily into the darkness, their heads shuddering as the glider, buffeted by the gale, dipped and lunged on its tow-line like a baited trout.

Henke sat with his eyes closed, his bruised face locked up tight like a sealed container. No sign of the jitters there, Spengler thought. No sign of anything at all. Henke might have been asleep. Something had happened to Henke since the fight on the mountaintop. His air of sadistic conceit had disappeared. To Spengler's surprise, he had shown no resentment at all, not even at Spengler taking command. Instead, he seemed intent on playing his subsidiary role to the best of his ability, as if, machine-like to the last, he was determined not to allow himself even a trace of human emotion. Beside him crouched Helene Rössner. Her face was pale and composed, but Spengler could see the tension beneath her calm exterior. A feeling of ominous foreboding swept him like the warning tremors of some imminent disaster. The glider was bucking wildly as the wind hit it, and he realised with terrifying perception that they could not last much longer in such violent turbulence. Sending them aloft on a night like this was little short of a death sentence, he thought. He peered down at the ice-stream zipping by below. It looked so smooth, so incredibly white. Hard to believe there were crevasses down there, hidden gaps in the ice which could open and close in a matter of hours. Trap the unwary. Swallow them whole.

The glacier curved, narrowing, flanked on each side by scarred outcrops of barren rock. It looked a harsh landscape, a nightmare world in which to lose oneself. There were twisting gullies formed by a horseshoe of ridges which slid down towards the glacier's edge.

The glider reeled and bucked like a wild animal and Spengler cast a glance at the pilot. He could almost smell the fear emanating from the man's pores.

'Everything okay?' he asked, keeping his voice low so the others wouldn't hear.

Häutle's cheeks looked shiny as wet rubber. 'I don't think we can make it, Lieutenant.'

'What the hell are you talking about?'

'This contraption isn't made for such punishment. We could disintegrate at any second.'

He paused as a fresh wind gust caught the flimsy plywood craft and tossed it sideways in a dizzy arc. Jesus, Spengler thought, what idiot dreamed up this lunatic escapade?

'We can't be far from the summit,' he said. 'Think we can hold on for a few minutes longer?'

Häutle swallowed, his adam's apple bouncing. 'It's thick as cheese up there, Lieutenant. I tell you, if we don't get down fast, we'll break into little pieces.'

Spengler felt his stomach tighten. He peered through the window. 'Let's try for a landing now,' he said.

'On the glacier?'

'There's nowhere else. It'll be like landing on frozen porridge, but anything's better than coming to bits in mid-air. Can you get us down?'

Häutle swallowed again. His eyes bulged, and Spengler could see sweat stains on the back of his flying jacket. 'Oh Jesus, Lieutenant,' he whispered.

I know how you feel, my poor friend, Spengler thought grimly, but win or lose, it's your show now.

'Disconnect,' he ordered.

The line parted, and Spengler watched the tow-plane vanish into the mist. The great sweep of ice and snow came zooming up to meet them. There was no sound but the gush of the wind on their wingspan. Mist drifted across the windscreen. They were enveloped in wads of the stuff, it was like drifting through an endless vacuum. Häutle's face was tense with concentration, his hands on the controls keeping them steady with blind pilot's instinct.

Then it happened. Suddenly a sharp crosswind caught them in its grip and the glider slewed wildly to the right, rotating swiftly. Spengler's stomach plunged, and he gripped the edge of his seat, fighting to control his dizziness. Behind, the men shouted in alarm. Spengler saw the glacier whipping by like an endless curtain unfolding at stupefying speed. They were skimming its surface, out of control. He thought: Let it come quickly – one swift crunch and then oblivion. Oh Jesus Christ.

Häutle pressed a button and the parachute brake whipped out from their tail. Their nose dipped, and they careered on through a vision of blinding white. Häutle was holding on to the controls like a madman, shouting in an impassioned senseless way. Something hit Spengler on the brow, a piece of the windscreen frame. He tasted the salty sting of blood. His body, held tight by the seat harness, jolted up and down like a pea in a rattle. Teeth clenched, knuckles white, he waited for the end. There was a roaring in his eardrums, a flashing intermittent roar that went on and on, driving needles through his brain. Would this damned skid never stop, he wondered? The glider was disintegrating as it went, scattering wreckage across the glacier's desolate surface. Snow churned in, pouring over their heads, engulfing the seats and the terrified passengers strapped inside. Then slowly, their momentum began to slacken. They felt the vibrations fading, the world steadying as they slithered bumpily to a halt. Spengler sat frozen with shock. Time seemed not to exist. He knew he was bleeding, but he could not say where. He saw the sky, pale as fresh milk, and the pale blue cornice of the glacier's rim, and nearer, much nearer, Ernst Häutle's face shiny with blood. Sounds reached him from the rear, sounds of pain – moans, whimpers, the hoarse croak of human voices. Reality came flooding back, and with relief he realised he was still alive.

Oh God, he thought, give me strength to do this right. He undid his seat harness, digging through the snow which covered him to the waist. His body felt stiff with pain. He ran his hands swiftly over his limbs. Genitals intact, thank God. No bones broken. The bleeding came from his brow where the windscreen frame had hit it. He turned to check the pilot. Ernst Häutle was still strapped in his seat, his head dangling forward on his chest. The front of the control panel had sliced through his abdomen and his guts were out in purple bloody loops. Spengler felt nausea sweep from his stomach and swallowed it back with an effort. Suddenly he thought of Helene.

'Oh my God,' he breathed. 'Sweet suffering Jesus.'

He clawed his way over the back of his seat into the cabin and saw Arno Richner digging himself out of the snow. Arno had been hit in the mouth and nearly all his teeth were gone. Bloody spittle oozed over his lips as he wrestled with his seat harness.

'Have you seen Dr Rössner?' Spengler gasped.

Richner shook his head. He seemed dazed.

Spengler spotted an arm sticking out of the snow and began to dig around it frenziedly. The arm was unattached. Oh Christ, he thought.

He felt someone else tunnelling their way to the surface behind him. It was Henke, his bruised face flayed raw by fractured ice.

'Are you okay?' Spengler asked.

'I think so.'

'Where's Helene Rössner?'

'Over here, Erich.'

Waves of relief flooded Spengler at the sound of her voice. She was huddled in the rear, intact. Thank God, he thought.

He could feel the gale buffeting what was left of their shattered fuselage. 'Start digging,' he ordered. 'We've got to unload the supplies and get the hell out of here.'

'Where to, Erich?' Arno murmured.

'Where else? The Jungfraujoch.'

'In this state? Look at us, for God's sake.'

'We've got to find shelter, otherwise we're done for.'

'But the Americans. We won't stand a chance up there.'

'To hell with the Americans, Arno. We either stay here and die, or we get up there and fight. Now dig.'

But the unloading proved more of a headache than Spengler had anticipated. In the first place, the glider's interior was a scene of total destruction. No part of the hull was completely intact. Bits of wood, glass and tattered canvas lay scattered along the full length of their route. In the second, the cabin was filled almost to the roof with thick snow. It took them nearly an hour to uncover the other members of the group, unstrap the sled and load it with their supplies. By the time they had finished, Spengler looked at his survivors with a sense of dismay. Of the original nine-man team (eleven, including Dr Rössner and Ernst Häutle) Häutle was dead, four others had been killed outright (one man torn completely in half) and Rolf Notz was dangerously wounded, a gaping hole gouged out of his belly. The other five, though bruised and bewildered, seemed generally in one piece. Spengler peered down at Notz who was gasping for breath, his cheeks beaded with sweat despite the intense cold. Helene was kneeling by his side, trying to staunch the outflow of blood.

'How do you feel?' Spengler whispered.

Notz tried to speak but the words would not come. His lips trembled with effort. He tried again. 'Bit stiff, that's all.'

'Numb?'

'That's it. I think . . . my arm is broken.'

'We'll strap it up once we're under cover. Try to rest.'

He turned to the others. 'Load him on to the sled.'

As they moved out of the fuselage, the storm hit them with maniacal fury. Spengler fastened his parka hood, but the gale tore at his cheeks, stinging his eyes, numbing his skin. God knows how far the summit is, he thought. Let's hope no more than a mile. In these conditions, that's all we're good for.

He took a compass reading and they started off, sliding across the snow on their short cross-country skis, tilting their heads into the wind as they hauled the sled behind them, watching for drifts and crevasses, trying to shut off the pain in their limbs, concentrating instead on the simple straightforward task of staying alive.

The train stopped. Major Lewis D. Shellburn, commander of the US Third Army's Unit D, woke from his sleep feeling numb and heavy. 'Where are we?' he demanded.

One of the soldiers rubbed his sleeve against the window. Dimly, Shellburn spotted a sign on the station platform: 'LAUTERBRUNNEN.'

'Jesus, what a night,' the soldier exclaimed. 'It's sheeting down out there.'

Major Shellburn staggered to his feet as around him, the men began to come awake. 'Everybody out,' he snapped. 'We have to switch trains here for Kleine Scheidegg.'

'Switch trains?' said Sergeant Bullock. 'Won't this take us right to the top?'

'No. The railroad runs in stages. First, we take a traction loco up to the plateau, then we switch to an adhesion job for the pull to the summit.'

The sergeant peered glumly through the rainstreaked window.

'I don't see any welcoming committee out there, major. You sure we've come to the right place?'

Shellburn hesitated, feeling uneasy. Sergeant Bullock was right. The station looked deserted. He glanced at his watch. Nearly four a.m. What the hell, he thought, surely they were expected?

Shellburn pulled on his parka and stumbled on to the platform, flinching as the full force of the wind caught him in the face. On both sides of the track, tree-covered hillslopes leaned into a swirling sky. Rain lashed at him solidly, driving into his mouth, forming huge puddles around his mudstained boots. Christ, what a downpour.

He ducked around the back of the ticket office, pulling up his parka hood. A light gleamed in one of the windows. Shellburn rapped the pane with his knuckles. A small elderly man in blue overalls slid back the panel and blinked at him through watery eyes.

'Speak English?' Shellburn demanded.

The man nodded. 'Not good,' he admitted, 'but I speak it. You must be Major Shellburn?'

'That's right. There's supposed to be a train laid on to take us up to the Kleine Scheidegg.'

'Not possible,' the man said bluntly. 'No trains. Power gone.'

Shellburn frowned. 'This is government business,' he protested. 'It's also highly urgent. I have top priority.'

'I tell you, no trains,' the man insisted. 'The storm has disrupted the power. I have message from Mr Dulles at American Legation. You sleep here till morning. Trains will run again tomorrow.'

Shellburn swore. His orders had been terse and explicit. Reinforce the OSS contingent on top of the Jungfraujoch at all possible speed, and under no circumstances allow the man Lasser to fall into enemy hands. Jesus, if this show ever got off the ground, it'd be a goddamned miracle. 'Where's the station master?' he demanded. 'Does he live nearby?'

'No station master,' the man said. 'Even if station master were here, trains cannot run without electricity.'

Shellburn spat on the ground. 'How far is it to Kleine Scheidegg on foot?' he demanded.

'On foot?' the man whispered. 'No one goes to Kleine Scheidegg on foot.'

'It's possible, isn't it?'

'Oh yes, you can follow the railroad track. But . . . it is up-grade all the way.'

'How many kilometres?'

'Sixteen,' the man said.

'You're sure?'

The man nodded and Shellburn sighed, peering at the sky. No sign of a let-up. The rain was pounding the valley with relentless fury. He strode back to the train, thankful for his slicker.

'Sergeant Bullock,' he snapped, 'I want that equipment unloaded pronto. We're going for a little walk.'

The sergeant stared at him with dismay, flinching as a shift in the wind hurled raindrops into his face. 'In this weather, sir?'

Shellburn shrugged. 'I know it's a bastard, Mitch,' he said, 'but every hour we waste down here is another strike in the enemy's favour. I want to be inside that tunnel before daybreak.'

It wasn't much to speak of, just a thickening of the mist ahead, but Spengler knew they were coming up to the tip of the glacier. There were rocks up there, the bare flank of the naked mountain. If he'd got his compass bearing right, then somewhere amid that cluster of shadows lay their only hope – the security of the research station and hotel. They had pushed relentlessly up the endless curtain of ice, testing the ground ahead, picking a delicate route around seracs and crevasses, straining their bodies in a constant battle against the blizzard. Dizziness had threatened to engulf them at every step, for the sudden switch in altitude had left them disorientated, and Spengler felt his body melting from him as if his life-force was dripping away drop by precious drop.

The snow made zig-zag patterns through the steel-grey mist. Here and there, outcrops of pulverised rock surged through the surface like billowing clouds. The wind was a thunder in their ears. There was nothing to see, and nothing to feel almost, for the gale was battering them to such a degree that their flesh had lost its sense capability. There was only the ice and fog and the inescapable skin-stinging snow needles driving in at them from all directions. It was nothing new to Spengler. He had been through such conditions before, on high altitude climbs where the weather had turned unexpectedly bad; then, it had meant a quick scuttle back to base and the muggy warmth of inns in the valley, but here, retreat was out of the question. Descending the full length of the glacier would be nothing short of suicide, and Spengler knew it. Their only hope was the Jungfraujoch. And what then? Hole up out of the storm, fine, but there was still no way off this godawful mountain, except down the railway tunnel, and that meant immediate capture. To hell with it, he thought. All he could think of was the misery of the moment. Nothing else existed.

He paused, clenching his muscles as he peered into the

driving snow. Twenty yards away, the smudges thickened and he saw the rock blocking their path. It looked menacing in the swirling gloom, an enemy bent on their destruction. The wavering lines fused into one and Spengler felt his heart leap as he saw, tucked high on the limestone flank, a solitary oblong. A window. Ice-encrusted and sunk deep inside a rocky crevice, it was indisputably a window. A balcony traced its lower rim. The Jungfraujoch hotel. They had made it. A few more feet, a brief scramble up the precipitous ice-slope, and then a blessed escape from this dreadful tempest.

According to Krassner, the hotel was unoccupied. Still, they could have posted sentries just for safety's sake, although in this blizzard, even the most cautious of men would hardly be expecting visitors. He would have to take a chance on it.

It was impossible for Spengler to make himself heard over the roar of the gale, so he waved ahead into the driving fog. The others stared at him blankly, their faces caked with snow. Spengler pushed forward, dragging on his ski poles, and sensed rather than heard the rest of the team begin to follow. The gradient steepened, and soon Spengler had to remove his skis, digging in his toes for the last heart-rending drag up. He reached the balcony and struggled over its rail. It was impossible to see through the window, for ice had traced intricate patterns over the surface, blotting out what lay within. The hotel had been actually constructed inside the rock, and only the reinforced glass and the observation balcony showed it existed at all. Fingers numb with cold, Spengler tried the door. It was locked, but it jimmied easily enough and in another second he was out of the gale and coughing and spluttering on the bare stone floor. The others stumbled in after him, caked with snow. They looked grotesque on the windswept threshold.

With intricate care, Hüsser and Richner unstrapped Notz from the sled and hauled him into shelter. Spengler's brain could not register the blissful cessation of pain and misery. Safe at last, he thought. Safe? He pulled himself together. Only for the moment, he realised grimly. No sentry, a good start. That was a bonus. It meant they had the advantage of surprise, but they were still hopelessly outnumbered.

He could hear the hullabaloo of the storm outside. He glanced around. They had entered the hotel through its restaurant. Empty tables lined the walls. Through a sliding hatch, he could see the kitchens beyond. Everything was shrouded in shadow. No sign of life. The hotel *looked* empty at any rate, unless there was a caretaker hidden away somewhere. How many OSS bodyguards did Lasser have? Thirteen? Not much of a contest, when you came right down to it. Thirteen trained experts against four battered men, one woman and a badly-wounded stretcher case.

The others had collapsed on the floor, spent and breathless, their punished limbs drained beyond belief.

'Get up,' Spengler choked, his voice almost non-existent. 'Up, damn you. There's no time for lounging about.'

They stared at him uncomprehendingly, their mouths slack, their eyes dead. Shock loomed there, shock, pain and misery. They needed time to readjust, but time was the one thing Spengler didn't have.

'Come on, you gutless bastards, we're not out of the woods yet.'

'Can't we rest?' Richner gasped wearily. 'Just a quick breather.'

'We finish the job, then we rest. Come on, damn it, we're wasting time.'

One by one, they struggled to their feet. Spengler watched them, his heart sinking. They looked little short of zombies. He hoped there would be no real resistance ahead.

'Leave Rolf here,' he ordered. 'We'll pick him up later.'

Cocking his Schmeisser, he beckoned the others to follow, hoping to hell the precariousness of their situation would set their brains working again. They filtered through the restaurant and into the corridor outside, cold air bathing their faces. The corridor had been hewn out of the solid rock. Only its floor was smooth. The walls were covered with cracks, crannies and shadows. Spengler hesitated. Which way, he wondered? As far as he could tell, right or left made little difference. He toyed with the idea of splitting up, but decided against it. No sense weakening ourselves further, he thought. Besides, for the moment at least, he couldn't trust any of them to think straight, and that included himself.

They tried the left side of the tunnel first. It ended on the platform of the Jungfraujoch railway station. They could see the metal rails disappearing into the darkness below. They retraced their steps, their breath leaving clouds of steam on the thin cold air, their boots clattering between the bare rock walls.

Spengler frowned. 'Boots off,' he ordered. 'We'll go the rest of the way in stockinged feet.'

Twenty yards further on, they spotted a luminous sign:

'JUNGFRAUJOCH SCIENTIFIC RESEARCH STATION – OUT OF BOUNDS TO GENERAL PUBLIC.'

Spengler waved the others to a halt and, with the Schmeisser ready cocked, scuttled forward, flattening himself against the granite wall. The tunnel opened into a cave of sorts, its entrance blocked by a heavy metal gate. Spengler opened it easily and slithered through. The corridor was wider here, the walls no longer carved out of the bare rock but neatly plastered and painted over. Moreover, it was warm. Thank God, Spengler thought. The heat brought some semblance of feeling back to his frozen limbs. Lights hung from the ceiling, but he made no move to switch them on. There was still no sound, no scrape or scuffle to indicate the presence of a sentry, nothing at all to show the place was occupied except the heating system and – Spengler's stomach jumped when he heard this – the rasp of a human snore. He turned to peer at the others and noted with approval that their glassy look had gone. Their faces were pale and alert. Action and warmth had infused them with life again.

Doors lined both sides of the corridor. Spengler tried one. It opened easily into a comfortable lounge. There were soft chairs, sofas, a coffee table strewn with magazines and a metal stove, its belly grey and cold. Unwashed cups littered the armchair rests. Cigarette ends choked the ashtrays. Two men sat beside the window, Thompson machine-guns across their knees. They were both asleep, lulled into a sense of impregnability by the storm outside. Spengler shook his head in wonder. Two only, and none at all in the deserted hotel. They must feel secure indeed in their mountaintop refuge.

He nodded to Hüsser who leaned over and pressed his fingers against the first sleeper's lips. The man came awake without a sound, and his eyes widened with disbelief as the muzzle of Spengler's Schmeisser pressed against his ear. The second sleeper was seized by Richner who clamped one hand across his mouth and shook him unceremoniously by the hair.

Spengler struggled with his English. 'No one speaks, no one dies,' he whispered. 'If you are sensible, we have no reason to kill you. Nothing will happen if you do as you are told. But make a sound, any sound at all, and you will both be shot. Understand?'

He moved on to the next room. It was unoccupied. He tried the handle of the door opposite. It opened into the dormitory. It was large and oppressively warm, and filled from end to end with narrow bunks and the tell-tale bulges of sleeping figures.

Spengler took a deep breath. If it comes to a fight, we're done for, he thought. You'd better get them confused and keep them confused. Now.

Hurtling inside, he swung up his Schmeisser and fired a burst at the ceiling. The noise was deafening in the confined area. Chips of plaster whirled through the air. The men in the bunks jerked up, blinking stupidly. They stared in amazement at the sight of enemy troops scurrying into their dormitory.

'Who's in command here?' Spengler shouted.

It was an anxious moment. If the Americans realised his true strength, they would undoubtedly resist. He knew everything depended on bluff.

They sat staring at him in silence, their eyes still glazed. Damn them. Had they been shocked completely out of their wits? He fired another burst into the air and the room filled with the odour of cordite.

A small stocky man with crewcut hair gave a resigned sigh and slid from his bunk. 'I guess I'm in command, Lieutenant,' he said gloomily. 'My name's Hayes.'

Spengler studied him, keeping his face as inflexible as possible. 'The Jungfraujoch is in German hands,' he said. 'Your men will leave their weapons where they are and assemble in the doorway. If you wish to avert bloodshed, you have sixty seconds in which to obey.'

For a moment, the man stared at Spengler as if he couldn't make up his mind whether to fight or submit. Then he sighed again, and Spengler knew that he had won.

'Looks like you caught us with our pants down, Lieutenant,' the American said wearily. 'Okay, we surrender.' It took less than thirty minutes to establish that no other room was occupied, and to secure the captured Americans to their bunks with climbing rope. A quick scout around the building produced a huge assortment of mountaineering equipment, including a cable system for rescue attempts on the Eiger's North Face. Spengler examined it, reflecting wryly that the Eiger, the source of his torment, was barely a stone's throw away. A mile or two, no more, he thought. But he put that from his mind and concentrated on the problems in hand. Dr Walter Lasser was easily identified, not only from his photograph, but also because he was the only man in the dormitory over the age of thirty. He was grey-haired and slightly built, but carried a hint of wiry toughness that made Spengler resolve to watch him carefully, despite his diabetic handicap.

Lasser spoke excellent German. 'I don't know what you hope to achieve, Lieutenant,' he said, 'but if you have any ideas about persuading me to work for the glory of the Reich, you'll find me a very stubborn man.'

'You're a scientist,' said Spengler. 'What difference does it make who you work for?'

'It makes a difference to me.'

Spengler studied him thoughtfully.

'I was hoping you'd be a little more amenable, Dr Lasser. I don't wish to tie you up like the others. Will you give me your word you won't try to escape?'

'Why should I?'

Spengler shrugged. 'It would make things easier all round. For you as well as us.'

'You might as well know, Lieutenant, I despise everything you stand for.'

Spengler smiled coldly. 'Then think of it like this. As long as you co-operate, you're a valuable commodity. Give us trouble, any trouble at all, and we'll finish you off without a second thought. Either way, we still win. At least you'll be no further use to the Americans.'

Without waiting for Lasser's reaction, Spengler turned and walked into the next room. The stretcher bearing Rolf Notz stood on the floor. It had been collected from the deserted restaurant by Hüsser and Henke. Notz's face was shiny with sweat. His eyes were glassy and there was a strange smile on his lips.

'How's it feel?' Spengler asked.

Notz looked puzzled for a moment. With some difficulty, his gaze focused on Spengler standing there. 'Not bad,' he whispered, 'doesn't hurt any more.'

'We're moving soon, down into the valley. The glacier's out of the question in these conditions. We'd never escape that way.'

'How will you get past the Swiss guards?'

'We're going the hard route,' Spengler smiled, 'down the Eigerwand.'

Notz stared at him in amazement. 'You're out of your mind.'

'I don't think so. There's a gallery window which looks out from the railway tunnel. It's only eight hundred feet above the screes. We can rope down from there.'

'What about Lasser?'

'We'll lower him like a sack of laundry.'

'In this weather?'

Spengler shrugged. 'It shouldn't be too bad. The bottom eight hundred feet are the easiest of all. I'm sure we can do it. Once in the valley, we'll steal a truck or something.'

Notz studied him thoughtfully. 'Are you sure it's Lasser you're thinking of, Erich?'

'What are you talking about?'

'You know damn well what I'm talking about. Are you sure you're not looking for some excuse to get yourself back on that damned mountain?'

Spengler was silent for a moment, then he said: 'If I had any choice in the matter, I wouldn't go within a thousand feet of that cliff, Rolf. But in this storm, the Eiger's the only hope we've got.'

'Then I hope you make it,' Notz said, his chest rising and falling as he struggled for air. 'I think you're crazy, but I really hope you do.'

Spengler took out a handkerchief and mopped Notz's glistening cheeks. 'Rolf,' he said gently, 'we're leaving you here. Those Americans are bound to break loose sooner or later. They'll get you to a hospital.'

Notz closed his eyes, relaxing. 'I'm sweating,' he whispered. 'That's funny. I've felt cold all bloody morning. Sometimes I thought I was sleeping, but I couldn't be sure. I dreamt I saw my father standing right where you are now, clear as day.'

'How did he look?'

'Disapproving.' Notz smiled weakly. 'He always disapproved of everything I did. Mountain-climbing, he hated that. When I joined the army, he accused me of being rabbit-brained. And seeing him just now, he looked as though he even disapproved of my dying.'

'Don't talk such rubbish,' Spengler said.

Notz chuckled. 'Good old Erich. Let's not mention the unmentionable. Let's not say it out loud. Help, I'm bleeding to death.'

Spengler did not answer. He wanted to say: you're right, it's just a game we're playing. A sordid game with no true ending except the inevitable one, an end to everything.

A racking cough shook Notz's thin frame. Watching, Spengler felt his stomach contract. Death was a belittling thing when it came so slowly.

'What a balls-up it's been, Erich,' Notz whispered. 'A balls-up from the very beginning.'

Spengler squeezed his arm. Failure was too painful to bear, for failure wiped out the reasons for dying, took away point and purpose. 'We've taken control of the

Jungfraujoch,' he murmured. 'We've got Dr Lasser. As soon as the storm slackens, we'll escape into the valley. We're not done yet, Rolf.'

Notz was silent for a moment. He lay so still that Spengler wondered if he had passed quietly away. But Notz spoke again.

'I envy you,' he whispered. 'You know what I hate most about . . . about dying? It's the thought that I'll never get to do the Eigerwand. I dreamed about it all through my boyhood. I nearly cried when they scaled it in 1938. I promised myself that as soon as the war ended, I'd come back to the Oberland and make the second ascent. It was the one thing that kept me going on the Russian Front. I used to think, I can't let them kill me, I haven't done the Eiger yet. I used to feel I was immune in some way, as if the Eiger was protecting me, like a guardian angel keeping me out of harm's way.'

'You're wasting strength,' Spengler said. 'Try to rest, I'll come back later.'

Notz peered at him, shivering like a man in a fever.

'Erich?'

'What?'

'Give me your gun.'

Spengler hesitated. Notz's eyes were dim with pain. He stared at Spengler with desperate entreaty. But Spengler shook his head and walked away.

He wanted to hammer his skull against the wall, to bellow senselessly into the storm outside. It was a world without reality, this miserable crow's nest in which they found themselves. Nothing real existed, only Notz, filling their souls with the stench of his dying.

Spengler forced himself to go through the motions of normality. He checked the dormitory and the prisoners inside. He looked in on Dr Lasser who was snoring on the lounge sofa under the watchful eye of Arno Richner. He closed the door and was making his way towards the library when he spotted Henke coming down the passageway pushing Helene Rössner in front of him. She was struggling and dishevelled, lashing out at his shins with her feet. He held her in a vicious grip, her left arm twisted behind her spine. His eyes glittered with malevolent fury.

'What's going on here?' Spengler demanded.

'I caught her in the caretaker's office,' Henke said. 'She was on the telephone, talking to Grindelwald police station.'

Something turned in Spengler's stomach and began to throb. It's not possible, his mind screamed, not Helene Rössner.

He stared at her accusingly: 'What the hell is he talking about?'

'What do you think he's talking about?' she snapped. 'I've just put paid to your mad little escapade. You're finished, Lieutenant, you and your lunatic friends. You were finished from the first moment you started.'

She was glaring at him with angry defiance. If he had any doubts about her guilt, the look in her eyes convinced him. There was no quarter there. No submission. Their intimacies of the past were forgotten. He was staring directly and indisputably into the face of the enemy.

Suddenly it all slotted into place like the final gap in a jigsaw puzzle. The night he had caught her wandering in the corridor. Her husband who'd died in a Nazi concentration camp. How could he have missed the obvious tell-tale signs? She'd never belonged, not from the beginning.

A bitter sense of betrayal engulfed him. Even when she'd helped him it had been nothing more than a strategy, a little game of subterfuge to cement her cover. She'd made fools of them all, blind, silly, contemptible fools.

And now, he told himself, she'd probably scuttled the whole operation. When the police got word to the troops at the tunnel mouth, they'd be up that track like a swarm of locusts.

He watched Henke release Helene and take out his Walther, slipping off the safety catch.

'What the hell d'you think you're doing?' Spengler demanded.

Henke looked surprised. 'She's a spy,' he said.

'You bloody *dummkopf*! You can't bump off our doctor.

Who's going to look after Lasser? She's the most important member of this team, Henke. That little man's going to need careful nursing if we're to get him out of Switzerland alive and well.'

Henke hesitated, then he slipped back the safety catch and slid the Walther into his holster. 'You're right, I wasn't thinking,' he admitted. 'But as soon as we get back to Italy, I'm going to make damned sure she faces a firing squad.'

Spengler's brain worked quickly. Four-and-a-half miles down the tunnel. It would take an hour or so for the Swiss to organise themselves. Still time to make their escape, but they daren't postpone any longer. Storm or no storm, they had to move at once.

'Henke,' he snapped briskly, 'sort out the equipment. Make sure each man has pitons, crampons, iceaxe, sleeping sack, food and overgear.'

'*Jawohl*,' Henke said. 'We are going to try the glacier?'

'No,' said Spengler. 'The glacier's out of the question in this storm. We're going down the Eigerwand.'

'What?'

'It's our only chance, Henke.'

'You're crazy. We'll never survive.'

'I think we will. We can rope down from the gallery window. It's eight hundred feet, no more. Would you rather fight your way through the tunnel mouth?'

Henke shook his head blankly, like a man in a state of shock.

'What about Lasser?' he whispered.

'He comes too. Make sure he's properly kitted out, and we'll lower him on the ropes.'

'He's a diabetic, Spengler, he could die out there.'

'He could,' Spengler admitted grimly, 'but we'll all die if we stay here. Carry out your orders, Henke, and make it fast. By the time those troops pull themselves together, I want to be down that tunnel and on to that cliff.'

At seven-thirty in the morning, after hiking for more than three hours up the railroad track, Major Shellburn and his men arrived at Eigergletscher Station, wet-through and weary, to find the little detachment of Swiss troops milling about in great agitation. Their commander was a sallow-faced young man who seemed more intent on contacting his superiors on the field telephone than in making any decisions which might, in the long run, damage his army career. He seemed delighted to see Shellburn, as if with the Americans' arrival his responsibility had come to an end. In halting English, he blurted out the news which had reached him from Grindelwald, and as Shellburn listened, his face grew pale. God Almighty, so the stinking Krauts had done it.

Major Shellburn was not a career officer; before the war, he had been a civil engineer, but with the draft he'd been transformed in a way he could not easily explain, not even to himself.

Shellburn liked to think of that period as his rebirth, for the army had been a revelation to him in those early weeks of basic training – never in his life had he felt so completely at home, so utterly and positively rejuvenated. While the rest of the platoon moaned and bitched about the miseries of boot camp, he had to admit that not a single day had passed when he hadn't looked forward to the next with eagerness and anticipation. Major Shellburn had realised rather belatedly that the army was what he'd been born for, and when this war ended he intended to do his damnedest to see that he stayed around. Which was why, in strictly personal terms, this mission was so important. If the Germans got away with Lasser, it would hardly enhance his future prospects. Son of a bitch, he thought as he glanced around.

'Is there any other way out of there?'

'None,' the Swiss commander answered positively.

'You're quite sure?'

The Swiss shrugged. 'They could escape across the summits, but in this storm that would be suicide.'

'So there's only the tunnel?'

'Yes. Apart from the gallery windows, that is.'

'Windows?'

'Openings on the Eiger Wall. They were used for the disposal of rubble when the tunnel was being constructed.'

'Jesus Christ,' Shellburn breathed.

The Swiss shook his head. 'No, Major,' he said firmly. 'No one in his right mind would come down the Eigerwand in such weather.'

'Maybe they're not in their right minds,' Shellburn maintained. 'Maybe . . . for Christ's sake, we don't know what the hell they're capable of. Listen, can you deploy your men along the foot of the Eiger's face?'

The Swiss stared at him. 'For what reason?' he asked dumbly.

Shellburn grunted with exasperation. 'Because we might have a bunch of mad bastards on our hands,' he said, 'because they might just be dumb enough to try it. Who knows? Maybe they're clambering down that stinking cliff at this very minute.'

'And what about you, Major?'

'I'm going up,' Shellburn said. 'We've got to spook them out of there somehow.'

'In a narrow space like that, one man could hold off a regiment.'

'I know. Christ, don't tell me, I know.'

'Will you need help?'

Shellburn shook his head. 'Best keep out of it,' he advised. 'Remember Swiss neutrality? Just make sure those loopholes are plugged, that's all I ask.'

Despite his concern, the Swiss commander seemed delighted at avoiding an armed confrontation. 'Good luck, Major,' he said.

Shellburn squinted into the fog and rain. The thought of leading his men up that gloomy bolt-hole was not an alluring one. The Swiss was right. There'd be no room to move, no room to manoeuvre. If the Germans had a mind to, they could hold out for days. Still, the job had to be done. He turned, his face gleaming softly in the early-morning light. 'Okay,' he snapped, 'Let's go.'

And with carbines held loosely across their chests, Unit D trotted up the incline towards the tunnel entrance.

The opening to the gallery window was so narrow Spengler almost walked right past it. He was feeling his way down the tunnel wall when Hüsser aimed his flashlight beam at a chalk mark on the rock: *Km 3.8.*

'This is it,' Hüsser whispered.

The tiny tributary passage was black as pitch, and Spengler's flashlight picked out the rough-hewn walls, disappearing into a curtain of gloom. He inched forward, the others following, ducking beneath the ceiling of chipped hanging rock. Spengler saw a heavy metal sheet held in place by wooden pegs. He thrust his flashlight into Richner's hand, then with his iceaxe began to prise open the timbered struts. Getting his shoulder against the metal door, he struggled to force it backwards.

'Weighs a ton,' he grunted. 'Give me a hand.'

Hüsser handed his flashlight to the man behind and joined Spengler, heaving and grunting as they slowly eased the massive shield back against the rock. Mist rolled into their aperture, bringing with it wild snow flurries which danced into their faces, chilling the skin.

'Christ,' Henke breathed, 'it's like a tornado out there.'

Spengler nodded grimly. 'I'm going out to take a look,' he said.

He inched carefully on to the shelf, flinching as the gale whipped at his cheeks and throat, spewing spindrift out of the chasm below. The storm raged around him in billows of swirling white. He stared across the Eiger's massive wall, gazing speechless at the biting outcrops and slabs of blotched ice. It looked like some monstrous eruption heaved up from the bowels of the earth. He peered down, struggling to see the bottom. Fine particles of churned-up snow lashed at his brow, driven by the gale. The crest of grey cloud parted momentarily to give a view of the valley below, and Spengler felt his nerve-ends jump. Along the foot of the massive cliff, between the scree-slope and the pastures lower down, he could see the scattered heads of helmeted figures. They looked small and indistinct, toy soldiers, insect men in insect uniforms. He tumbled back inside the tunnel and leaned against the wall, breathing deeply.

'What's up?' Henke asked.

'Troops.'

'Below?'

Spengler nodded, and Hüsser spat angrily into the dust.

'How could they know we'd try this way?' he snarled.

'They're plugging up the gaps, that's all,' said Spengler. 'They're thinking faster than I gave them credit for.'

'What now?'

Spengler considered for a moment. The truth was, he didn't know. He had gambled everything on this one escape route. Now his brain seemed to have gone into neutral.

It was Hüsser's voice which brought him back to reality.

'Someone's coming,' Hüsser hissed.

They stood quite still, listening hard, each man holding his breath. From the tunnel, they heard the sound of trotting feet, the muffled drone of distant voices. There were men coming up the track.

'We're trapped,' somebody whispered.

'Shut up,' Spengler snapped. 'Keep still and switch those flashlights off. Maybe they'll go right by.'

He was filled with a terrible premonition. What chance did they have, stuck in this narrow hole with only the storm-tossed precipice behind them. The entire operation had been stricken with disaster from the word 'go'. First the glider crash, then Helene Rössner's treachery.

Helene Rössner, he thought. He'd imagined he knew her. Soft, feminine, gentle. He'd trusted her completely, confided in her, confessed his innermost secrets. He had bared his soul like a witless schoolboy. And all the time she'd been laughing behind his back.

Laughing at him.

She was not the woman he'd thought she was, but a different being. Cold. Dangerous. Hard as nails.

He gripped his Schmeisser tightly, listening to the clump-clump-clump of approaching feet. Voices reached him, faint at first, then growing louder, American voices. His eyes widened. They weren't Swiss out there, they were Americans. That made things ten times worse. The Swiss weren't participants in this war, and would be less inclined to make a fight of it if it came to a shooting match, but the Americans had too much to lose. To save Lasser, they'd blow this whole damned tunnel to kingdom come if need be.

He heard their footsteps clattering up and down the track, sending shock waves into their tiny fissure. Then, with a shrillness that startled them all, Helene Rössner bellowed at the top of her voice. Henke had his hand across her mouth in an instant, but he was too late. The Americans had stopped, frozen into immobility. Damn the woman, Spengler thought, and damn himself for not realising she would give them away.

Hüsser let off a burst with his Schmeisser, and in the narrow corridor it sounded like an artillery barrage opening up. The Americans scuttled for cover and opened fire in a fusillade of sound. Spengler felt his eardrums quiver under the force of the din. Bullets screeched and pinged, ricocheting off walls and ceiling. Spengler heard Hüsser cry out with pain, and saw him writhing on the floor, clutching furiously at his leg. The noise came in waves, growing louder with each second, echoing backwards and forwards between the limestone walls, barking and reverberating up and down the corridor, deadening their senses with its intensity, spreading itself like an oppressive cloud that fed on its own vile discord, an ear-splitting uproar that went on and on until Spengler felt it would never stop; and then, above the tumult, he heard a man's voice barking orders and, as abruptly as it had begun, the racket rattled to a halt.

Spengler shook his head to clear it. He glanced around, looking for casualties, but in the entire impassioned burst, only Hüsser had been hit, and that had probably been an unlucky richochet. At least their position seemed secure.

Henke was still holding on to Helene Rössner, though what good that would do Spengler could not imagine.

'We should have killed the bitch when we had the chance,' Henke snapped.

'You'll get plenty of opportunity for killing now, Henke,' Spengler murmured.

'It's hopeless, Erich,' Arno Richner said. 'We'd better surrender.'

'Not yet.'

'We're done for, any fool can see that.'

'Not yet, I said. There's still one way out.'

Henke let Helene go and reached for his Schmeisser. 'We could fight our way back up the tunnel to the Jungfraujoch,' he said.

'Too dodgy,' muttered Spengler. 'If those OSS men have worked themselves free, we'd be caught like rats in a trap.'

'What's on your mind, then?'

Spengler hesitated. The idea seemed preposterous, even to him, but he knew there was no other way.

'We can no longer go down the cliff,' he said softly, 'but we can still go up.'

Henke's eyes widened. 'Up the Eigerwand?'

Spengler nodded. 'If we can reach the summit, we can get down the Mitellegi Ridge. There's a hut built on the mountain's rim. We can hole up till the storm passes, then escape into the valley before they can figure out where the hell we've gone.'

'Have you gone completely mad?' Henke asked.

'It's our only chance, Henke.'

'Call that a chance? We've got as much hope of sprouting wings and flying to the moon.'

Arno Richner said: 'Erich, that's the North Face of the Eiger out there. No one could climb that Face in these conditions.'

'No one's ever had to. No one's been as desperate as we are.'

'We'd be throwing our lives away,' said Henke.

'I'm hoping that's what the Americans will think. I'm hoping once we get out there they'll figure we're done for and leave us alone.'

Richner was watching him carefully. 'Are you sure it's not some personal vendetta you've got with that mountain?' he said quietly.

'I'm thinking about survival,' Spengler said. 'Getting out of this bloody mess, nothing else.'

'What about him?' Henke asked, nodding at Lasser.

'We pull him up on the ropes.'

'He'd never survive,' Helene Rössner said coldly. 'He suffers from diabetes mellitus. Do you know what that means? It means just the stress of our being here is disturbing the sugar balance in his blood. Take him up that Face and the physical exertion will disturb it even more.'

'You can moderate his sugar level. You've got his insulin supply.'

'That's true, but to counteract the insulin he needs regular meals and rest. If Lasser burns up too much sugar through exercise or too little food, he could sink into a coma. Then there'll be no way on earth we can save him.'

'He'll have to take his chances like the rest of us,' Spengler said flatly.

'If he dies, which he almost certainly will, won't it make your heroic gesture rather pointless?'

Spengler looked at Lasser. The scientist was watching him closely, no expression on his weatherbeaten face. Lasser knew his choice was simple: co-operate or die.

'At least dead he can't help the enemy,' grunted Spengler. 'We'll have achieved that, if nothing else.'

For a moment Helene was silent. Then she said: 'I was wrong about you, Spengler. You're really quite a ruthless bastard, aren't you?'

'I'm a soldier,' he snapped, 'a German soldier, can't you get that into your head? You're alive now only because we need you. Let Lasser die, and I might find some difficulty in justifying your existence to Henke. Remember that.'

To the others, he said: 'Leave your weapons here. We must keep our weight down as much as possible. Check your equipment, and get Lasser roped up. Hurry.'

He shuffled forward to the mouth of the gallery and knelt over Hüsser who was lying with one leg doubled beneath the other, the wounded one stretched out along the dusty floor. His Schmeisser lay beside his chest.

'See anything?' Spengler whispered.

'They've pulled back below the bend,' Hüsser said. 'It'll take them a while to figure out what to do.'

'How's the leg?'

'Throbs a bit.'

Hüsser's face was white with pain. 'Bullet's made a right bloody mess of my knee,' he said. 'It's put paid to my climbing for a while.'

Spengler shifted his machine-gun into a more comfortable position. 'Kurt, do you think you could keep those Yanks back long enough to give us a start up that cliff?'

'From this position, I could hold out until the cows come home.'

'No need for that. Give us twenty minutes, then surrender. Once we're clear of the window, we'll be okay. I don't think they'd be crazy enough to follow.'

Hüsser was staring into the darkness, frowning fiercely like a man expecting a divine visitation.

'Aren't you going to wish us luck?' Spengler asked.

'You don't need luck,' Hüsser said. 'What you need is a bloody miracle.'

Spengler didn't answer. He stared at Hüsser for a moment, then turned and scurried off. He had a terrible feeling Hüsser was right.

'Looks like they're surrendering, Major.'

Crouched in the darkness, swathed in an odour of dust, rainsoaked clothing and cordite, Major Shellburn felt a momentary twinge of unease. Too simple, he thought. Those Krauts were socked-in tight. They knew damned fine he could lose half his men trying to winkle them out. Why quit now?

'Take it easy,' he warned. 'Could be a trick.'

'They're waving some kind of white flag,' the soldier shouted. 'Handkerchief, likely.'

Shellburn considered the situation. A minute ago he'd been cursing himself for his own stupidity. Walking straight up the tunnel had been an invitation to disaster. Those Germans had found themselves the perfect defensive position. When they'd started shooting, it had been a miracle nobody'd been hit. Now he was faced with two alternatives – either he could rush the gallery, which seemed certain suicide, or negotiate. He made up his mind.

'Fuller,' he said crisply, 'move in slow and hug the wall. Stay out of our line of fire, and we'll give you cover.'

'Okay, Major.'

Shellburn waited, his heart pounding, as Fuller moved

off. He did not like the situation one little bit. It was the goddamned-awfullest place to be stuck in. Like fighting a war in the middle of a sewer, for Christ's sake. Climbing crags hadn't been doing a hell of a lot for his military career, but right now he wished like crazy he was back in Sicily, back in the sun-warmed pure clean air instead of cooped up inside this shithole with a bunch of crazy squareheads ready to cut loose at anything that moved or breathed.

Fuller shouted to him out of the gloom, his voice harsh and startling. 'Major Shellburn, you'd better get up here quick.'

Shellburn scrambled to his feet and ran up the incline, stumbling over the metal rails. He saw Fuller standing at the gallery entrance, he saw the shadowy figure of the German who had waved the surrender flag sprawled across the limestone floor. There was no one else. The gallery seemed empty.

'Where the hell is everybody?'

'He's the only one, sir. He's wounded, hit in the knee.'

Shellburn felt his left boot stumble against something in the dark. He picked it up, studying it in his flashlight beam. A Schmeisser submachine-gun. Several others lay about in the shadows.

'Ask him what happened to his friends,' Shellburn commanded.

'I can't seem to get any sense out of the bastard, sir. He just lies there grinning, like there's some kind of joke only he understands.'

Sergeant Bullock had eased himself through the narrow window and was peering down from the gallery ledge. 'Major,' he called.

Shellburn joined him, flinching instinctively as the wind sent needle-sharp ice granules into his face.

'They can't have come this way, sir,' the sergeant said. 'Snow's as clear as frosting on a Christmas cake.'

Shellburn stared down through the swirling mist. It was impossible to see the valley below, but he could discern enough to realise the sergeant was right. No one had made a descent in the past hour or two. And yet . . .

'Somebody's been on this ledge,' he exclaimed. 'Look at the bootprints.'

Shellburn studied the cliff-face again. There were runnels in the snow where something had scraped its surface. Could have been the wind of course, but he didn't think so. He glanced up. Above, the cliff was obscured by an overhanging ceiling of rock, but protruding from its edge he spotted the tip of a solitary piton. The realisation hit him like a physical blow. Goddamnit, they weren't making for the valley at all, they were heading for the summit. They were going straight up the sheer North Face of the Eiger.

The sergeant followed his gaze. 'Holy Christ,' he breathed.

Shellburn stumbled back inside, his brain reeling. No one could survive up there, not in those conditions. But supposing they did? What if, against all odds, they managed to fight their way to the top? It was crazy, but if they pulled it off he would have lost them, Lasser too. He didn't dare leave them to the Eiger. He had to finish the job himself.

'They're heading for the summit,' he announced.

The men stared at him, their faces pale blurs in the dusky light.

'They've gone *up*?' somebody breathed incredulously. 'Right.'

'That's crazy. Even if they made it, what good would it do?'

'Plenty,' said Shellburn. 'They could come down the west flank maybe, or the Mitellegi Ridge. Or back across the glacier to the Jungfraujoch. Who the hell knows? If they can reach the Eiger's peak, they'll have a choice of a dozen different routes.'

'They'll never do it, sir,' the sergeant said. 'That mountain will gobble them alive.'

'Maybe, but we can't afford to take the chance. If they smuggle Dr Lasser into German hands, Hitler could end up winning this war. We've got to get to the top first.'

Pfc Duffryn, tall, lean and cadaverous-looking, chewed dolefully at his gum. He came from the tobacco belt of northern Virginia, and had the big hands and weatherbeaten face of a dirt farmer. 'How d'you figure on doing that, Major?' he asked.

'We'll go up the tunnel to the Jungfraujoch. From there, we can traverse east across the summits until we reach the Eiger. This storm'll freeze our butts off, but the route is essentially a traverse and not a climb. We should get there long before our German friends, so even if, by some miracle, they do manage to reach the top, we'll be ready and waiting.'

Pfc Duffryn scratched himself. 'Maybe they'll turn back, sir. Head for the valley instead of the summit. Then we'll be stuck on top of that mountain like a bunch of limp pricks.'

'I know,' said Shellburn. 'That's why somebody's got to go after them.'

There was silence for a moment. They stared at him unbelievingly. 'Up the Eiger?' somebody breathed.

'Listen,' Shellburn snapped, 'there's a helluva lot of cliff out there. Unless somebody keeps on their tail, they can still end up giving us the slip. If it wasn't so goddamned important, I wouldn't even consider it. But we've got to get Lasser, understand? It's probably the most vital objective any of us will face in this whole lousy war. Now you're all climbers, you know the Eiger and its reputation. Once you set foot outside that window, you'll be fighting for your lives every inch of the way. I want you to think carefully. And I'm calling for volunteers.'

The men stood in silence, the rancid odour of their sweat hanging about them like a blanket. Boots scraped on the rocky floor. There was the muffled clump of a carbine being dropped. Pfc Duffryn spat in the dust. 'I reckon it's always been kind of an ambition of mine to have a crack at that mountain, Major,' he drawled.

'Me too, I guess,' said a bull-shouldered man called Scribbs.

Shellburn looked at them. 'You realise what's waiting for you out there?'

Scribbs grinned and patted his heavy belly. 'Shit, Major, I got natural protection against the cold.'

'Okay, two of you should be enough. Leave your carbines behind and stick to hand guns. Get your weight

157

down as much as possible. Go through your packs and give anything you don't need to the sergeant here.'

'What if we catch up with them Krauts, sir,' asked Duffryn. 'What do we do, blast their asses off the mountain?'

'Just concentrate on Lasser,' Shellburn grunted. 'He's the important one. We can't afford to leave him prisoner.'

'We'd be lucky to pull off a rescue on that cliff, Major.'

Shellburn looked at them, shrugging glumly. 'Forget the rescue,' he said. 'I'm sorry, boys, but you'll just have to kill him.'

Eight

Helene wedged herself hard against the cliff and played out the rope as Spengler led off. They were at the foot of the 'Difficult Crack', the first real testing point on the Eiger's Face. Mist swirled everywhere. It looked like great puffs of smoke, and Helene thought: If ever there was a human conception of hell, this must be it. She felt the wind hit her, sweeping in from east and west, and pressed herself even harder against the cold rock, letting the rope slide expertly across her shoulder as Spengler, deft and sure, picked his way from crack to cranny, from knob to wrinkle, never tiring, never pausing, lost in his own private world, a no-holds-barred contest between the mountain and himself. She watched with admiration. He moved like an athlete, yet with economy of style, always studying the route ahead, picking his holds with an expert eye, testing them briefly before pressing on, inching upwards with a satisfying rhythm. Even the howling gale, tugging at his anorak hood, seemed little more than a minor irritation. Spengler ignored the wind, just as he ignored gravity, exposure, or the awesome void yawning out below. Helene shook her head in wonder. She saw now where Spengler's reputation came from. If she lived to be a hundred, she could never learn to climb like that. Spengler was born to the rock, he belonged here, as if no other part of his life could have any meaning except this, the ability to pit his nerve and skill against the challenge of impossible pitches.

At the top, he belayed himself to the cliff and took up the rucksacks on the rope. In a moment, it was Helene's turn.

'Climbing,' she shouted, though it was a pointless gesture, for the wind plucked the word from her mouth and hurled it into the empty mists, but she knew Spengler could feel her coming through the tautness of the rope.

The wind picked up force, lashing at the rock like an

angry sea, its roar obliterating everything, voices, snaplinks clanking, boots scraping – there was nothing to hear but the wind, and nothing to see but the mist and snow, and a few bare feet of ice-glazed limestone. Slowly, carefully, making each move as deliberate as possible, she eased herself up the massive wall, digging in her toes, taking care not to hug the rock too closely, leaning out as she picked her route steadily upwards until her feet were poised on a narrow ledge. The wind tugged at her clothing, but she thrust her fingertips into a narrow crack and perched there, numb and breathless, gathering her strength for the next move. Gingerly, she removed her left hand from its hold and reached out as far as she could. Her muscles were screaming from the strain, and as the gusts continued to batter her spine, the worrying thought occurred to her that she might end up with cramp. She shuddered. She was on the rope, of course, and would not fall far, but the thought of plummeting downwards into that swirl of mist made her feel sick to her stomach.

She shook her head to clear it, and let her fingers scurry across the rock like a spider, searching for a new crack to get a grip to. She found one and held tight, easing her foot a few inches higher. Her spirits began to rise. She would be all right as long as she could withstand the gale. She heard it coming in a fresh assault, stampeding up the cliff towards her. Gritting her teeth, she jammed her fingers into fresh holds and waited. The blasts hit her in successive bursts, tugging and pummelling, trying to whip her from her perch, but she held on grimly until the bombardment subsided.

If Spengler thought they could reach the summit in such conditions, she reasoned, he was a bigger fool than she'd imagined. Still, she owed him something. Her life, for one thing. Spengler could have killed her back there, and hadn't. He'd stopped Henke too. Henke would have finished her off at the drop of a hat. He was like that, mean and merciless, but Spengler was different again. Helene could not put a name to the way she felt in Spengler's presence. She had thought herself dead for so long now, sustained by neither conviction nor hope, that she found it difficult to understand the urges Spengler aroused in her. He was not at all like Karl, neither physically nor emotionally. Where Karl had been explosive and reckless, Spengler was thoughtful, cautious, even at times uncertain. And yet, she had to admit Spengler was the first man since Karl's death who had managed to take her out of herself, produce in her something she hadn't known for a very long time, a kind of calmness, a feeling that the darkness of the past might yet lead to a liveable future. What a shame they had to be on different sides.

Disregarding the void below, she moved on, inching up as swiftly as she could, reaching out with her left hand and following with her right foot, taking care always to keep three points of contact with the rock, but doing it with a breathless haste which, in different circumstances, she would have deemed reckless and foolhardy.

Below, the mists suddenly parted, and she caught a glimpse of rolling pastures a thousand feet down. She saw rivers, and miniature cow-huts, and just for a moment she spotted the little cluster of hotels at Kleine Scheidegg. A trick of the wind brought sounds to her ears. Cowbells and human voices. There were people down there, talking, chattering. It seemed impossible to believe that life could go on, maintain its normality, while they battled their way up this terrible mountain.

The fog slipped back, obscuring her view, and she balanced upwards like a gymnast, trying to recall from memory the holds Spengler had used, enjoying the comforting pull of the rope, the knowledge that whatever happened, Spengler would hold her from his stance on that good secure ledge at the top of the crack.

She paused for breath, sweating hard. The sky hung heavily down, wrapping the upper reaches of the Face in impenetrable gloom. Below, it formed a curtain beneath her feet. She supposed she ought to feel grateful for that. It had shut off the valley again, the great immensity of space down there, destroying that nerve-tingling sense of exposure. She thought of Dr Lasser. Sooner or later, the stress and strain of climbing this mountain would push him into a coma. She was doing everything she could, but if he died it would be Spengler's responsibility, not hers.

And – though she hated herself for thinking this – the fact remained that it would be better to have Lasser dead, than alive and in German hands.

She pushed Lasser out of her mind and pressed on, reaching, testing, heaving, scrambling, and by the time she reached Spengler's position, the war and their reasons for being here were utterly forgotten. The exhilaration of scaling a difficult route had wiped from her brain the notion that Spengler was still the enemy. Only the mountain mattered. The mountain, and the fact that they were fighting it together.

There was room to move around on the ledge, and Helene stood gasping for breath, sweat streaming down her face and throat.

'You handled that crack with excellent style,' said Spengler and, idiotically, she felt herself swell with pride. Is that all it takes, she thought, a casual compliment, a bit of flattery to start me preening myself like a silly schoolgirl?

'We'll need more than style to get us to the top,' she grunted.

'It's a start.'

She studied him in silence. There was something different about Spengler on the mountain. The uncertainties of yesterday were gone. He looked as sure of himself as a tiger.

'You really think we can do it, don't you?' she said.

'No. But I'd rather die up here than spend the rest of the war locked up like a squirrel in a cage.'

Beneath his coating of wind-blown snow, he looked pale and determined.

'Richner was right,' she said. 'You're not doing this for Germany, not for the Reich. It's for yourself. You and this mountain. It's all you've thought about for years. I might have known you couldn't come so close without being drawn to the Face like a moth to a flame.'

He scowled. It was as though she had found his weakness.

'There was only one way to escape those Yanks and we took it,' he snapped.

'We could have given in.'

'You'd have liked that, wouldn't you? You'd have gone back to your friends a hero.'

'Don't talk like an idiot. I want to stay alive, that's all.'

There was a look on his face that was half-angry, half-accusing, and she knew he was about to confront her. The shock of her treachery had penetrated deeply, and he needed things out in the open.

'You lied to me,' he said.

'That's right.'

'You were lying all the time.'

'It goes with the job,' she said.

'That night in the surgery, you were lying then.'

'Not altogether, Erich. What I did was directed at the German Reich, not you.'

'But why?'

She shrugged. 'Partly my husband, partly . . . well, call it conviction, if you like.'

'Or treason,' he said.

She smiled thinly. 'Not treason, Erich. I'm German in name only. I was born a Swiss, remember?'

He glowered at her. She saw him take a deep breath and haul hard on the rope, sliding it around his shoulder for purchase. His stance was so sound he'd used only the flimsiest of belays, and with a sense of wonder she watched the top of Dr Lasser's head bobbing towards them between the bulges of rock. Spengler's strength seemed boundless. Lasser was climbing as best he could, scrambling at fissures and projections like a monkey on a string, but it was Spengler who was taking most of the strain, pulling him upwards with a steady relentless pressure. She saw the rope tighten across Spengler's spine as Lasser came off and swung away from the crack, dangling helplessly in space. He swayed back and forth, rotating slowly, clinging to the rope with both fists. Gritting his teeth, Spengler heaved hard, pulling with his right hand while he played out slack with his left. She leaned forward and helped, adding her own strength to the line. Dr Lasser's head bobbed level with the ledge and she squatted down, thrusting her hands beneath his armpits, heaving him up and over the rock, gasping and spluttering in the wind.

Anxiously, she checked his pulse rate and peered into his eyes, while Spengler re-coiled the rope and glanced over the edge. Already, Henke and Richner were at the base of the 'Difficult Crack'. In a minute or two, the ledge would become too crowded for comfort.

'Let's push on,' Spengler ordered. 'We'll freeze to death if we hang about here.'

For the next hour they moved freely up easy ground, skirting the foot of the mighty 'Rote Fluh', that smooth wall several hundred feet high, down which spasmodic salvoes of stones came winging their way earthwards. Spengler tried not to think about the stones, tried to keep his mind on the push and pull of the upward haul, not enjoying it much, this breathless scramble, wishing instead for the more delicate pitches which tested a man's skill and made it feel more worthwhile. He had supposed that his return to the Face would be painful, or even macabre, and yet his mind was too busy to think of past memories, and even the sight of the odd piton, rusty with age, or the discovery at midday of a pair of ancient wool mitts had no more effect upon Spengler than they had upon the others. The girl moved well behind him, keeping up the pace. Good, he thought. This was no place for the jitters. One old maid on the rope could turn the whole thing into disaster. Their chances were slim enough with Lasser, without having to worry about stragglers. Henke and Richner had negotiated the 'Difficult Crack' with remarkable ease and were now hot on their heels as he headed towards the vital passage to the 'First Icefield', the smooth featureless slab which, years before, had so savagely and effectively shut off his friends' escape. When they reached it, he felt a surge of dismay. The rock was glazed with ice; it looked utterly un-climbable, a pitch of seemingly contourless smoothness. He remembered how Anderl had struggled again and again to forge a path across its slippery surface. The condition of the rock was as bad as Spengler had ever seen, and yet he knew there was no other way available. The traverse was a key point on the Eiger Wall, the gateway to the upper reaches of the Face above. He pushed his fingers into his mouth and sucked hard. The wind was picking up again. Snow came whistling into his cheeks, blinding his eyes, chilling the muscles around his lips. There was no time to waste. The traverse had to be negotiated now, before the storm blotted out visibility altogether.

'It's like a sheet of glass,' Helene muttered. 'Will it go?'

'It might,' said Spengler. 'If we put our faith in Hans Dülfer.'

She stared at him. 'Who on earth is Hans Dülfer?'

'Discoverer of the "rope-traverse" technique. He used it on the first ascent of the West Wall of the Totenkirchl. You fix the rope as a diagonal support. I'll show you.'

Instructing Helene to keep the line as taut as possible, Spengler inched upwards several metres. A cluster of rusty old pitons peppered the rock. He tested them, discarding the ones which seemed shaky with age, driving in fresh pegs where he could and attaching the rope for the delicate move across. When he was satisfied the pegs would hold, Spengler climbed back down and eased himself on to the slab. That was a terrifying immensity down there, and he tried not to think of it as he chipped away with his ice-hammer, tearing the shiny crust from the rock, balancing precariously like a steeplejack as he leaned out from the wall and edged steadily to the left. The world closed in, wrapping itself around him like a choking blanket, and he saw outcrops rearing through the mist like strange monsters from a mystic vision. Nothing was real any more. The whole world was a nightmare. He felt sick and his body ached. He knew only the rope was giving him the purchase he needed to get across, and even then it was a battle every inch of the way, a fight against gravity, against spindrift which swirled into his face, against the glazed-over rock which threatened to slide him off into eternity like a graceless vulture, and against his own underlying fear, for such conditions filled him with a dangerous flush of panic.

'Erich, come back,' Helene shouted.

'Not yet. There's a cranny here. Might get a peg in.'

'It'll never hold.'

'Better than nothing.'

'You'll slip, Erich.'

The wind hammered his back, buffeting him mercilessly. In the clamorous din, his body seemed to lose substance, as if he were floating, a bubble dancing on the storm's tumult. Sometimes the Face loomed out of the fog, dark and foreboding, like an ephemeral vision of God, but in a second the storm would close in, snuffing out sight, sound, reason, an invisible enemy that wracked and tore from an invisible refuge. The wind ripped up again. Spengler saw it coming in a great whorl of white, like a foam-crested tidal wave sweeping in from the sea, but this whorl he knew was of snow and ice whipped up at hurricane force and whirled around in a moving funnel. He pressed himself flat against the slab. The whorl hit him like a tornado and Spengler felt his body being rolled around as if a giant invisible hand was trying to pluck him from the cliff. He fought for breath and hung on tightly, praying he could stand the strain. And then the whorl passed, and like a shipwrecked seaman who finds himself drained, exhausted, but within sight of land, he raised his head cautiously, scarcely daring to believe he was still alive.

'Are you all right?' Helene called.

'I think so.'

He didn't know if he was all right or not. He didn't know if there was a scrap of feeling left inside his body, but he moved off again, inching his way gingerly sideways, and bit by bit, with the awesome void yawning below and the storm whirling around his skull, he fought his way across the delicate slab of rock. Helene, watching from the platform at the starting point, was overcome with admiration. Look at him go, she thought.

When Spengler had reached the other side, she made the traverse herself, finding it relatively easy with one rope holding her from above, and another guiding her into Spengler's strong sure hands. It took a little longer to bring Lasser across, but he too managed without too much difficulty, and they sat belayed on a narrow ledge, waiting for Henke and Richner.

'We'll leave the rope attached,' Spengler grunted. 'It'll give us an escape route if things go wrong.'

Helene nodded. She did not say what she was thinking. If the weather worsened, having an escape route wouldn't make a damned bit of difference.

'We'll have to eat,' she said.

'We have a long way to go. Best conserve rations.'

'Dr Lasser needs food,' she insisted. 'He must keep up his intake. Also, I want all the glucose tablets in the emergency packs.'

Spengler frowned. 'Can't you use his insulin?'

'I'll administer that when the time comes. The glucose tablets I need now.'

Spengler sighed and shrugged. 'You're the doctor,' he admitted.

He sat for a while studying their position. Above lay a vertical crack, seventy feet high, and beyond that, he knew, lay the opening to the 'First Icefield'. Soon they would be back in the direct line of fire, the 'Eiger Artillery', the salvoes of stones which dropped without warning all through the day, sweeping away the unwary. He tried not to think about that, not to listen to the ominous rumblings, not to shudder when the rocks went whistling by, to concentrate instead on the next move, the next pitch, the next belay.

All afternoon they climbed steadily upwards, sometimes pausing while Spengler tackled some delicate problem, sometimes retracing their steps when he got the route wrong. Despite his handicap, Dr Lasser climbed ably and competently, with Spengler hauling him up the really difficult sections, and by late evening they were above the 'First Icefield' and well up the rocky cliff which led to the second. Against their wildest hopes, the wind began to drop as they peered around for a bivouac spot. There was nothing but sheer rock and ice on all sides. Nevertheless, they managed to discern a ledge, barely five inches wide, with a comforting overhang above it. The overhang would protect them from falling stones, and the ledge would give them at least an illusion of security. Lying down was out of the question. There was not even a reasonable sitting space. But they drove in a few pitons and hung up the rucksacks. Then they manufactured strong seats with the slings, pulled on padded jackets and overtrousers, and settled down for the night with feet dangling in space.

The storm was definitely slackening. Their spirits rose as the wind dropped and the swirling curtains of cloud parted suddenly in front of them. Across the valley, the mountaintops looked flat and hard, their outlines silhouetted against the evening sky. Below, mist rose from the trees. Helene Rössner attended to Dr Lasser, who looked, Spengler thought, not very much the worse for wear in spite of his day's ordeal. The prospect of several hours dangling from the vertical Face was hardly a pleasant one, but Arno managed to brew up some coffee, balancing the tiny mini-stove on his rucksack, and afterwards they all felt better. They hung from the cliff, swaying gently in the breeze like sacks of barley, while far below, night fell.

The two Americans, Duffryn and Scribbs, moved swiftly and easily up the 'First Icefield'. They were climbing well, their twelve-pointer crampons making short work of the crusty surface, though in places, as Duffryn said, the ice was like porridge, sometimes giving way beneath their weight so that crampon, boot and half a leg would disappear without warning. Still, they had no complaints, and they knew the ice would harden when the temperature dropped. From time to time they paused for breath, hacking out a good solid stance to rest on, then driving in their iceaxe shafts for safety's sake.

Both Duffryn and Scribbs knew they would never have made it across the 'Hinterstoisser Traverse' if the Germans hadn't left their rope intact. That treacherous slab was an insurmountable barrier when its surface iced over. Only a climber of the highest calibre would have dared to attempt it. Whoever was leading those Krauts had to be somebody very special.

Duffryn paused briefly, balancing on his crampon points while he scanned the cliff above. Darkness was gathering fast. In an hour the Face would be swamped by night. They would have to bivouac soon. Visibility was bad enough as it was. With the light gone, they'd be totally helpless. Should they retreat to a bivouac perch on the Icefield's lower rim, or push on a few more feet in the hope of finding a sanctuary higher up, he wondered? Duffryn did not relish spending the night on this shield of ice. Too exposed for one thing. They were in the direct line of fire for the avalanches from above. Moreover, he did not care for the texture of the snow. It seemed too loose, too ready to dissolve. He could never free himself from the fear that it would suddenly give way and let him slide off into eternity, an experience which had indeed once happened to him on a scramble in the High Sierra. He had been scaling a snow gully in early spring, and the snow, with its soft underbelly, much softer than he had expected, had gone away from under his feet leaving him dangling from the rope like a carcass on a butcher's hook.

He was remembering this when suddenly, in the gathering gloom, he spotted something flicker on the cliff above. A light. Small, barely distinguishable, it flashed once, twice, three times, making a ruddy glow against the dark forbidding rock. Duffryn knew what it was. The party above had bivouacked early. That light was the glow from their cooking stove.

'Bo,' he whispered, keeping his voice down despite the wind, 'up here, quick.'

Scribbs clambered swiftly up to join him, using his iceaxe as an anchor. He followed Duffryn's pointed finger.

'We've caught them,' he hissed.

'I guess so.'

'How far, d'you reckon?'

'Hard to tell in this light. Can't be much though.'

'What the hell do we do now?'

Duffryn rubbed snowflakes from his nose. 'Well, goddamnit, I don't know what you're going to do, Bo, but I'm going to finish off that egg-head and get back down to the gallery window.'

Scribbs stared at him. 'In the dark?' he whispered.

'Why not? Better than tackling the bastards in broad daylight. The night'll give us cover.'

'Jesus, Frank, I hope you know what you're doing.'

Duffryn took out his pistol, snapped it open and checked the cartridge clip. He knew Scribbs was scared, but Christ, he was scared himself. Anybody would be scared on this bastard mountain. If they could finish the job tonight, they could retreat to safety with a clear conscience; it was worth a try. He slipped the pistol into its holster and picked up his iceaxe.

'Are you with me or not?' he asked.

'Do I have any choice?' Scribbs demanded.

Duffryn grinned. 'I guess not,' he said softly. 'Let's go.'

Spengler peered at Helene Rössner. 'Feel okay?' he asked.

'Bit sick,' she admitted.

'That's the altitude. Sip some coffee. Tastes foul, but it'll settle your stomach.'

She looked at the mug in her lap. 'It's barely hot.'

'The air's too thin for the water to boil, but cool coffee's better than nothing at all. Drink.'

He watched her sip, obeying his command not so much because she wanted to, but because protesting would have taken a monumental amount of effort. She was exhausted after the storm. They all were, he thought, Lasser most of all.

'Better?' he asked.

She nodded, her face slack and weary. She looked about finished, and no wonder. It had been a hard pull-up today, not a climb he would have chosen in happier circumstances. Nor were they through the worst of it, not by a long stroke. Even if the storm cleared, there was still an awesome expanse of cliff to scale.

To his surprise, he no longer felt any anger. Helene Rössner had lied, it was true – she had schemed and plotted their destruction – but against the reality of the Eiger, that seemed trite and unimportant. His anger had gone, just as the war itself had gone. All that mattered now was survival.

Spengler eased himself back against the rock. He had chosen the most inhospitable perch of all, a point where the ledge was so narrow that he kept sliding off into space, dangling furiously in his rope-sling like a bag of potatoes.

'Ever bivouacked like this before?' he asked.

She twisted her face, stretching her limbs uncomfortably.

'Never so exposed,' she admitted. 'If I had the energy, I'd be terrified.'

'Relax. These pegs are good and strong. If you feel cold, try flexing your muscles. Flex and relax, that's the secret. Movement generates heat.'

She looked at him, a strange smile playing on the corners of her mouth. 'Don't you feel angry with me?' she asked.

'For what?'

'Being the enemy.'

Spengler shrugged. 'On the Eigerwand, there's only one enemy, and that's the mountain.'

The night was growing colder, turning their breath into clouds of vaporous steam. Mist still swirled beneath their feet, but, glancing upwards, Spengler caught a glimpse of the stars and thought: that's a good sign for tomorrow. He felt relaxed for the first time that day. It was a phenomenon he had never ceased to wonder at, the way he could feel suddenly and peacefully at rest, even on the most precarious of positions.

'Where did you live before the war?' he asked conversationally.

She looked at him and shrugged. 'Mainz mostly,' she said, 'on the Rhine.'

'Will you go back there, when it's over?'

She stared hard, as though seeking some hint of mockery on his face. 'Haven't you forgotten something?' she said. 'Henke wants me shot.'

'Don't worry about Henke. A lot can happen between here and the Italian border.'

'What do you mean?'

'Just deliver Lasser intact. After that . . .'

He shrugged.

She folded her arms across her chest. Surprisingly, she felt no relief at the prospect of release. 'You don't really imagine we'll ever get off this wretched mountain?' she murmured.

'I have to,' Spengler stated simply. 'It's the only thing that keeps me going.'

He wondered why, after her betrayal, his resentment had failed to incubate, but the fact remained that he felt no animosity whatsoever. No place for it, he thought. Up here, each needed the other. But it was more than that. After the emptiness of the past few years, she had wrought in him a kind of tranquillity, a notion that life was good and satisfying.

He said: 'Was it in Mainz that you met your husband?'

'No. That was in Paris.'

She leaned back against the rock, smiling softly at memories of the past. He felt a sense of pain that there were things about her he could never know or even begin to guess at.

'He was on his way to Chamonix,' she said. 'The weather was bad. It had been bad for almost a month. Karl decided to stop off in Montparnasse and indulge in a little social drinking. The police brought him to my surgery at six in the morning. He'd been hit by a car on the Boulevard St Germain. He wasn't badly hurt, but I had to stitch up a nasty cut on his cheek. He'd been on a bender for nearly three days. I learned later that was typical of Karl. He never did anything in half measures. Climbing mountains, getting drunk, it was all the same to him. He went at the world like a bull in a china shop. No restraint and no compromise.'

'Is that why you married him?'

'I married him because I loved him,' she said and, absurdly, he felt a pang of jealousy.

'Oh, not the story book love,' she added. 'I never believed in that. Karl and I were the kind of people who fitted together like old shoes. He needed my stability, I needed his recklessness.'

He stared into the mist. 'How did he die?' he whispered, thinking: Is it necessary to know? Can a corpse be a rival? The man is dead, the past is over.

'He was a lawyer,' she murmured, resting her head against the rock. 'A good one. We would have had a comfortable life among Mainz's bourgeoisie, except that Karl hated Hitler and everything he stood for. What was more, being Karl, he couldn't keep his hatred to himself. Every opportunity he got, he attacked Hitler's policies, Hitler's excesses. I could see his behaviour was madness and tried to stop him, but stopping Karl was like stopping a bulldozer. I began to notice our friends were avoiding us. That only made Karl a thousand times worse. His hatred of Hitler developed into an obsession. When they took him away, it was almost a relief. At last I had something I could face.'

'Did you try to get him released?'

'Every day. In spite of his idiosyncracies, Karl still had lots of friends in the legal profession, and some of them were willing to stick their necks out for old times' sake. Also, I was a respected member of the Nazi Party myself by then. At first, I tried the Kriminalpolizei. I visited the Reichskriminaldirektor with a letter from one of the top judges in Berlin. He informed me that Karl's fate was already out of his hands. Karl had become a ward of the Gestapo. After a great deal of negotiating, I managed to get an interview with the SS Reichsführer himself.'

'Himmler?'

'He promised to look into Karl's case personally. Three days later, I received Karl's ashes in a cardboard box.'

Her voice had hardened. It was like the onset of some vague hysteria. Spengler felt uncomfortable.

'I knew then,' she said, 'that for Karl's sake, and for the sake of my own sanity, I had to devote myself to destroying Hitler and everything he stood for.'

Staring into the darkness, Spengler seemed caught in a kind of haze. He scarcely dared admit, even to himself, what it was he was thinking. Its very nature made his breath quicken, his heart flutter.

'Do you ever wonder if you'll marry again?' he asked with studied casualness.

She stared at him curiously. 'That's a funny question. I never considered anything beyond the war. There wasn't anything left to consider. I was glad the war existed because it gave me an excuse for existing also.'

'The war won't last for ever,' he muttered, and watched her shudder.

'I try to forget that,' she grunted. 'When I think about that, it makes me . . . uneasy.'

Spengler picked a pebble from the ledge and hurled it into the darkness. 'You'll have to face it sometime.

A world without Karl. A world without war. The longer you put it off, the harder it'll be to pick up the pieces again.'

She blinked rapidly, her eyes glistening. She seemed on the brink of laughter or grief. 'What about you?' she asked. 'Have you never married?'

'No.'

'Why?'

'I got near it once or twice, but . . . due to one thing or another, it never came off. I suppose, when you come right down to it, I didn't want it badly enough.'

'Well,' she said, 'it's hardly a state of grace. Some people were born to be single.'

'I used to think I was, but not any more.'

She was watching him closely, her expression unreadable. The feeling persisted that he had set in motion an inexorable chain of events, a chain which she herself recognised and identified, so that she was waiting now, with apprehension and anticipation, for him to make his next move.

'Supposing we get out of this?' he murmured hesitantly, 'I mean, supposing we make it to the summit, and supposing I manage to let you escape before we reach the border . . .'

His words trailed away. He felt caught in a helpless drift of time.

'What are you leading up to, Erich?'

He shifted uncomfortably. 'You said before that Karl needed your stability, you needed his recklessness. Has it occurred to you that we have something in common too? We both have ghosts to be exorcised.'

She was crying. He could see the tears glistening on her cheeks.

'We're on opposite sides,' she said, 'enemies.'

'Only for the moment.'

She shook her head slowly, wiping her eyes with the back of one hand. 'You're thinking of a future that doesn't exist,' she protested.

'You're living in a present that doesn't deserve to,' he insisted.

'I can't afford this to happen . . . I daren't. I need . . . I must think only of the job in hand. It's the only way I can survive.'

Spengler nodded, understanding. He felt that some-thing had been settled between them, though he scarcely knew what.

'Then concentrate on Lasser,' he murmured. 'That's all you need worry about for the moment. Later, when this is over, we can talk again.'

He glanced beyond her to where the scientist sat perched against the rock, staring into the murky darkness.

'How is he?' he asked.

'Recovering,' said Helene. 'I've given him a shot of insulin.'

'He looks pretty tough at any rate.'

'I haven't heard him complain yet,' she admitted.

Spengler studied Dr Lasser thoughtfully. The scientist *did* look tough, he decided. From his nose to the swell of his chin, his face appeared as if it had been pounded flat. His eyes were narrow, and the lids jutted from the protruding brow like cornices, leaving only the lower halves of the pupils visible, hard and unyielding.

Spengler filled his mug with coffee and passed it over. 'Drink?' he offered.

Lasser turned to look at him, and Spengler saw a ragged scar running from his left ear and disappearing beneath the folds of his anorak collar.

'Who are you, Lieutenant?' Lasser asked in his thick Danish accent.

'The dreaded Hun,' Spengler said with a grin.

Lasser did not smile back. At close quarters, his nose seemed to glow like the prop of a music-hall drunk. It was a nose that had been broken at least twice. Altogether a face to steer clear of, Spengler thought, a face that had at one time or another tried to enforce its will upon others.

'No normal man could climb like you did today,' Lasser whispered. 'With my own eyes I watched you go up pitches which were a physical impossibility. Who *are* you?'

Spengler hesitated. 'Lieutenant Spengler,' he said, 'of the 5th Gebirgsjäger.'

Lasser's eyes flickered. 'Erich Spengler?'

'That's right.'

'I've read about you. You made the first ascent of the Maztagh Pike. I read about those climbs with Vorg in the Himalayas too. I used to be a climber myself, in my younger days.'

Spengler's eyebrows lifted with new interest. 'I didn't know,' he murmured.

'Nothing as fancy as the North Face of the Eiger, mind you. But this is no new experience for me.'

Spengler stared at the beat-up leathery face and felt a glimmer of understanding. No wonder Lasser had managed so well today. He'd come up that cliff like a veteran, out of condition and out of practice, but with a certain amount of style nevertheless.

Lasser eased himself back against the rock and stared pensively into the night, as if somewhere beyond the darkness he could see the future, or the past. 'I devoted years of my life to climbing,' he mused. 'When I was eighteen I used to think nothing else in the world mattered.' He laughed humourlessly. 'Look at me now. I'm like this old cliff here. Dried-up and hammered flat.'

'You've got memories, though,' Spengler protested.

'I've got nothing. I'm a fossil, like the mountain. Don't talk to me of memories. You can't buy peace with memories.'

For a moment, Spengler saw Lasser as a kindred spirit, a creature stretched on a rack of his own making, not realising it fully, not understanding it, but teetering on the rim of the same abyss.

'We'll never make it, you know,' Lasser said softly, 'not to the summit. We were lucky today. Luck like that doesn't come twice in one lifetime.'

'We've got to make it,' Spengler asserted, and Lasser smiled thinly.

'Are you sure you're doing this out of a sense of duty, Lieutenant, or is it something else?'

'What d'you mean?'

'I watched you climb today. You're not like the others, simply trying to escape. I think you're sick, up here . . .' He tapped his forehead.

Spengler was silent for a moment. He felt an urge to

turn his soul bare. 'You don't know what happened to me on this mountain,' he breathed.

'Oh, yes I do. I read about that too, about what happened to the people you were with. And now, no doubt you feel guilty.'

Spengler hesitated. 'That comes into it, I suppose,' he said. 'The guilt bit.'

'Don't let it,' Lasser advised. 'It'll eat you up inside. There isn't time for guilt.'

He smiled. 'You think about time when you get to my age.'

Spengler wanted Lasser to understand, though he couldn't say why. It was like seeing a reflection of himself sitting there, a caricature of his own unrest. 'You don't know all of it,' he said, 'not really. The people I was with, they only died. But with me, there was something left. You see it sitting in front of you. It looks like a human being. It performs the functions of a human being. The only difference is, the insides have been taken out.'

Lasser chuckled. 'We make a good pair, you and I. A German officer who thinks he's carrying the sins of the world on his shoulders, and a worn-out old hack planning to blow mankind to bits. Let me tell you something about myself, Lieutenant. I should've died years ago, when I was thirty-five. Nothing much happened after that. If I'd had to go then, I wouldn't have shed any tears.'

His pupils gleamed like dark coals. 'That's something a woman could never understand,' he said. 'Women cling to life with all the fury they can muster. Suicide is alien to them. When a woman commits suicide, it's seldom a premeditated act. A woman sees life as a valuable commodity. She would rather live it in second gear than not live at all. A man now, he can never stand the second-gear bit. Once he stops being functional, he's happy to go. He wants to blast away like a roman candle, and when it's done he just sits back and waits for it to end. He doesn't exactly court death, but it doesn't worry him much either.'

'Don't talk about death,' said Spengler. 'It's bad luck.'

Lasser's eyes twinkled. 'Tomorrow we'll make our own luck,' he said. 'Tomorrow we'll beat the mountain, or the mountain will beat us. Either way, for you and me, Lieutenant, the outcome will be the same. We carry death inside us like a secret affliction.'

Fifty feet away, the American, Duffryn, paused in his ascent to peer, sweating, through the gloom. It had been a difficult climb, coming up through the dark, leaving the icefield behind and mounting the lower reaches of perpendicular rock. He was thankful for the wind which had blotted out the sound of his boots and the clinking of the pitons which dangled from his waist. He'd been reluctant to drive in pegs in case the clump of their hammers had reached the ears of the people bivouacking above.

From his perch, he could now see their outlines clearly. Five altogether, all dressed in the sage green anoraks of the German Gebirgsjäger, except one who wore a bright yellow parka and loose-fitting climbing breeches. That had to be Lasser, Duffryn thought. No German soldier looked like that.

Duffryn reached down and gently removed his pistol. He cocked it silently, easing back the hammer with his thumb. The light was bad, but at this distance he couldn't miss. Static target, and handguns were his specialty. Before the war, he had been a carnival sharpshooter.

Carefully, he took aim. Lasser couldn't move far, fastened as he was to the rock. Duffryn squeezed the trigger, but nothing happened. Cursing softly, he squeezed again. In the bitter cold, the firing mechanism had frozen. Swearing, Duffryn pushed the pistol back into its holster and peered back at Scribbs.

'Give me your gun,' he hissed urgently.

Scribbs looked puzzled, but without a word he took out his pistol, clipped it with a snaplink to the rope and slid it across. Duffryn examined the weapon carefully. Both guns were caked with ice, and useless.

A chilling truth dawned upon Duffryn. Without guns, there was only one way to get the job done. They would have to climb up and finish off Lasser by hand. Jesus Christ, he thought, that was bare rock up there. The slightest scrape could give them away. Duffryn thought for a moment, then unhooked the ironmongery from around his belt and let it drop into the night. The string of snaplinks and pitons fell vertically, vanishing into the cloud like a plummeting swallow. Scribbs watched in disbelief.

'What in hell's name are you doing?' he whispered.

But Duffryn did not answer. With a sense of grim purpose he untied himself from the rope, and began to pick his way delicately up the cliff in the dark.

Spengler shifted on his stance, trying to jolt some of the stiffness from his limbs, trying to will some blessed warmth back into his frozen body. He had known happier bivouacs, he thought, this one was an abomination. There wasn't even room to sit properly. Every time his muscles relaxed, he slid from the ledge and hung helplessly in his rope-sling, peering into the emptiness below.

He grunted, easing himself back against the rock, turning his mind from the cold and discomfort. There were always things to remember at times like this, with death only a breath away. He'd never minded death, he thought. It was not something he truly feared. His fear in the past had generally been for others, for once you were up here, just you and the mountain together, death seemed to lose its significance, somehow. The mountain became a living force, you could feel its strength through your fingers and feet. Its strength was sustaining, not in any way fearful. Death became a phase, unwanted, but certainly not unpalatable.

Spengler sighed and hunched his shoulders, trying to tuck his head against the cliff. He could feel the chill surface of the rock against his ear. He saw the narrow ledge, and the coils of rope, and the slings, and the rucksacks dangling. He saw Helene Rössner's climbing breeches, coated with a thin sheen of ice. He saw the hand.

Spengler blinked. Was he losing his mind? Had reality gone drifting away somewhere beyond those cracks and pillars and twisting chimneys?

He stared. It was indisputably a hand, human and alive.

It came creeping over the lip of their ledge like a cautious insect, the fingers slithering, exploring, seizing.

Despite the cold, sweat broke out over Spengler's entire body. His mind in a daze, he watched as the hand took a firm grip, the tendons standing out around the wrist. Then slowly, the head rose into view. It was a head without features, a blob of grey against a murky sky.

Spengler felt dizzy. The incongruity, the sheer unlikelihood of finding another creature on this unspeakable mountain made his senses reel. Pull yourself together, he thought. That is no friendly head you see there, but the enemy bent on his kill.

Still, Spengler did not move. The others were dozing, and the man crept with such perfect litheness that the wind obliterated his approach. His shoulders rose above the level of the ledge, and his face was no longer obscured. Some trick of the night, a pool of watery greyness gave an outline to his nose and the deep sockets where his eyes should be. His breath steamed on the mountain air. Spengler saw his other hand raised high, saw the faint gleam of an iceaxe blade. And Spengler moved.

His own iceaxe dangled from a piton above his head. With one jerk, Spengler snatched it free and rammed it out as far as it would go. There was a metallic clanking sound as the two blades met in mid-air. Sparks showered the night. Spengler felt the strength of the blow ripple down his arm, heard the man curse loudly in surprise. An American voice, his brain registered. Helene Rössner jerked upright with a short sharp scream. Along the ledge, the others began to stir; he could hear their voices, startled and alarmed.

The man swung his arm for another try, Spengler tried to get at him but the rope-sling held him back. He saw the iceaxe poised for the kill, he saw Dr Lasser's startled leather face. He swung his own iceaxe with all the strength he could muster, not aiming outwards this time, but down, driving the blade deep into the hand on the ledge. The tendons contracted wildly as cold steel bit into the flesh. Two fingers shot like arrows off into the darkness. Frozen against the mist, with one arm raised to strike, the man screamed in agony. Still strapped to the mountain,

Spengler swung up his legs and lashed out with both feet. He felt his boots drive solidly into the man's chest, felt the ribcage give, and then the man was gone. It was as quick as that. One second he was there, the next he had disappeared. There was nothing to see but mist, and nothing to hear but the wind's howl and the sickening crunch of the body striking outcrops on its long drop down.

The force of his kick had taken Spengler clear of the ledge, so that now he dangled in the rope-sling, swaying in the wind. It was the fall which saved him, for the blade of a second iceaxe missed his skull by inches, striking the rock in a ragged arc, sending a trail of fiery sparks into the night. Spengler had been so absorbed with the first intruder that he had not even seen this second figure climbing up to the ledge on his left. Oh Christ, he thought, the bastards are crawling all over the place.

The man was edging along the narrow ledge, hugging the cliff. Spengler could see his face clearly. It was clean-cut and youthful, the features twisted into a mask of fearful determination. Sweat streamed down the man's cheeks, tracing rivulets of white through the dirt which had caked there during the day. He reached out, steadying himself, holding on to Spengler's belaying piton with one hand while he took careful aim with the other. In that second, Spengler realised what he was after. It was not he who was the target, but Dr Lasser.

Desperately, Spengler seized the American's trouser leg and tried to drag him from the rock. The man moved. As his iceaxe curved in a vicious swing, Lasser ducked his head, grunting with alarm. The blade scoured the cliff, sparking furiously. With a curse, the man drew back his arm for a second try. Spengler could see Lasser struggling to wriggle backwards. He was unable to move however, for the slings held him fast. He was, Spengler realised, a sitting target. Jesus, he thought, this time the Yank can't miss.

Thrusting his feet against the cliff, Spengler leaned out against the pull of the rope and rammed his iceaxe shaft into the intruder's testicles. The man squawked out with pain. Spengler thrust again, missing the target this time, but jabbing hard into a defenceless stomach. The man dropped his own iceaxe and doubled over, retching in agony. Slipping, he made a desperate lunge for Spengler's rope, and next second, the two of them were dangling wildly over the yawning void.

The wind shrieked in Spengler's ears as the other body hugged him furiously, struggling for purchase. He could feel the blind terror in the strength of the man. My God, I hope that piton holds, he thought. A face slipped into view, barely an inch from his own, Young, unshaven, streaked with dirt, it stared directly into Spengler's. I've got to break the bastard's grip before he rips out that peg altogether, Spengler thought.

He tried to bring up his iceaxe, but the man seized his wrist, forcing back the arm. Face to face, they tore at each other savagely, kicking, twisting, writhing. Spengler's skull cracked against the cliff. Lights flashed in his eyes and, dazed, he let go his grip on the iceaxe. Instantly, the American swung it in a tight arc, holding it by the shaft, high up. Spengler tried to stop him, but his arms were still caught in the intruder's desperate bear-hug. Spengler felt the steel blade bite deep into the muscle above his left elbow, and he cried out in pain. Blood spurted the rock. Waves of agony lanced his upper shoulder. He felt his senses reeling. I'm passing out, he thought. He'll finish me off and that'll be the end of it.

He squirmed, spinning slowly on the rope. Where the hell was everybody? Spengler felt abandoned.

Chunk. The impact of the blow vibrated through Spengler's body, but this time there was no pain. He was beyond pain, lost in that never-never land where pain and time had ceased to exist. If he wants to kill me, let him kill me, he thought. But to Spengler's surprise, the grip around his body began to slacken. A pair of yellowish eyes flickered close to his, desolate and filled with despair. Spengler could see in them the glimmer of approaching death. A stream of scarlet slithered down the man's dirt-streaked face. Someone's iceaxe – Henke's probably – had bitten deep into the crown of his skull, and now a gaping wound pulsed blood and bone fragments through the yellow close-cropped hair. Spengler felt death seeping through the man's upper limbs. Slowly, unwillingly, he slid down the length of Spengler's body, making one last attempt to save himself by holding tightly to Spengler's left leg, but dying, his strength gave out and he had to let go. Spengler watched him plummet earthwards, the thick body in the khaki-green anorak vanishing swiftly into the drifting waves of mist. There was no cry, just a strange gripping silence. The silence, Spengler thought, was worst of all.

He felt strong hands hauling him up to the narrow ledge. Someone was peering anxiously at the wound on his arm. He sat back, relieved to be still alive, letting himself drift, lost in delirium while his blood trickled with alarming insistency down the surface of the dark cold Face.

Nine

Major Shellburn and his men had spent the night in the dormitory of the Jungfraujoch research station. Shellburn had felt there was little chance of the Germans making the summit before the end of the second day (if indeed they made it at all) and it had seemed pointless to expose Unit D unnecessarily to a night on the mountain while the storm was still raging.

On arrival at the laboratory, they had discovered the body of a German soldier (it was Rolf Notz, who had died less than an hour after Spengler's departure), and the little detachment of OSS bodyguards still strapped securely, and red-faced with embarrassment, to their bunks.

Unit D had dined in comfort, using the provisions from the Berghaus Restaurant (for which Shellburn had left an official IOU) and even rounding off the evening with a few bottles of Swiss beer, which Shellburn had insisted his men pay for with American money. Now, as dawn spread its greyness across the eastern sky, the men gulped their mugs of hot coffee and prepared to face the blizzards outside. Shellburn stood at the window and peered into the snow. Though the storm had slackened during the early hours, he realised it had been only a temporary respite. A cold wind blew across the mountain. Heavy clouds scurried ominously by. It would be no picnic out there, he knew. And no picnic either on the dreaded North Face. Already, he regretted having sent Duffryn and Scribbs on that maniacal climb, but there'd been no other way. The Germans had to be stopped, Lasser either rescued or neutralised.

He turned with a sigh, and peered again at the mountaineering equipment his soldiers had unearthed in the caretaker's storeroom.

'We'll take the stretchers along,' he announced. 'They may come in useful if anyone gets hurt out there.'

'What about this, sir?' a soldier asked. He was holding the assortment of heavy cables used for rescue attempts on the upper reaches of the Eiger's Face. They were built into metal frames, with attached couplings, rollers, brakes and winches. Shellburn pursed his lips. With a cable like that, they could, if necessary, lower themselves down from the summit.

He nodded. 'Those too,' he said.

Thirty minutes later, laden down with equipment, their faces almost hidden beneath their parka hoods, the men of Unit D stepped out of the comfort and security of the research station into the driving storm.

Spengler watched his hand. He was perched with his face against the rock, his left arm jutting out from his body at a curious angle. He could see his fingers piercing the mist like anti-tank posts. It had taken him quite some time to figure out who the hand belonged to, an hour or two at least, he estimated, for he remembered a snow shower which had seemed to go on interminably. The hand, however, was indisputably his own. He had identified it by the zig-zag scar at the base of the thumb. Recognising the hand as his own was, he felt, something of a victory. It proved for one thing that his senses were still functioning, he was still alive, still intact as a human being. I can feel the rock, he told himself, and think with a certain remnant of understanding. Up there is the sky, the cloud, the summit.

Towards sun-up, the air seemed to freeze, wrapping itself around them like a choking blanket. Their clothes felt brittle from a thin coating of ice, Inside their nostrils, the tiny hairs froze into needlepoints.

Spengler sniffed the wind. The weather was worsening, not improving. They would be lucky to last another day on this Face.

He touched his arm with his fingertips. Beneath the bandage it seemed swollen. There was no pain any more, only a disturbing numbness. It was a nasty wound, he knew that, though Helene Rössner had dressed it as best she could, and yet already his flesh felt like a block of fudge. He held the arm in front of his face and clenched his fist. It moved hesitantly, but at least it moved. The question was, for how long?

A roll of thunder seemed to rip the sky apart above his head. With teeth chattering, they brewed up fresh coffee and began to prepare for their second day's climbing. The bitter night had had a devastating effect upon them all.

'How's the arm?' Helene Rössner asked.

'Stiff,' he said.

'I hope it holds out.'

'It'll have to. No room on this mountain for a one-armed man.' She pushed something soft into his hands.

'Eat this,' she ordered.

'What is it?'

'Last of the cheese.'

He grimaced and tried to pass it back. 'Give it to Lasser.'

'He's got enough,' she said, shaking her head.

'Save it for later then. I thought he had to eat regularly.'

'He'll survive.'

'Not if the Americans have anything to do with it. You saw what they were after?'

She nodded, not looking at him directly.

'He's too important to live,' Spengler said, wondering – now that the implications of what they were doing were out in the open – how far he could trust her. He added quietly: 'In the wrong hands, that is.'

She stared at him wryly. 'Don't worry,' she said, 'I haven't sunk that low yet. Not even in the name of duty.'

Breakfast over, they repacked the rucksacks, strapped on crampons and started up the 'Second Icefield'. The surface, which had looked from below as smooth as glass, was pock-marked with boulders, a grim testimony to the 'artillery barrages' from the heights above. They must be climbing directly up the line of fire, Spengler thought, grateful that it was early morning and the rocks were still anchored to the cliff by ice. The gradient was almost perpendicular, but the twelve-pointers gave them good purchase on the brittle crust, and only occasionally did Spengler pause to hack away steps with his good arm. There was no time for slow steady climbing. Every hour spent on this terrible cliff was draining them of life, heightening their chances of disaster.

They moved through a grey world without colour; even the snow looked grey, and sometimes the different shades merged so that it was impossible to tell where the ice ended and the mist began, and impossible too to maintain any sense of depth or distance.

Spengler looked behind and saw for a second a tinge of scarlet through the gloom. The sun, he thought. It must be out there. He would write it a hundred odes if he ever saw it again.

The snow whirled across their route like drifting sand. In half an hour their trail would be covered. There would be nothing to show they had been there except themselves, if they lived. One step at a time, and keep up the pace. It was easy to believe that nothing else existed, to imagine that the blanket of mist down there extended for ever, a dream mirage inviting them to defy the wind and float off like swans into eternity.

Such illusions were dangerous, he told himself. The two Americans hadn't defied gravity. They'd gone all the way down to the *Bergschrund*.

Spengler wondered how it would feel falling through the atmosphere. Would a man die before he made contact with the earth or would the sheer breathless drop take away his consciousness, render him insensible? Climbers who'd fallen and survived claimed that the brain separated from the body, bringing a feeling of euphoria, a glorious release. Spengler liked to believe that. He found it reassuring.

By mid-morning, he had reached the stance below the overhanging cliff which was known as 'Death Bivouac'. He brought the others up to join him, then called a halt while they lay and rested. Sprawled in the snow, their bodies displayed the hopeless, passive air of people carried beyond the boundaries of endurance. Lasser especially, Spengler thought. The strain of the past twenty-four hours showed plainly on his face.

'How's he doing?' he asked Helene.

'Not good,' she said. 'He needs rest, shelter, decent food.'

'We'll give him what we've got.'

'Not enough, Erich. He's a tough old bird, but keep this pace up and you'll surely kill him.'

Spengler smiled bitterly. 'Well, we can't push on until the gale slackens,' he said. 'That should give him a chance to get his strength back.'

'How's the arm?' she asked.

'The arm's fine.'

'Want me to change the dressing?'

Damn the woman, he didn't want her concern. A little too much at the wrong moment and he might crack altogether.

'Leave it,' he growled, 'let me rest. It's all I'm good for.'

They shivered as the wind began to hammer their perch with a relentless persistence. Soon it was hitting them in a continual barrage, sometimes ramming them head-on, sometimes blasting its way in to catch them from the rear. Spengler began to see the wind as a living force intent on their destruction, heaving and straining like some tenacious animal struggling to get at them in their lair. He knew there was no hope of climbing on unless it dropped, and little hope of surviving either. Like the two German climbers who had given the bivouac its macabre name, they would be found weeks later, frozen in their tracks like useless clay statues. It seemed a bitter end after having come so far, but the decision was no longer Spengler's. Everything now depended on the wind. If it eased, they still had a chance. If it didn't, they were doomed.

He began to think about his life, not in any logical way. He recalled the past with a flavour and intensity that had never really existed. He was a child again, running home from school on dark winter nights, over the narrow iron bridge which straddled the tree-lined ravine and up the alleyway to the blessed light and safety of the terminus where the tramcars turned. He was a boy again, waking in the night to hear his mother call, and getting up and going into his parents' room to find his father dying. Holding the powerful shoulders, seeing the calloused neck, the cropped hair, listening to the death-rattle in the razor-scraped throat.

Sometimes Spengler felt there was a judgement a man knew in his heart was more utter and terrible than anything he could put a name to. It bubbled clear and clean in his brain, yet he must be blind to it. Blind of necessity, though his eyes turned inwards could see it plain. He thought about the war, which, in the beginning, they had prophesied would end by Christmas. It had not ended though, it had gone on, a confused blur of attacks and counter-attacks, breakthroughs and counter-breakthroughs, stretching through January, February, into spring. Victories had lost their excitement. They had come to accept them as their right; you advanced, you overcame. But that had changed, he told himself bitterly. The victories had ended like everything else. Four years later, weary, footsore and on the brink of exhaustion, they had shuffled through Tuscany watching the yellow-white puffs in the sky as the enemy had shelled their rear positions. Spengler had lost count of the days and nights of continual bombardment, of the blackened bodies which had lain tossed about the mustard-coloured scrub, or the burnt-out shells of tanks which had littered their path. He had lost count of the burned villages, of the frightened refugees who had choked the dusty roads, and the starving children, their bellies swollen from malnutrition, their eyes hollow with the intensity of their need. Wholesale murder had become an integral part of their lifestyle, not as excesses practised by individuals in the front line, but on the express command of the generals themselves. Prisoners of war had been summarily executed. Civilians suspected of subversion shot out of hand. As the weeks had spread and the killings had gone on, Spengler had given up even the pretence of caring. He was simply a soldier, a tool in the hands of faceless strategists, a solitary figure in the lines of red-eyed beard-stubbled troops whose first preoccupation was no longer victory for the Reich, but the simple fundamental urge to stay alive.

He thought about Helene Rössner. What makes you think Helene Rössner would be interested in you, he asked himself? What have you got to offer a woman like that? A common soldier who never got above the rank of sergeant in his life, until now. No education, or none to speak of, and slow on the uptake too; if it hadn't been for the army, you'd have spent your life in the Hamburg shipyards, while she is indisputably a lady of learning.

Henke's voice woke him from his reverie.

'Wind's slackening,' he said.

Spengler sat up. 'Are you sure?'

'Listen.'

Spengler nodded. He had been almost afraid to believe the truth, as if the easing of the storm was a cruel fancy wrought by his own exhaustion. It *was* true, however, he saw that now. The massive gusts had already subsided to such an extent that the first timorous rays of hope began to revive inside him. They were alive. Battered, dazed, half-smothered with snow, but unquestionably alive. He tested his arm. Between shoulder and elbow it had lost all feeling, but miraculously the hand and fingers still obeyed his brain's command.

'Get up,' he ordered, his voice a painful croak. 'Up, all of you. We've got to . . . move.'

Their route lay, Spengler saw, diagonally across the 'Third Icefield' towards the foot of the 'Ramp', the rocky buttress which leaned out against the sky like a minister's pulpit. It would be no easy rock climb at the best of times, and certainly not for a one-armed mountaineer nearing the end of his tether.

It took Spengler six hours and five rope-lengths to reach the chimney in the upper reaches of the 'Ramp'. It was ugly beyond belief, its walls smooth and black, free of holds, free of anything at all that offered even a hint of purchase, and worse, there was a waterfall tumbling down inside its crack. Spengler felt his spirits drop. Leading off, he balanced precariously up the miserable sliver. Water ran through his clothes, oozing down his neck and sleeves, trickling into his breeches, filling his boots. Despite the need for speed, he moved with agonising slowness, his breath coming in short bursts. He was shivering from head to foot, his arm no longer part of his body. When he reached out and took a grip, no sensation communicated itself to his brain. It was as if the arm had become a separate organism, hand and fingers operating in-dependently. By the time he had reached the top and brought up the rest of the team, they were drenched to the skin and beginning to freeze in the chill mountain air.

'Keep moving,' he told Helene, 'don't let your clothes ice up.'

She studied him anxiously, brushing the drops from his cheeks with her fingertips. 'Stop worrying about me,' she whispered. 'Concentrate on yourself.'

Spengler felt his insides dissolve. To change the subject, he said: 'Lasser?'

'He's fine.'

'Good. We're still alive at least. That's something in our favour.'

'I don't think I'm alive at all,' Helene said, 'I'm sure I've been dead for ages now.'

Spengler smiled thinly. 'If we hang about here, you soon will be,' he said. 'Come on.'

He set off again, and a few drops of rain pattered on his face, then a few more, then suddenly the heavens seemed to fall apart and rain shot down the cliff in a frenzied deluge. His toes would not grip on the slippery surface. Crazy, he thought. Rain at this altitude? His fingers were washed from their holds. Rocks and shale, caught in the tumult, whistled narrowly past his skull. He was fighting for breath, fighting for balance, fighting every inch of the way until, nearly an hour later, when the downpour finally subsided, it was with a sense of both surprise and wonder that he realised he was still climbing.

He heard Helene call up to him.

'Erich, we've got to stop. It's Lasser.'

Spengler looked around. There was no reasonable resting place, but he found a narrow defile that offered a flimsy refuge, and hammered in a peg to fasten himself on. Then he brought the others up to join him. Lasser looked done in. His face was grey, his eyes lost and bewildered. Helene examined him anxiously, testing his pulse rate, his temperature. Spengler watched them in silence. 'He looks ill,' he said presently.

'Can you blame him? He's not built for this kind of assault course.'

'We can't stay too long,' Spengler told her. 'Daylight's vital.'

She shook her head. 'He needs an hour at least.'

'Thirty minutes,' Spengler insisted, 'that's all we can spare.'

She looked at him, her eyes calm and composed. 'If he dies, Erich, it'll make a nonsense of this entire climb.'

Spengler shrugged. 'I'm sorry,' he said. 'All our lives are at stake now. Thirty minutes, no more.'

He hated himself, but there was no alternative. As soon as the scientist looked able to climb again, he pushed remorselessly on. The only way to survive, he thought. Keep moving. No room for stragglers.

After the deluge, they seemed to have reached a lull in the storm. To the east, the clouds began to break up. There were rainbows, and mottled blotches of shadow on the distant hills, and a deep rim of scarlet tingeing the horizon, casting the tips of tiny firs into sharp relief.

Spengler felt unimaginably cold. Nausea started in his chest like a tight little ball, growing and swelling until he knew it would have to explode. The mountain seemed to see-saw. He felt his insides lurch, and as he held himself choking against the rock the vomit burst from his lips, shooting down the cliff face. Below, Arno Richner tried to lean out of the way, but the bile caught his shoulder, streaking his anorak. Spengler hung helplessly, retching again and again, forgetting his exposure, swallowed up in an abyss of misery. He went on retching until there was nothing left, then lay gasping against the wall.

'Sorry,' he murmured. 'Sorry about that.'

Arno forced a grin. 'What's a little vomit between friends,' he called.

Spengler pushed himself weakly back from the cliff and looked around. His slobber seemed to be everywhere, on the rock, the ice, on his chest, waist and breeches. He scooped up a handful of snow and painfully washed his face. Then he moved on, his hands numb, not so much from the cold as the sheer nonstop groping and scrabbling and heaving. He balanced like a dancer, shifting his weight, measuring distances, gaps, risks, moving without feeling or nerve. He longed to stop and drink from the trickles of water which pattered down the mountainside, but somehow the conviction had lodged in his brain that to stop meant to die.

In the late afternoon the storm, by some trick of the day, some quirk of nature, suddenly cleared, the clouds parting to reveal the valley far below. Spengler could see rolling pastures studded with pine trees, the scattered buildings of Grindelwald township and the tiny ratchet railway climbing up to the Kleine Scheidegg plateau. The mountains seemed almost to lean back, their contours coming into sharp and vivid relief until he noticed with a sense of shock that they were not totally sheer, totally vertical, totally blank, but that they sloped and slithered, curled and wriggled, their lower slopes tinged with yellow, green and russet brown. Above the treeline, the jagged peaks formed a great circle that ringed the valley, making it softer by their very hardness. Ribbons of ice spread from the tips like tentacles, turned blue by the watery sun.

He searched about until he found a line of rubble-strewn ledges traversing horizontally to the right. Above the start of the traverse was a sheltered platform a yard or so wide, seven or eight feet long. It was carved into the mountain, protected from above by a bulging shield of rock. Spengler called a halt and watched the others flop exhausted on to the rubble-strewn perch. He knew that beyond the traverse lay the 'Spider', the infamous inverted bowl of ice which would lead eventually to the difficult exit crack to the summit icefield. The 'Spider' was the funnel down which more than eighty per cent of the mountain's avalanches streamed, sweeping the ice clean almost hour by hour. Rocks peppered the crusty surface at all moments of the day, It would be like crossing an anvil and waiting for the hammer to strike.

Spengler looked at his party, wondering if they still had the strength to make it. He could see in the clumsy way they moved, and in the slackness of their faces that they were operating by instinct only. He stared at Helene, experiencing a stab of dismay. Her face had the texture of melted wax. Her mouth was a hole through which spittle dribbled. She crouched forward, her arms folded across her chest, sustained only by some curious phenomenon within her.

'Storm's coming back,' Arno croaked miserably.

He peered across the valley, his eyes like a pair of marbles thrust into an expanse of grey putty. It was true. The clouds were thickening again. The great overhanging blanket was sliding in to shut off what meagre light there had been. Even the immediate outcrops were already blotted from sight. A heavy humid smell replaced the chill with a suddenness that can only happen in high mountains.

'We ought to press on,' Henke murmured. 'Still two hours of daylight left.'

Spengler hesitated, peering again at Helene. She's finished, he thought, at least for the moment. Lasser too.

'We'll stay here,' he decided. 'Right now, none of us would be capable of getting up that exit crack.'

'But Spengler,' Henke protested, 'if the storm builds up, we could freeze to death. I don't know about you, but I'd rather die out there, climbing free, than huddled on some ledge like a helpless sparrow.'

'We daren't venture on the "Spider" tonight,' Spengler said. 'Better to try at dawn, when the cold freezes everything solid. There'll be no rockfalls then.'

'And no climbers either, the state we're in. Good God, man, look at us, we'll never survive the night.'

'Of course we will,' Spengler said mildly. 'A good sleep is what we need. You get the stoves out and brew some coffee. Arno and I will fix a line along the traverse so we can save time in the morning.'

Henke shook his head, sighing with exasperation as Spengler began to coil the rope. Arno peered at the traverse ahead, his face drawn and set. His eyes looked flat, without expression.

'Let me lead,' he said suddenly.

Spengler looked surprised. 'You?'

Arno nodded, and Spengler hesitated. Maybe I owe him that much, he thought. If he wants to prove something – to himself or to me – then okay.

'Right, Arno,' he said, 'but take it slowly.'

Richner set off, picking his way delicately across the narrow rock band, Spengler playing out the rope as he edged along, inch by painful inch. Behind them, the others were busy assembling the tiny stove. It was, Spengler knew, a beauty of a traverse, quite safe really, with good ledges and plenty of handholds. Thinking it over afterwards, he could never understand why the thing happened at this particular point. They had covered so much more difficult ground, had surmounted hazards of the most insurmountable nature that by comparison the traverse should have been a walkover, and yet, when disaster struck, they were taken completely by surprise.

Sweat bathed Arno's face. His hands shook as he groped for holds. Spengler watched, thinking: poor bastard, if he comes off now he'll never forgive himself. I can hold him all right, it's a good strong belay with no more than twenty feet playout, but he's got this crazy notion about proving some damned thing or other, and is ready to bust his neck doing it.

Arno paused. 'I'm going to put a runner on,' he called.

Spengler watched as Richner painstakingly drove in a peg and fastened on a sling, clipping it to the rope. Spengler thought: I don't know if he even knows what the hell he's doing any more, he's moving by numbers almost. Maybe he's gone crazy. It happens sometimes, temporary insanity brought on by fear and extreme fatigue.

Arno glanced over his shoulder and moistened his lips. 'Keep the rope tight,' he said hoarsely.

'Okay, Arno, I've got you held.'

Richner moved. His leg snaked out, disappearing from sight inside a narrow defile. He swung right, shifting his weight, one hand tracing a rapid arc across the rock.

The wind blew up, scattering dust into Spengler's face. Gently, Arno, he thought. What the hell is he trying to do? He's scrabbling at the limestone like a dog burying a bone, disregarding footholds, handholds, gravity. Oh, Jesus.

The piton went first. Spengler heard a metallic ping, then a sharp whistle as it zipped like a bullet past his ear. He heard a startled cry, saw Arno's shocked face bright with alarm, and then Arno was dropping down the sheer cliff-wall.

Spengler rammed himself hard against the mountain, waiting for the strain. The others sat frozen, transfixed by the terrible inevitability of the scene before them. Spengler realised suddenly he had moved too far to the left. His stance was now so narrow and his strength so depleted, that line or no line, there was no hope on earth of halting Richner's fall. The rope zipped taut, and for a fraction of a second Spengler remained straining backwards, teeth clenched against the sheer power of the thing that was trying to tear him from the cliff. Pain lanced his wrist as the line gouged deep into his palm, oozing blood between his fingers. He could see Arno dangling fifty feet below, his eyes bulging with fear. Spengler felt giddy; he dug in hard with his heels, wanting to cry out with the pain as his bad arm was almost wrenched from its socket. Then something seemed to give inside his body, and in another second, he too was over.

The wind rushed past his head and he experienced a detached sensation of floating on air. His vision was obscured by a great spray of snow, and he realised with no sense of alarm or dismay that he was falling rapidly and there were rocks everywhere, cascading around him like raindrops. He had the impression of being whirled dizzily around. Like Alice in the rabbit-hole, he thought. It was like riding a motorcycle at a very fast speed.

Then suddenly there was a jerk. He felt a sharp constricting pain around his chest. The world stopped spinning. It steadied, coming into focus. The belaying piton at the top of the cliff must have held. He was jammed hard against the rock, caught helplessly in the twisted rope, but alive.

For a moment he hung motionless, his senses numbed; it was like coming up for air after swimming underwater – he needed time, time to get things in perspective, time for his brain to assimilate what had happened.

He heard a groan and looked down. Arno was suspended below, his spine pressed against a limestone bulge, his skull covered with blood. Blood was running from his own head too, trickling into his mouth with a strange saltiness. He tried experimentally to move. His left arm seemed paralysed. His right was caught in the rope at his chest. When he attempted to pull it free, sharp stabs of pain shot through his limbs.

His first surge of hope at being still alive began to fade. What a mess, he thought. Hanging from the rock in the teeth of a howling gale. Can't climb up, can't climb down, can't do a damned thing to help either myself or Arno. As he realised the impossibility of his situation, he was filled with a curious peace. There was no need to struggle. No need to hope. Everything was moving towards an inevitable climax. He was going to die.

Henke watched the bodies fall, Richner's first, so far below that his bulk looked strangely diminished, then Spengler's, turning gracefully on the wind, both legs spread wide as if to guide his dreadful descent. Gritting his teeth, Henke seized the slipping rope and held on fast, hoping to God his own belay would hold. The line zipped madly through his fingers. Helene leaped forward and added her own weight as a secondary anchor. Muscles wobbling, Henke gripped hard, braking the line with both hands. All feeling seemed to drain from his flesh and sinew, then slowly the rope's progress began to slacken, and bit by bit, with both Henke and Helene holding on hard, it slithered to a halt, stretched like telegraph wire over the rocky lip.

'Get fresh pegs in,' Henke croaked. 'Quick.'

Helene hammered in pitons and secured the end of the line. Gasping, Henke let go. His palms were shredded, and blood dripped copiously on to the rocky platform, but he scarcely noticed. He peered over the rim, struggling to see through the swirling strands of mist. Nothing, he thought. Not a damned thing. Below, the cliff bulged like a galleon prow, shutting off whatever hung on the end of the line.

Henke shouted: 'Spengler, are you all right?'

A grim silence echoed across the mountainside, broken only by the howling of the wind. He tried again. 'Spengler, are you still alive? Richner?'

There was no animosity left in Henke. Against the

Eiger, such an emotion seemed trivial and absurd. Spengler and Richner were down there, they needed help, and they had already gone through too much together to think of anything so petty as resentment or revenge.

'We'll have to pull them up,' he said.

Helene looked doubtful. They were exhausted already. To make matters worse, the gale was pounding their flimsy ledge in a relentless tattoo.

'Both at once?' she whispered.

Henke pulled a face. 'We'll never do it as a dead weight. We'll have to spread the load a bit. That means rigging up a pulley system with the karabiners. It's dangerous. There'll be too much friction. The rope will get red hot, but there's no other way.'

'Then let's give it a try,' said Helene.

Henke drove in fresh pitons, placing them as best he could in parallel lines, then he clipped on karabiners and threaded the rope through them in zig-zag fashion to diminish the strain of the pull. When he was satisfied that the pressure had been evenly distributed, he took one of the spare slings and tied it to the line with a sliding friction knot.

'It'll serve as a brake,' he explained. 'The knot allows us to pull upwards, but locks tight if the rope begins to slide.'

They peered at his makeshift pulley-hoist dubiously.

'I know it's primitive,' he admitted, 'but it's all we've got, so we might as well make the best of it.'

Crouched together, they began to haul on the rope, with even Lasser adding his own badly-depleted strength, but despite the pulleys, the line wouldn't budge. It had caught in a narrow crack thirty feet below. No matter how they struggled to jerk it free, it remained firmly embedded in the rock.

'I'm going down there,' Henke said.

Helene stared at him. 'In this wind, Henke?'

'It's their only chance.'

She was close to tears. Damn it, what was she crying for? Spengler was nothing to her. He'd been nice to her, kind certainly, he had even – though she couldn't be sure – tried to propose to her, but what was that in time of war?

She had no right to even think of him as a human being. He was the enemy, a German soldier. And yet she couldn't bear to think of him dead. She couldn't imagine that life snuffed out like a candleflame. Other people died, but not Erich Spengler. She shook herself. Damned fool that she was. Men were dying every day, in Italy and France. Life was too transient a thing to build around one person. You left yourself open for moments like this, when the world tore you apart with a single unexpected thrust. She had decided with the death of her husband that she would never again put all her eggs in one basket. It made you too susceptible to despair. Above all, she had to stop Henke before he killed himself.

'Wait a while,' she urged, 'let the wind drop first.'

'They'll die of exposure.'

'Maybe they're dead already. You could be risking your life for a couple of corpses. If you go down in this gale, we might not get you back. Then what happens?'

Henke thought for a moment, his pale face calm and composed. He looked as if the end of the world would merit no more reaction than a raised eyebrow.

'You're right,' he agreed at last. 'We'll all die if I try to bring them up in this lot. They'll just have to stick it out for a bit longer.'

Spengler looked down. He could see the top of Arno's crewcut head bobbing from side to side. Arno had regained consciousness but appeared to be out of his mind. He was singing in a shrill voice that sounded flat and discordant on the stormladen air. That singing was more than a ditty hurled into the wind, Spengler thought, it was an indictment, a proof positive of perfect guilt. But he would not think about that. He moved through a secret land of long-lost dreams and memories; he recalled colours, smells, feelings, plucked them out of the air.

The wind whipped up and snow came leaping in, a whirling shroud from out of nowhere that caked his face and froze his eyes, and dimly through its blanket he could see the few square feet of rock and ice against which they hung coated with a thin white film like the interior of a defrosting icebox. The thrust of the cliff against his spine seemed to chill him to the marrow, yet he was grateful it was there for, had they been dangling free, he knew the rope's constriction would have strangled their innards, killing them both within the hour. Still, he had never experienced such cold. He tried to move his arms and stabs of pain shot up his spine. He moved his legs. That was better. He moved them more vigorously. What did the manual say? Exercise generates heat.

Arno's monotonous mumbling had stopped. He was staring up at Spengler with a grave expression. 'Where's Henke?' he asked, his voice now intelligent.

'Above, I think.'

Arno thought for a while. He seemed to be concentrating very hard. At length, he said: 'My head hurts.'

'I'm not surprised. You probably bashed it against the rock. How bad is it?'

There was no reply. Arno had noticed that his breath left clouds of steam on the frosty air. He pursed his lips and blew a series of short blasts, then looked up at Spengler, laughed, and did it again. Presently, he grew quiet.

He said: 'I think I am going to be sick.'

The wind changed, hurling spindrift into Spengler's face. He twisted his head from side to side, fighting for breath. Below, Arno was vomiting down the mountain.

I must breathe, I must think, I must savour these last frozen hours. I will not hang defenceless like a lump of putty or lie remorseful on the fishmonger's slab. Yet he was lucky in one respect, he realised, to be dying slowly, for it gave him time to think. It was good to look back on his life at the moment of dying, like a satisfying or unsatisfying meal; it was all there, a veritable library of memories, and not one had been misplaced, not one had been forgotten.

After a while the wind dropped, and through a gap in the cloud Spengler caught a glimpse of the valley. Night was falling. The Americans would be down there, no doubt. Or would they have made for the summit, traversing across the peaks from the Jungfraujoch?

Spengler wanted to laugh at that. It would have been the final irony, the most bitter joke of all, to have arrived at the top to find the enemy already waiting. At least, he thought, they will bring our bodies down. For some reason, it was a relief to know he would not be left on the mountain when he died.

'Erich?'

Arno was blinking up through the mist. His face was black with caked blood, his lips smeared with vomit. 'Erich, are we going to die up here?'

Spengler coughed. The wind swung him savagely to one side, and he clenched his teeth against its chill. 'I think so,' he replied gently.

Arno thought for a moment. He said: 'What about my mother? Who will look after her?'

The vacant look was back in his eyes. Maybe he's been smashed about so much he's ready to take anything now. Explanations, gestures, confessions of remorse. 'Arno, I just want to say that I'm sorry as hell that this thing happened. It was mainly my fault. We should never have attempted the Eigerwand.'

'That's all right, I don't mind dying. I always thought I would, but now I find that I don't. The only thing that worries me is my mother.'

Spengler let that one go. 'We should never have attempted it,' he repeated, 'the whole idea was crazy.'

'The weather beat us, not the Face. Why don't you cut yourself loose? They say it's like floating on a cloud, doesn't hurt a bit.'

'I can't,' Spengler said. 'My hands are trapped.'

'I can't either. I'm a Catholic.'

Later, Arno lapsed again into semi-consciousness. He talked a great deal, sometimes intelligently, sometimes not. He talked about a man called Heini, and a girl called Ulla. Sometimes he had long stretches of silence when he hung limply from the rope and Spengler thought he was dead, but then he would start to talk again, and as the evening wore on, his ramblings became more absurd, more illogical, more outrageous.

Occasionally, the mist went away and the moon came through, a great soft moon that startled Spengler with its gentleness, but it never lasted longer than a moment; the storm would sweep back with a fury that took his breath away. He felt he was not a man any more, he was an object, a piece of clay, a crucible in which all the hopes and fears of his life had simmered and distilled until there was nothing left.

Let me keep my reason at least. Let me salvage some semblance of an ill-begotten and highly-dubious dignity on this stinking mountain.

The snow flurries whipped by like wild birds, and he clenched his teeth and closed his eyes and tried to make his brain go blank, but it didn't work, and when finally he peered down again he saw that Arno was dead.

Arno's head was thrown back; his mouth, stained with blood and vomit, hung open. His eyes too were open. They were coated with frost and glistened sadly in the fog.

Spengler sighed. His own eyes were sore and dry. His body seemed an inert shell of pain, and he waited for death expectantly, almost reverently, as a child might wait for an imminent and much anticipated treat.

'I'm going down,' said Henke. 'The wind seems to be dropping. It's probably the only chance I'll get.'

'Watch yourself,' Helene warned, 'It's still dangerous. Remember you have to climb back.'

Henke started off on a double rope, dropping earthwards like a spider on a thread, leaping out from the cliff in ten and fifteen feet jumps. He hated abseiling at the best of times, and this was going to be one hell of an abseil. There were too many dangers over which he had no control. There was no real contact with the rock. If things went wrong, his chances would be slim indeed.

He wondered what he would find below. It was hard to believe they could have lived through the last few hours. The wind had lashed the mountain with an unbelievable force. He did not envy them their solitary ordeal. Better to go all the way down, Henke thought, than freeze to death like a turkey in an icebox.

He had been surprised to see Helene Rössner cry. It was something alien to him, a woman's tears. He was a fatalist, a stoic. In mountains, you lived or died according to the weather, your own judgement, and your luck. It had been a damned shame for Spengler and Richner to have come off like that, after all they had gone through, especially since that traverse should have been a piece of cake. But that was the way it happened sometimes. Fatigue, exhaustion, they played funny tricks. More accidents occurred coming down than going up, that was a proven fact. Coming down, a man's concentration wavered, he missed the small essential points which made the difference between survival and disaster. He, Henke, felt sorry for them both, but crying wouldn't help. A woman's tears were as useless as spitting in the ocean.

He lowered himself gently over the overhang to where the bodies hung motionless against the rock. One was dead, he could see that at a glance. It was Richner. His eyes were wide open, coated with ice.

Henke called to Spengler, 'Spengler, are you still alive?'

Dimly, almost imperceptibly, he heard Spengler reply: 'Help, help me, for Christ's sake.'

He was lying like a sausage in the hinterland of silvery winter moonlight. What a dreadful commotion, what an awful bloody clamour. Death was surely a soothing relief, a peaceful oblivion, a sweet chariot swinging low with sweeter voices calling him in, a prodigal sinner. But he heard Henke coming, heard the sound of boots on rock, the hiss of rope on ice, the chunk-chunk of pegs being driven in, and his eyes closed, his body trembled.

Henke will vanish into the drifts of forgetfulness, he thought. Yet he heard the incoherent racket of that resolute approach, far away at first, growing louder, insistent, sensible.

In his mind there were rainbows and rocky islands, and the smell of tar and the sea. And sometimes it was blue and he could see the bottom, and there were swans drifting like flocks of cumulus. Men and women were mystic wonderful beings, and in the sunlight, starlings turned above the dawn. It was the chorus of life, a thousand birds whirling like smoke above a hundred thousand acres of Eden.

Then Spengler heard a sinister sound. It came from far off, a weird and mournful call that grew steadily louder, swelling in the wind, until at last he recognised it for what it was. He was screaming.

He screamed and screamed, unable to stop, and then a hand gripped his shoulder and a voice murmured soothingly into his ear: 'There, there, I've got you now. Calm down, you'll be okay.'

Henke cut Richner loose with his iceaxe. Richner's body dropped like a stone, vanishing silently into the mist and snow. Henke pushed his feet against the wall, took Spengler's rope in one hand and jerked hard. Nothing happened. He gritted his teeth and jerked again. The line came free of the crack.

Using spare slings, Henke fashioned a chest and seat harness around Spengler's body. He knew it was essential to ease Spengler's weight off his waistline during the long haul up, otherwise he could die from the constricting pressure of the rope. When he was satisfied the harness was secure, Henke began to fight his way back up towards the platform. He climbed more by instinct than from any conscious effort. He liked it that way. To climb or do anything else which took over a man's brain removed the need for thought. He was not much of a thinker, and was always happiest when it wasn't necessary.

It took forty minutes to reach the ledge, and by the time he did, his body felt like bruised jelly. He collapsed coughing and spluttering, while Helene waited in a fever of impatience.

'Spengler?' she hissed.

'Alive,' he gasped, and she felt her body flood with relief.

'And Richner?'

'He's gone. I had to cut the rope.'

Henke pulled himself together. The job was only half done. Spengler was still lying helpless below. 'Come on,' he snapped. 'The line's free. Let's get him up.'

Bit by bit, using Henke's makeshift pulley system, they dragged Spengler's inert weight up the icebound wall. Gasping with effort, racked by dry tearless sobs, they heaved and hauled until at last Spengler's head bobbed level with the ledge and they were able to drag him over the rim to safety.

Helene struggled to bring him round, wiping away the blood on his face and throat. Spengler opened his eyes. They were curiously out of focus as he gazed at the snowflakes whirling wildly around him.

'We're going to tie you to the rock,' Helene said gently. 'Then you can rest.'

'Rest?' he murmured. 'That's good.'

They looped the rope around a projecting nobble of rock, and fastened Spengler firmly on.

'He'll be okay,' Henke said, 'let him sleep.'

'What about you?'

'I'm fine. Shattered a bit, that's all.'

'That was a brave thing you did, going down there.'

Henke shrugged. 'We need each other if we're going to survive,' he said. 'All of us, even Lasser.'

She frowned. 'Lasser?' she echoed.

It was then, for the first time, they realised Lasser was lying prone on the platform, staring at the sky. Helene felt a shiver run along her spine. On his face was a strange rigidity; his pupils slanted upwards at some point above the tip of his skull, and his limbs were writhing like angry snakes.

'His breath smells funny,' Henke said, lifting Lasser's head with one hand.

Helene felt her heart sink. After all they had gone through, it was the final calamity. 'Ketosis,' she whispered.

'What?'

'The first stage before a coma. He hasn't had enough food to balance his insulin injections. That last bit of effort must have pushed him over the brink.'

She peered anxiously at Lasser's dirt-streaked face. He looked dreadful, almost demoniacal, as if he'd been possessed by some exterior force.

'It can't be ketosis,' she decided. 'He must be suffering from hypothermia. He'll die when the shivering stops, unless we can infuse some heat into his system. The sleeping bags, quickly.'

With breathless haste, they unpacked the haversacks,

but to Helene's dismay the bags were as drenched as the rest of their clothes. They're useless, she thought. My God, think of something. In a few minutes, he'll be beyond redemption.

An idea occurred to her. It seemed ludicrous in the extreme. Insane even. She didn't even know if it would work. But one glance at Lasser's face warned her there wasn't time to debate the point.

'Help me get his clothes off,' she snapped.

Henke looked at her in amazement.

'What?' he whispered.

'They're wet through.'

'Where the hell do you think we are? In the honeymoon suite of the Bellevue Hotel? Take off his clothes at this altitude and he'll die in seconds.'

'He'll die anyhow if we don't do something fast,' she snapped. 'Stop arguing, for God's sake, and help.'

Swiftly, they tugged at Lasser's buttons and fasteners, stripping away the sodden undergarments. His skin looked startlingly white in the darkness. When he was naked, they pushed him, teeth chattering, into one of the damp sleeping bags.

Helene looked at Henke and Spengler, caught in a dilemma between embarrassment and necessity. She was filled with an uncomfortable physical awareness, but there was no alternative she could think of. What had to be done, had to be done.

Keeping her face averted, she tugged her anorak over her head and began to strip off her own garments. This is crazy, she thought, whoever heard of undressing three thousand feet up the North Face of the Eiger? If my idea doesn't work, we're both finished.

She pulled off her sweater and wriggled out of her breeches, moving with a tense angry energy as if half-fearing the loose swing of her breasts, or the soft smoothness of her belly might somehow arouse even their spent bodies, imbuing them both with that terrible longing that was the essence of life itself.

Spengler, fastened to the cliff, watched her disrobe in silence, staring with wonder at this amazing sight, the strong beautiful figure of a naked woman gleaming like alabaster in the swirling snow. Weighting her clothes with a rock to prevent them being blown away, she wriggled into the sleeping bag and gathered Lasser, still trembling, into her arms.

Dazed with fatigue, pounded by the gale and drugged by two days on the mountain face, they crouched on their ledge and waited dumbly for the dawn.

Ten

Major Lewis D. Shellburn stood on the Eiger's summit in the late afternoon and peered down into the maelstrom of mist and snow. It had taken almost eight hours to traverse the two and a half miles from the Jungfraujoch research station, curling around the peak of the Mönch, crossing glaciers, crevasses and treacherous cornices and finally ascending the last fifteen hundred feet to the snow-covered tip. It was not a hospitable peak, Shellburn realised, for the snow came together in a razor-sharp ridge, making it possible to stand with one foot on the northern flank and one on the southern, with no place at all to shelter. High winds lashed their faces. Their position seemed frighteningly exposed.

'Think they've beaten us, sir?' the sergeant shouted, his face clogged white by blown snow. Shellburn shook his head.

'Not a chance,' he yelled. 'They'll be somewhere down there, if they're still alive.'

Sergeant Bullock shuddered. 'I don't envy them, major.'

'Me neither. Let's see if we can find a place to anchor the cable. We might be able to spot the bastards if we lower ourselves down a piece.'

But it turned out to be a more difficult job than Shellburn had anticipated, for the few outcroppings of rock they were able to uncover were split and fractured by wind and weather. Pitons fell out at the first hint of strain, and the stone surface crumbled like lump sugar under their hammer blows. In the end, Shellburn had to order his men to dig out a wide platform on the ice-cap, driving the cables deep into the cornices and anchoring them as firmly as they could with heavy metal grappling hooks. The job took three hours. When it was finished, Shellburn stared dubiously at the big drum-like winch which perched on the ice like a monstrous insect.

'Think it'll hold, Major?' the sergeant asked.

'Only one way to find out,' Shellburn said. 'Strap me into that harness.'

The sergeant's eyes widened. 'You fixing to go down there, sir?'

'Just a little reconnaissance trip, Sergeant. I want to see what those Krauts are up against.'

'Think that's wise, sir?'

'We'll know soon enough. Keep your fingers crossed, Mitch. I don't relish dropping off into that tub of black porridge if I can help it.'

Buckling on the canvas harness, Shellburn stared around at the men. They watched him silently, their faces blank. He knew what they were thinking, and maybe they were right, maybe he *was* crazy, but he couldn't resist the opportunity of seeing and experiencing the North Face of the Eiger at close-hand.

'Start lowering,' he ordered.

Leaning against the cable, Shellburn began to back down the precipitous slope of the summit icefield. He watched the men above growing smaller as he made his descent. Their silent faces, caked with snow, looked glumly apprehensive.

Despite his short height, Shellburn was heavy-boned and thick-muscled; he was acutely conscious that he weighed almost two hundred pounds, and hoped like hell that the quarter-inch cable would prove strong enough.

Backing carefully over the icefield's rim, he peered down the awesome sweep of the North Wall. His stomach plunged as an onset of panic bubbled up in his chest, and he controlled himself with an effort. Mustn't crap out, he thought, not in front of the men.

He backed down the menacing cliff, easing out against the harness, hoping the winch at the top would hold, hoping those thickheads up there knew what they were doing, struggling to refrain from peering into the dreadful mists below.

The rock looked split and broken, peppered here and there by little ledges of fleecy white. Outcrops bulged around him, caked with ice. Shellburn went on wriggling his way downwards, making for a shadowy gully he could see to his right, and it was then, at that precise moment, that the wind hit him. There was no warning. He had been pounded by its blustery gusts for so long that he'd thought the wind had no surprises left, but when the blast struck, it came with such violence that he felt as if his whole body was about to be torn apart. Terror gripped him. He hunched forward, trying to tuck his head into the cliff, clenching his teeth, holding on to the cable for dear life as the wind hammered his spine and neck, driving ice particles into every opening in his clothing. Snow lashed his cheeks, thundered against his skull, rammed into his eyes in blinding freezing veils. The cable writhed and twisted under the strain, sliding him sideways across the rocky wall.

The first wave lasted for well over a minute. When it momentarily subsided, Shellburn grabbed the tiny radio set around his neck and bellowed into its mouthpiece: 'Pull me up, for Christ's sake, get my ass off this mountain.'

He scarcely felt the cable's pull, for by then the second wave had hit him with a stupefying ferocity. Keeping his eyes closed and his head doubled forward, he moved his legs instinctively as the winch eased him upwards, the wind pounding his body every inch of the way.

When he reached the summit, the men hurried to unstrap him from the harness. He wiped his cheeks, peering back over the empty gap from which he had come. Snow was spurting out of the Face, lashing across the icefield in wild twisting jets. He shuddered.

'Forget the cable,' he snapped, 'it's a death-trap. Tell the men to hack snow caverns in the ice. We'll make camp for the night.'

Sometimes, through the long hours of darkness, Spengler thought he had already died. It felt like that, as if his spirit had somehow come apart from his body and was floating somewhere up there among the snow flurries, peering down with a compassionate sadness. Sometimes he forgot where he was, imagined the storm had moved away leaving the warm softness of summer sunshine; he saw green fields and steep valleys and cows grazing in the meadows. Nothing lasted however, neither illusion nor reality. He drifted between the two with a strange defenceless longing.

It was a miserable ledge on which they found themselves, he thought. A sad and lonely place for a man to die. Though protected from the rocks above, it caught the full fury of the storm, and the sleeping bag in which Helene and Lasser lay was now completely covered with snow.

Henke too, thought Spengler. He looked like a carnival snowman, swathed in the stuff from head to toe, the wind tracing patterns in its fleecy surface. Pretty, Spengler thought, a blueprint for a century of Christmas cards. But his heart was beating wildly and his spine felt like ice, for he did not believe that morning would ever come.

Strange that Henke of all people should have risked his life to drag Spengler up the mountain like a helpless puppy. You never knew about people. There was good in the most evil of men, given the right stimulus.

Spengler shifted uncomfortably on his stance. Hard to imagine a different world existed down there, some immeasurable distance below, hard to believe that people lay snug in their beds, listening to their roofs rattle, their windows shudder. Oh, you're a clever bastard, he told himself. You thought you were so damned smart in running up this Face, escaping from the enemy behind, escaping from the enemy below, but there's no escape now. The others are finished, all of them. You too. Except with you there's still that awful stubborn pride. He wanted to rest, to lie still and let oblivion take him, but he knew he was the only chance they had. If the Americans had traversed to the summit, if he could somehow get to the top and reach them, there was still a flimsy shred of hope. Get to the top, he thought? Who are you fooling? The state you're in, you couldn't climb a ten-foot stepladder. That arm is gone for sure. If you want to move from this ledge, you'll have to crawl on your belly. Okay, then I'll crawl, he told himself. For Helene, for Henke, and for Dr Lasser. I'll crawl up that bloody 'Spider' and, if I have to, up that bloody exit crack too.

It was a curious thing, here on the mountain, the war

seemed diminished somehow. Helene Rössner was not his enemy any more than Henke was. The Eiger had brought them down to size, forced them to unite against a common enemy. They were bound by the same driving force, the instinctive human need for survival.

How old do you think Helene Rössner is, he wondered? Thirty-five, thirty-six? They'd finished off her husband in a concentration camp, sent his ashes home in a cardboard box. No wonder she hated them like she did. You couldn't blame her for turning traitor. Not traitor, he corrected, she was Swiss. She had the right to choose her side in this war.

How beautiful she was, he thought. There was a strength there that was impossible to ignore. Do you think, if things work out, we might yet get together, he wondered? He grinned painfully to himself. There you go again, he thought. 'If'. The most overworked word in any language.

When morning came, it took Spengler by surprise. He wasn't sleeping, but his eyes, open, seemed no longer capable of registering the difference between light and shade. The sky had been grey for almost a full hour before he realised it. Startled, he peered around. The storm was subsiding somewhat, leaving them battered, covered with snow, but able at least to gather together some semblance of feeling again.

No movement came from the sleeping bag. Helene and Lasser were in there. Lucky old Lasser.

Henke looked like a massive ball of snow. Spengler didn't bother to speak. Talking would use oxygen and he needed all the strength he had for the hours ahead. Slowly, painfully, he began to move around on the platform, gathering his belongings and packing them into his rucksack. He moved to the start of the traverse and peered balefully at the series of narrow ledges which had claimed the life of Arno Richner. In the early morning, they were caked with snow. He paused for a moment and glanced back. Inside their pure white mask, Henke's eyes were open. They stared at him in silence, registering nothing, not hope, not fear, not even resentment that he might be deserting them. He wanted to explain he was going for help, but somehow the breath lodged in his throat, so in the end he gave it up and turning, began to inch along the snowpacked traverse, moving as carefully as he could. When he reached its end, he stood and stared into the breathtaking sweep of the 'Spider'. It looked almost perpendicular, its shiny surface sliding away into nothing. There were no falling stones, it was too early in the morning, but the awesome silence which hung across the icy bowl seemed strangely overpowering, and he moved on to its surface with more confidence than he felt. Despite his crampons, Spengler cut steps with the iceaxe, not the usual one-chop jobs of the high-alpine mountaineer, but great bucket-holds, carving out massive chunks for his feet to nestle in. What the hell am I doing, he wondered? At this rate it'll take me all day. I'll still be fiddling around when the temperature rises and the stones start falling, and then they'll have you cold, you bastard.

He forced himself to balance on his crampon points, teetering upwards, using his axe-blade as an anchor, oblivious to the pain raging through his left arm. On three sides, black rock bulged menacingly against the sky, coated with a rippling curtain of ice. The surface on which he moved was studded with fallen stones, a sobering reminder of what the day would bring if he tarried too long.

An hour passed, and then another. The light disappeared as the cloud grew thicker. Occasionally, he thought about Helene, but only in an ephemeral way. He no longer felt even half-way sane any more. Images swept through the jingle-jangle wonderland of his mind like fragments glimpsed from a moving train. The mountain was his only reality. It was there beneath his feet, beneath his fingers. He could feel its vitality on his palms and toes. He had come back like an ancient enemy, and this time, this time he knew the mountain would reward him. He had paid the price, God knew he had paid with everything he had.

He moved by instinct almost, feeling his way by touch and luck. He felt dreadfully tired. When he leaned to the right, his body seemed controlled, but when he swung to the left he was filled with a dangerous sense of instability.

That was the arm, he thought. It had grown worse during the night. His head felt bad too. The blood that had flowed so freely after his fall down the mountain face had caked into a brittle shield as far as his brow. If he touched it, the crust gave slightly, sending a searing pain zig-zagging across his eyes.

A new feeling began to move in his veins, a feeling that was taut with a senseless yet long-deferred resentment, a frightening feeling that left him dazzled by its intensity. Hate. It filled him with a strange vibrating power, pushing him upwards and onwards. It was the Face he hated, as if it was human, as if it could be crushed like an antagonist, battered and subdued through the sheer force of his anger. He was determined he would climb it or die.

For three solid hours he battled on, making for the 'Spider's' left-hand edge. The damned icefield seemed to stretch for ever. And then at last, his fingers touched rock and, drugged, limbs numbed with fatigue, he crouched breathless beneath the narrow defile which led into the final exit crack.

Time had no meaning for Spengler. The hours ran one into the other as if he had reached some strange infinity, freed from the confines of past, present or future, a never-never land where the complex cycles of minutes and seconds had ceased to exist. Beneath his hands the rock felt soft, almost like living flesh. He opened his mouth to laugh at that, but somehow the laugh wouldn't come. He was beyond such things. He had been clambering up this dreadful little gully for what seemed an immeasurable period, climbing, pulling, climbing, pulling. Sometimes he would stop for a while, passing into a dreamless sleep from which no succour ever came. Each time he woke, he felt more drained than ever, and yet the remarkable thing was, he never fell. Wedged in the rock he defied gravity, distance, space, reaching up, finding new holds, testing their strength, moving on. Maybe, he thought, the crack continues for ever, zig-zagging its way to heaven itself, like Jacob's ladder.

The Face mocked him, standing out against the storm, hiding its features in swirling snow, sombre and eternal.

Where had it come from, his obsession with this mountain? Deep down, the fragments of his old self were united in a cry of emptiness and desperation. It was not a living thing, this heap of unspeakable limestone.

He thought wryly: what I am trying to say, if I may be allowed to say it, is that here in this miserable little gully I have come to a bitter conclusion, that my life has been a waste of time, which is a sad thought for a man on the threshold of death. Don't think about death, he told himself, not even to acknowledge its existence. Just keep pushing on and up.

Suddenly, the gully lost its steepness. Spengler felt puzzled. His hands touched hard snow. He had emerged on to the lower rim of the summit icefield. Had he really come up that tricky exit crack blind? It seemed impossible, and yet here he was, and here indisputably was the icefield. How far now, he wondered? An hour, two? He knew the final stretch could be deceiving. After the harsh gradient lower down, it seemed almost a doddle, leaning back against the sky enticing him to quicken his pace. Almost there, it seemed to say, hurry and get it over with. But he wasn't fooled. This was where the avalanches came from. A man could be swept to his death with the summit within his grasp.

Deliberately, and with great care, Spengler began to hack out steps with his iceaxe. He went on up: cutting, stepping, cutting, stepping, afraid to trust to crampons alone. A couple of hours passed and still he was moving, lost in that strange mystic tranquillity created by aching muscles, stultified thought processes, and wretched fatigue. He wondered how the others were faring. It was fearfully cramped on that little ledge. Helene, was she still alive? She seemed like a picture glimpsed in some glossy magazine; he knew her face, but it was as meaningless as plastic. Where was the blasted summit? This icefield was never-ending. He paused. Voices. Clear and articulate. People up there. He felt a burst of wild exhilarating hope. The Americans. They'd traversed across from the Jungfraujoch, as he'd anticipated. Thank God.

Remember they're the enemy, he thought, and this time succeeded in grinning. The mere idea of an enemy, the mere idea of the whole bloody war seemed too absurd for words. He laughed. What are you laughing at? The war, he thought, his head spinning, that was something to laugh at.

He turned in their direction and realised he'd reached the summit ridge. Why didn't they spot him, for Christ's sake, why didn't they raise a hullabaloo, drop him a toprope? He'd give his eye-teeth for the comforting feel of a line around his waist; to rest, to sleep, to let them haul him senseless to the top of this bloody mountain. Then he saw a young face caked with snow peering down at him in astonishment. He heard a voice whisper: 'Jesus God,' and closing his eyes against the wind, he collapsed unconscious into a cluster of willing arms.

It was warm in the snowhole, Spengler found. A sheet of stiff canvas had been draped across the opening to shut off the wind, and the combination of huddled bodies and little cooking stoves created a fug of hot air which breathed life back into his battered limbs. He lay on a khaki groundsheet, the metal plate from which he had eaten still resting in his lap, the cigarette Major Shellburn had given him dangling from his lips. Three other Americans crouched in the snow-hole. One of them was tinkering with a small two-way radio set. The only light came from a flashlamp perched on top of a biscuit tin. Major Shellburn's face was almost obscured by shadow. His cigarette tip glowed redly when he inhaled.

'How the hell you ever managed to get up the exit crack with that arm of yours, I'll never figure,' he muttered.

Spengler touched his elbow. The Americans had stripped off the old bandage and dressed it properly, and now his entire left shoulder felt as if it was held in some kind of vice. He grinned, trying to hide the nauseous feeling which threatened to engulf him.

'It's getting better every minute,' he said.

Shellburn shook his head. 'That's an illusion. You've got a nasty wound there, Lieutenant. You need hospital treatment, and fast. You stand a good chance of losing that arm.'

'I think it can hang on a little longer.'

Spengler leaned his head against the wall. It really was remarkable how warm you could be under snow, he thought, and how quickly your body could recuperate with nourishment and rest. Outside, the storm raged madly on, but here in their cavern under the ice-cap, Spengler felt as comfortable as he would have done in any hotel.

Shellburn smiled to himself. He was watching Spengler with an air of reluctant admiration. He felt intrigued by this battered German who spoke English with such a peculiar accent, and who had just accomplished what seemed to Shellburn the most amazing climbing feat of the century.

'I was thinking,' Shellburn said, 'you've made mountaineering history today. Nobody could have come up the North Face of the Eiger through a storm like that, it's impossible. If anyone asked me, that's what I'd say, impossible. Yet you did it. But here's the rub, my friend. We're not supposed to be here, none of us. The Germans will deny this ever happened, the Allies will deny it ever happened, the Swiss will deny it. I'm afraid you're a born loser, Lieutenant. Your achievement will never be recognised.'

'To hell with my achievement,' Spengler grunted, 'just concentrate on those people down there.'

Shellburn nodded, peering at Spengler through half-closed eyes. 'How many did you say are on that ledge?'

'Three, when I left. Including the man you tried to kill.'

'I had no choice, Lieutenant. He had to be rescued or silenced, one or the other. When you took Dr Lasser on to that Face, rescue was out of the question. There was only one option left.'

'And now?'

'Now it's a different ballgame. You're not taking him any place, not any longer. If the storm eases, we'll try and bring them up before dark. If it doesn't . . .'

He hesitated, trying not to look at Spengler directly.

'I've got to get my men off this mountain, Lieutenant. They need warmth and shelter and rest. I don't like this any more than you do, but unless conditions improve,

217

your friends will have to stay on that ledge until they die.'

For a long time, Helene Rössner couldn't remember where on earth she was. Then her brain unclouded, and reality came rushing back. This suffocating darkness was the sleeping bag, and this naked body entwined in her own was the man Lasser who, although he had never fully gained consciousness, was unquestionably alive, his pale beard-stubbled face barely a centimetre from her own. There was no further sign of the coma into which he had been sinking. His breathing was slow and regular, and he looked, if not exactly refreshed, at least unharmed.

'Dr Lasser?' she said.

His eyes opened and he stared at her without comprehension. It was not ketosis, she realised thankfully, but shock. Dr Lasser had withdrawn into the recesses of his brain, hiding from the real world as if reality was just too much to bear.

She had no idea how long they had lain like this, for her only memories were fractured ones. She remembered sleeping, waking, sleeping, waking; she remembered the thunderous roar of the storm outside, the invisible hand pummelling their flimsy perch, but it seemed like a dream, lacking substance.

She tried to move. Her limbs responded. A good sign, she thought. She eased her head up the sleeping bag, peering through its narrow opening. Her view was obscured by snow. Reaching up, she brushed the flakes away, glimpsing a sliver of rock bordered by an angry sky. Daylight. She shook herself. Which day, she wondered? How long had exhaustion claimed her? To have slept through such a tumult was little short of a miracle and yet her body had been carried beyond the limits of its endurance; small wonder she had sunk so deeply or so completely.

Gently, she disengaged herself from Lasser's grasp and wriggled upwards until her head poked through the sleeping bag top. Their little ledge was thick with snow. Snow whirled steadily around her cheeks, blotting out vision, blotting out the void beyond the platform's edge. The rucksacks, coated with a blanket of white, looked like boulders in the pale sheen of day. Belayed to the rock crouched Henke. He too was covered in white, even his face.

Helene dug through the snow until she found her clothes. They were stiff and frozen, brittle with ice. She pulled them into the sleeping bag and held them against her body until the chilled material became malleable again, then she dressed herself as swiftly as she could. Crawling out, she brushed the snow from the silent figure huddled in the corner. Henke's face was coated with a thin sheen of ice. Beneath, the texture of his skin looked waxlike. His limbs were stiff and immoveable. He was plainly dead, frozen solid. She studied him thoughtfully. Where on earth was Spengler? Had he toppled over the edge, swept off by the storm? Or had he decided to end it all by taking the swift way down? Helene crouched, shivering in the cold. She did not intend to die like Henke, freezing slowly into a glassy statue. Far better to go like Spengler, one swift plunge and then oblivion. But not without a fight, she decided. She peered at the sleeping bag. Somehow she had to bring Lasser out of his reverie and get him dressed. They had stayed too long on this miserable ledge. She did not know what lay beyond the traverse, but anything was better than waiting meekly for the end. She would revive Lasser, then together, storm or no storm, they would make one last bid to reach the summit.

Major Shellburn looked at the sky and made his decision. 'I'm sorry,' he said bluntly, 'I wouldn't send a polar bear down there in this weather. We're heading back to the Jungfraujoch.'

Spengler felt panic rising in his chest. 'You can't just leave them,' he shouted, screwing up his face against the wind-driven snow.

'They're dead, dammit. Nobody could live through this without shelter. My men are exhausted. I'm not risking their lives for a bunch of frozen corpses.'

'You don't know for certain they're dead. How can we leave while there's still a chance?'

Shellburn spat into the blizzard. Around him, the

Americans were gathering their equipment together. The cable drum, still anchored to the ice-cap, was furred with white. It looked grotesque in the fading afternoon.

'Lieutenant,' Shellburn shouted, 'may I remind you that you're my prisoner. I make the decisions here, and I say we're going back. Do you seriously think I'd send a man down that cliff with the wind tearing our balls off?'

'Send me,' Spengler yelled. 'I'm the enemy, that makes me expendable.'

Shellburn's face was caked with snow, but Spengler saw the eyes widen with astonishment. They seemed to be the only living things in that pure white mask. 'You?' he bellowed, 'with that arm? You'd be as useful as a water pistol at a skeet shoot.'

'At least let me try. One hour, major, that's all I ask. If we haven't located them within one hour, you can call the whole thing off.'

'You're crazy, you Kraut bastard.'

'Two of them are your people, major.'

'We don't even know if the cable will stretch that far, god-damnit.'

'Then let's find out, let's at least give it a try.'

Shellburn rubbed the snow from his cheeks. He peered into the storm, at the greyness beyond. The flakes were driving in at them from all directions. What kind of asshole am I, he thought, taking orders from the enemy? But the German's eyes were fixed on his in desperate entreaty.

'Okay,' Shellburn shouted, 'if you want to risk your ignorant hide, go ahead, but one hour is all you've got. If you're not back inside that time, I'm going to leave your ass dangling on that mountain, understand?'

Spengler nodded.

Quickly, they cleared the winch and tackle of snow, then strapped Spengler into its harness. At a signal from Shellburn, he leaned against the cable, backing slowly down the steep incline. He watched the figures above sink into the mist, vanishing almost instantly, leaving him alone with the tempest and only the thin metal line to give him comfort. The major's right, he thought, this is a crazy thing I'm doing, but I can't leave them there, Helene,

Lasser, Henke. We've come through too much together. Two days, they seem a lifetime.

Spengler licked his lips. His mouth tasted bad and his arm felt numb from loss of blood. Still, the cessation of pain was a relief. The radio dangled clumsily against his chest, crackling with static from the clouds. He hoped he could remember how to operate the thing. Shellburn had given him instructions at the top, but the howling gale made concentration difficult.

He reached the edge of the icefield and stepped over on to the perpendicular cliff. He could see the opening of the exit crack to his right and tried to veer away from it, picking a route down the overhanging slabs to its left. Suddenly, the cable jerked to a halt. Taken by surprise, Spengler lost his foothold and spun wildly, hitting his chin. The steel line whined in the wind like a guitar string. He dug his crampons against the ice-coated wall and shook his head to clear it. What the hell was going on? Shellburn's voice crackled on the radio.

'Hold it there, Lieutenant, we're fitting on another roll of cable. Won't take a second.'

The line began to move again and Spengler went on stepping downwards, driving his feet against the mountain's frozen surface. His chest strained as he struggled to inhale. What an irony it would be, he thought, if he ended up suffocating to death, dangling on this cable like a ludicrous puppet.

He tried to quicken his descent, sweat dribbling from his cheeks as he slithered diagonally down, sometimes missing a step and stumbling, then finding his balance and moving on again.

Once more the line jerked to a halt. Patiently, he waited as they fitted on another cable. Half an hour gone. Soon he would have descended almost a thousand feet. Could the line take the strain?

Spengler cupped his hands to his mouth and bellowed downwards. His voice echoed across the fractured slabs, lost in the frenzied roaring of the wind. He listened. Nothing. He tried again. Again, his voice seemed to be sucked into a vortex of noise. This time, faintly, almost indiscernibly, he heard an answering voice calling back.

His heart jumped. Someone was alive down there. Directly below.

The cable began to move again and Spengler went on kicking his way down. The journey had taken on a curious unreality now. The mists parted and he spotted, barely thirty feet below, the ledge he had left that dawn. He could see figures huddled on its surface. One of them was standing, waving to him through the snow. Too far to the right, he decided. Have to readjust. He radioed to the summit.

'Stop the cable.'

Instantly, he was jerked to a halt. Gripping the line firmly in one hand, he kicked at the cliff with his feet, sliding sideways across the ruptured rock. When he was satisfied he had reached a point directly above the bivouac shelf, he radioed the summit to proceed.

Four minutes later, his crampons touched the rocky floor and Helene Rössner came into his arms sobbing.

'Thank God, oh, thank God.'

He pulled her upright, peering anxiously at her face. Her cheekbones looked sharp and projected, the skin sinking into deep hollows on each side of her mouth.

'Who's left?' he asked.

'Only Lasser. I managed to get him dressed, but he's in some kind of shock.'

'Coma?'

'I don't think so. I'm sure we pulled him back in time, but he just sits there like a cabbage.'

'What about Henke?'

'Dead. He froze sometime during the day.'

Spengler held her by the shoulders, staring into her face with what he hoped was an air of confidence. 'Listen to me,' he said. 'The Americans are on the summit. They're taking us back to the Jungfraujoch.'

She was crying, but no tears issued from her eyes. Her body shook with dry racking sobs. 'I thought you were dead,' she murmured. 'I thought you'd gone over during the night.'

'I damn near did,' he said grimly, remembering the nightmarish haul up the exit crack. 'More than once.'

'How did you . . .?' She pulled back suddenly, peering

at him with a look of wonder. 'Erich,' she whispered. 'You climbed it . . . the Eigerwand.'

He nodded silently.

'Alone?'

'There was no other way,' he said. 'We'd never have made it as a team.'

'You've beaten it at last,' she said excitedly. 'Oh Erich, you can forget the past. None of that matters any more. Now, there's only the future.'

'The future?' he echoed wryly. 'That's good. It's all right for you, they're your people up there. They'll probably give you a medal for bringing Lasser back in one piece. With me, the only thing to look forward to is some kind of prison camp.'

'Maybe not,' she insisted. 'This is still a neutral country. You could ask for asylum.'

'They'd never grant it. The Swiss authorities will want me out of their hair as quickly as possible. They'll let the Yanks take me.'

'Where?'

'England, I imagine.'

She thought about that for a moment. 'At least you'll be out of the fighting,' she said, 'and the war can't last for ever. When it's over, you'll be free. No more nightmares, no more guilt.'

He hesitated. The snowflakes whirled softly around them. He had the curious sensation of being encased inside a bubble, secure from the storm and the world outside.

'You remember what I said?' he whispered. 'On the bivouac?'

She touched his lips with her fingertips. 'Ssssh, not now.'

'I have to know,' he insisted. 'There might not be another chance. Once we reach the top, I'll be a prisoner.'

Her face looked troubled. She turned her head away, peering into the blizzard. When she turned back, her cheeks were glistening.

'You have to understand something,' she said. 'When Karl died, I never believed there could be anyone else. I thought no one could take his place.'

'I don't want to take Karl's place,' he said miserably. 'I want to make a place of my own.'

'Please listen,' she murmured. 'I shut myself off to everything except the war. It was the only thing that kept me sane. It isn't easy now to feel like a human being.'

'What are you saying?'

'That you'll have to be patient with me. I still have to convince myself I'm alive again.'

He stared at her, scarcely daring to believe his ears.

'Then the answer's yes?'

'Yes, yes, of course it's yes. Did you ever doubt it?'

Spengler felt his heart soaring. He kissed her hard on the mouth, and she relaxed against him, closing her eyes. The wind caught his hair, blowing it across his forehead. What am I doing, he thought? Every second we stand here increases the possibility of disaster.

Spengler unbuckled himself from the harness. He looped it around Helene, fastening it tight.

'I'm going to strap Lasser to your back,' he said. 'Think you can manage?'

She nodded, staring at him confusedly.

'He's only small,' Spengler explained, 'and the cable will take most of the strain, but you'll have to try and support the rest of his weight with your legs.'

'What about you?'

'The wire can't take three of us in one trip. When you reach the top, send it back down, understand?'

She nodded again, and he dragged Lasser to his feet. The scientist was fully dressed and wide awake, but he seemed oblivious to Spengler's presence. His eyes stared blankly into space.

Spengler strapped him to the cable with his arms around Helene's shoulders, fastening his waistline to the harness with snaplinks.

'How far is the summit?' Helene asked.

'A thousand feet or thereabouts.'

'My God.'

'Use your crampons to keep you off the cliff, but let the cable do the work, that's what it's for.'

'I hate leaving you here like this.'

'Forget about me. Keep your mind on what you're doing.'

He showed her how to operate the radio. 'Think you can manage?'

'Yes,' she said. Her eyes glistened. 'You were safe . . . you could have stayed . . .'

'Without you, there'd have been no point. We started this together, we'll finish it together.'

Spengler radioed the summit and ordered Shellburn to begin the ascent. The cable hummed and whined above them. With a jerk, Helene Rössner, Dr Lasser strapped to her back, began to rise from the snow-strewn ledge.

Spengler patted her bottom. 'Don't forget,' he shouted, 'when they send that cable down, tell them to keep it well to the right, away from the exit crack.'

She nodded to show she understood, hobbling painfully upwards as the wire tugged at her waist. The storm sprang in to engulf her, hurling spindrift into her eyes. Lasser's weight on her spine seemed to be forcing her into the rock. She couldn't believe such a small man could be so heavy. Stumbling she fell against the cliff but the cable pulled her remorselessly on. Thrusting back with her boots, she recovered, sucking in a little air as she clambered shakily upwards.

Once, she glanced back and saw Spengler far below, almost obscured by fog. He looked so small, so pitifully alone that she felt a sob lodge deep in her throat. In another second, the storm had swallowed him up, but Helene Rössner was to remember that glimpse of Erich Spengler for the rest of her life.

Eleven

Helene had no idea how long she'd been staggering upwards. Time had no meaning any more. Nothing had any meaning except the will to keep going, the dogged determination to put one foot in front of the other, bending against the cable's pull, crushed by the dreadful weight against her shoulders. One of the harness straps was digging painfully into her ribs, but at least she still had the power to feel; she'd imagined she was beyond that, beyond everything except merely existing.

The wind was pounding her savagely, tearing at her hair, screeching in her ears. She peered upwards, trying to see through the snowflakes, but only the cliff stared back, its surface coated with verglass, slippery beneath her feet. One step at a time, don't think too far ahead. She remembered Spengler's advice; let the cable do the work.

Suddenly she realised the gradient had lessened, and the pressure across her shoulders had intensified, which could mean only one thing. She had reached the summit icefield. The cable whined and hummed, vanishing into the fog. Not far now, she told herself. Not far.

Major Shellburn noticed it first. The others were too intent on operating the winch. They looked like ludicrous bundles of fluffy white fur crouching against the wind, peering downwards into the storm-laden air. You couldn't blame them, Shellburn thought afterwards, there'd been no warning. The scene was frozen into his mind like a macabre tableau from some strange waxworks show. He saw the men grouped around the winch. He saw the cable streaked with snow. He saw the clouds swirling in to engulf them. And then, with a sense of freezing panic he saw the couplings inching out of the ice-pack. They rose slowly, sliding from the crusty surface like fish coming up for air. Oh my God, he thought. With a ping, one of the belaying wires broke loose. A cleft opened up in the ice, widening, growing deeper, gouging out a furrow where the couplings and pitons had formed their anchor. Shellburn felt the ground lurch beneath his feet and saw with a stab of horror the massive grey drum rearing upwards.

'Stand back,' he yelled, 'the cable's going.'

It was a miracle no one was hurt. They stood dry-mouthed and watched the wires snap, the final strands tearing themselves relentlessly free. The belaying pitons they had driven in with such care zipped out like ricocheting bullets. The massive drum seemed to vault into the sky, hovering motionless for a moment, its wires streaming in the wind like twisting tentacles, then with an almost reluctant grace, drum, cable, chocks and couplings plunged into the blackness, hurtling down the icefield in a trail of churned-up snow.

Helene Rössner felt her progress suddenly stop. She began to slide and dug in her crampons, clinging desperately to the slippery incline. What was happening? Why had the pressure ceased? Afraid to move, she peered up through the driving blizzard. Mist smudged the ice into a bleary haze that seemed to ooze into the sky with no dividing line. Then she saw the drum. It came rampaging towards her like a crazed beast, spewing out spray as it leapt and bucked down the precipitous ice-slope. Her face changed from bewilderment to terror, her stomach cringed. Too exhausted to scream, she watched breathless as, with a hiccupping roar, the mass of wire and metal thundered by less than four feet from her skull. Tiny particles of ice sprayed her cheeks. It disappeared over the edge, plunging down the sheer cliff wall, and a strange and subtle calm came over her, for she knew in that instant that they were finished. With the harness around her body, it would only take a second before the weight of the equipment dragged them both to disaster. She wanted to think of something comforting to die with, but the irony of their position was too strong. To have reached here, the summit icefield, only to be hauled back by this freakish accident seemed the cruellest joke of all.

She thought of Spengler. Poor Spengler. Would he

hear the crash of the winch as it thundered down the Face? Would he realise that was his last hope clattering away? Hers too. There was no justice in that, no justice anywhere in this mad frozen mountaintop world.

She felt the harness tear at her waist. There was no halting it. Desperate and defeated, half senseless, she dug her fingers into the ice, but her nails splintered as the downward haul went inexorably on. Despairingly, she tried to call for help, but the breath caught in her throat. She saw the glistening surface sliding by beneath her chin, saw the deep trough which her body had gouged stained with blood from her skinned hands, and then she was over the rim and falling, falling. The dark wall flitted past her face at a dizzy rate. Her stomach swooped upwards. She was caught in that blissful separation of body and mind she had read about. She couldn't breathe, but it didn't matter. Funny, her brain had gone blank. There were no memories tumbling in and out, no fleeting glimpses of a life past but not forgotten, only this strange absence of awareness, this lack of substance, this shutting off of nerve and sinew. Then there was a jerk. She swung across the Face, spinning wildly. A spasm of pain shot through her ribs as she hit the rock and bounced back. Desperately, she fought to make sense of it all, this new and bewildering sensation. She had stopped. She was falling no longer. She glanced up, squinting into the wind, and realised the answer. The cable had looped over the top of a protruding pillar and now the heavy drum and couplings were dangling down one side while she and Lasser were dangling down the other, balancing each other perfectly.

She heard a strangled gasp in her ear. 'My God.'

It was Lasser, shaken somehow into awareness. She could feel him trying to move against her spine, his limbs twisting under the line which bound them together. 'What's happening?' he muttered.

'Dr Lasser,' she gasped, 'for God's sake.'

He was struggling, pressing his knees against her buttocks in an effort to free himself. The peril of their situation had galvanised him back into life. Her feet swung backwards and forwards in empty space. There

228

was nothing to see down there, nothing but rock and ice and billowing mist. They had survived the fall, they were still alive, but were dangling helplessly over the yawning void.

'Stop struggling,' she hissed, 'you'll have us off.'

'Where are we? What happened?' Lasser demanded.

'We fell. We're hanging from the cliff.'

'Oh my God.'

He was still for a moment, his body inert as a corpse.

'Where's Spengler?'

'Trapped below on a ledge. We were almost at the top. Another few minutes would have done it. Now . . . now I don't know what we can do.'

'Well, we can't stay here,' said Lasser.

He began to struggle again, worming himself free. She heard the clink of snaplinks as he tugged them loose.

'Stop that,' she said, 'you'll tear us off, for God's sake.'

He grunted. 'There's a crack over to the right. I'm going to see if I can reach it. Just hold steady.'

She clenched her teeth as he fought with the straps. Backwards and forwards they swayed, the wind blasting their bodies with such force she felt her senses reeling. Beneath her feet, the Face rippled and blurred. Spengler was down there. Lost and helpless. Waiting for the end.

She felt the final snaplink come away.

'I'm free,' Lasser hissed. 'Don't move. I'm going to jump. Whatever you do, remain absolutely still.'

She waited, swaying hopelessly. She no longer cared if he made it or not. Nothing seemed to matter any more. Soon she would rest; that was all she wanted, to rest, to dream, to lose herself in the defenceless realms of slumber.

Lasser moved. She felt his weight leave her as he made his desperate leap. In a daze, she saw his shape flung out against the storm, arms outstretched reaching for a hold. He hit the rock, slithered downwards, stopped, slithered again, then held firm.

Helene felt something tugging at her waist. She was rising, the harness was dragging her upwards. No, that wasn't right. The winch was gone, dangling over the cliff as helpless as she. It had to be an illusion, a trick of the storm. I'm tired, she thought, my brain is tired. She closed her eyes and opened them again, and still her body had that strange buoyancy. It was no illusion. She was floating up the mountainside, climbing into the sky. It didn't make sense, unless she was dead already. Was that possible? Dead, and on her way to heaven? But that couldn't be, for the very thought accelerated her pulse-beat and now she could feel it quite distinctly, throbbing in her throat and chest. She was not dead, but alive, her torso supported, rising slowly, steadily, indisputably.

With a chill of horror, she realised what had happened. With Lasser's weight no longer maintaining the balance, the heavy drum-winch was dragging on the other end of the cable. She was being hauled upwards for the moment, but as soon as she reached the top of the pillar she would catapult over the other side. Her skin crawled. Oh God, she thought. She had to get out of this damned harness or nothing in the world could save her.

She wriggled forward, clawing at straps and fastenings with frozen unfeeling fingers. Damn Lasser. By saving himself he had sentenced her. Terror filled her body, translating itself into movement, concentration. A minute ago she had scarcely cared if she lived or died. Now there was no longer any doubt. She wanted desperately to survive.

The rock face slid implacably by, its endless angles and edges slashing at her chest, skinning her knees. She dared not look up, for up there the trap waited, towering above her, the final ledge that would jerk her into the chasm below. And why wouldn't her fingers work, for God's sake? They were like fat swollen sausages, no longer obeying instructions. She writhed and stretched in her efforts to undo the heavy steel buckles. Doubling forward, she tried to wrench at them with her teeth. There was no time for this, got to . . . get . . . the damn thing loose. In a frenzy, she tore and twisted. A buckle parted. Good. Two to go. How much longer did she have?

Her ascendancy was quickening. She could hear the cable sliding over the rock above with a sickening swish. Almost there. I'll never do it. Sobbing desperately, she thrust out with her feet, pushing them against the wall in an attempt to slow her progress, but the upward pull continued. Blinded by snow, she dragged the second buckle open. One left. Just one. The air was full of ice particles showering down from above. The swish of the cable had become a whine now as she was dragged up with flinty persistence. Her fingertips stung, the flesh seemed reduced to shreds. Oh, this is ludicrous, she thought. Am I to die now, with only one buckle to go?

Slowly, the pillar rose in front of her face. She saw its top, strewn with snow and rubble. She saw the cable sliding over the other side, sending a fusillade of stones clattering down the mountain. The harness tilted her forward, she felt herself skidding over the flat hard surface. Panic streaked through her. She was going. Going now.

Then her knee jammed hard inside a rocky fissure. It was only a momentary halt, but it gave her the respite she needed. Hauling frantically at the final buckle, she tore it loose and the harness whipped from her grasp, clattering across the top of the pillar to vanish into the vaporous fog.

Sobbing, Helene Rössner dragged herself over the granite platform, glad to be still alive. She had no idea how long she lay. There was no way of telling, for time had retreated to some distant point where hours, and minutes lost their meaning. She felt bloodless, lifeless, part of the mountain itself, as though she had taken root, sprouted incongruously like some dark plant. She dozed, and in her dreams she saw herself fastened naked to the pillar. I am stone, she thought. I have been absorbed into these lifeless walls. Unfeeling, I can't be hurt any more.

Then she heard Lasser coming, heard the scrape of his boots on the rock, the rasp of his breath against the air. She felt his hands on her shoulders, prising her up. 'Come on,' he hissed, 'we've got to keep moving.'

They were back on the summit icefield, following the deep scars in the snow which had marked their downward route. There were footholds, a line of evenly-spaced steps carved out of the crusted surface. Spengler's probably, she thought. She leaned against Lasser, moving stubbornly up, trying to estimate how far this immeasurable sweep of ice could reach. From time to time, when they paused for breath, Lasser would shout into the storm, but no answering cry came back.

She wanted to quit, to sink down where she lay, but Lasser refused to let her. She resented this body next to hers, this insistent figure that kept forcing her upwards. What was the point of it all? What was the point of anything, except rest? Leave me alone, she thought. I want to be left. Left to sleep. To drift away on the clouds. No pain, no cold. Nothing. Only sleep.

She heard Lasser's voice ringing in her ear, and this time there was an answering shout, dim and distorted, from somewhere above. A minute passed, and a rope came snaking down towards them. Lasser grabbed it, laughing out loud. He could barely control his laughter, so overcome was he with joy and relief.

She saw a cluster of figures taking shape through the mist, then strong arms held her and she felt herself lifted bodily into the air. Something was pressed against her lips. Brandy. She sipped. It burned her throat going down. They were strapping her into a stretcher. A voice, an American voice, said: 'Don't worry, lady, you're going to be okay.'

She tried to speak. There was something she had to remember, something terribly important. For a moment she could not recall what it was, and then the memory came back. A solitary figure swathed in fog. Spengler. Trapped on the ledge.

'Spengler,' she croaked, her voice barely audible against the wind.

'Sorry, Miss Rössner,' someone answered, 'the cable's gone and my men are exhausted. There's not a hope in hell of bringing that Kraut up alive.'

She opened her mouth in protest. They couldn't leave Spengler. It was outrageous. They belonged together, she, Spengler and Lasser. If one stayed, they all stayed, that was the way it had to be. She tried to tell them this, struggling to speak, struggling to form the words with her trembling lips, but the earth seemed to sway beneath her. A hand touched her forehead. She felt warmth flooding

232

her limbs. Then her body seemed to melt. She relaxed, unbending peacefully. And slept.

Spengler watched the heavy drum crashing down the precipice, trailing a cluster of wildly twisting ropes and cables behind it. He heard the roaring in his ears as it thundered down the ice-walls and bare trackless rock. He saw it grow darker, smaller, fuzzier, fading into the sheets of vapour and the gunmetal greyness of the eddying storm. No sign of Helene. Lasser either. They must have reached the top alive.

She'll be okay, he thought. Stop worrying. Worry about yourself. You're done for. You were done for when you left that gallery window. You were done for the second you set foot on this filthy mountain.

He grinned wryly to himself. What did you expect, he wondered? Some magical future to compensate for the miseries of your past? Happiness had been too much to hope for. The Eiger had scuttled him in the final innings. But at least Helene was safe. Thank God for that. She would go back to her own side, pick up the tattered remnants of her life again. Well, she deserved to win more than he did. When you came right down to it, all the virtues in the world were meaningless without courage, and she had plenty of that all right.

The snow lashed stinging into his eyes, covering the rock with a thin white film, blotting out notches and crannies until the protuberances of the cliff had almost disappeared, and in their place was a series of smooth, featureless slabs. He felt neither sad nor dismayed. Instead, he wanted to laugh. It was funny when you thought about it. The Eiger had played the dirtiest trick of all. He saw the Face as a living force, thinking of it, not with hatred, but with grudging admiration as a fighter might regard an adversary who at the moment of triumph delivers a mortal deathblow. Give the enemy its due, he thought.

Helene Rössner, I wish you were here to tell it to, you were the one good thing in my life, the only freedom I ever found. He had certainly never found it anywhere else, not in his climbing and most definitely not on this godawful precipice. The things I might have had, he thought, all the stabilising comforting comfortable things, were all there in that sun-browned skin, that soft hair, those lovely eyes. So much for plans and hopes and dreams. Reality was the final equaliser.

At least he had done his duty, no one could fault him on that score. Well, not quite, he reflected. Looking back, he realised he ought to have killed Lasser, but he'd done all the killing he intended to do in this war. He was through with killing. To hell with the war, he thought. The war was behind him now. The Eiger had taken away his commitment as it had taken away his guilt.

He stared down at Henke, frozen to the rock like a macabre statue. The handsome face looked glassy in the fading daylight. The eyes were open but covered with snow. Henke had saved his life this day, had clambered down that awful patchwork of cracks and fissures at great risk to himself to haul Spengler up from certain death. If the woman had courage, then Henke unquestionably had it too.

Spengler knelt down, took the Knight's Cross from his throat and tied it around Henke's neck. It's not much, he mused, a piece of worthless old junk, but you deserve it more than I ever did.

He was about to straighten when something in the snow caught his eyes. It was a tiny locket, Helene Rössner's. He realised she must have dropped it when he'd been strapping her into the cable. On an impulse, he picked it up and looped it too over Henke's ice-glazed head.

Then he reached for his haversack and peered speculatively at the traverse ahead. I always was a bloody fool, he thought, never did know how to quit. But we must settle this thing between us, the Eiger and me. We must fight it out to a decision.

And for the second time that day, Erich Spengler, racked with exhaustion, his left arm a useless stump of rapidly darkening flesh, set out for the summit as evening faded behind the western crags, turning the Face into a contourless featureless vacuum where nothing moved, and nothing lived.

Epilogue by Laurence Hemsworth
BBC Research Assistant

What happened on Erich Spengler's last battle with the Eiger isn't easy to define after so many years. The Eiger as a mountain carries an allure that is all its own. It's impossible to gaze at that great chunk of rock and snow without feeling a strange uneasiness in the pit of your stomach. Though I've seen it many times and in many different weathers, I never cease to marvel that men actually venture on to its terrible crags and terrifying icefields. What Spengler did was astonishing, not merely because of his physical endurance or his incredible will to survive, but because it happened in the days before climbing techniques and equipment had been properly perfected. The only thing he understood was to start at the bottom and keep on going until he reached the top – or died trying. Sadly, his achievement can never be recognised, for time has distorted everything, including memory. The events leading up to his climb, I was able to piece together from interviews conducted with ex-members of Otto Skorzeny's special commando force in Munich and Mannheim. Some of the incidents on the Face itself, including the accident at the 'Traverse of the Gods', were described to me by Dr Walter Lasser, now living in a home for the elderly in Flensburg, Denmark, and by Lewis D. Shellburn, who remained in the army long enough to reach the rank of general and then retired to Norfolk, Nebraska, where he now runs a highly successful roofing business. I learned that Helene Rössner had moved to England after the war, and discovered from an old newspaper cutting that she'd eventually married an ex-Polish army officer named Jacek Vaslav, but about Spengler himself I drew a complete blank.

Moreover, I didn't manage to trace Helene Rössner's whereabouts until many months after completing my research. Then, quite by accident, a friend at the British Imperial War Museum mentioned that they'd been using her for background material on a series of articles for *The Daily Telegraph*.

'Do you have her address?' I asked.

'It's somewhere in the Lake District, I think,' he said. 'I can get it for you, I'm sure.'

Two days later, I arrived at a charming whitewashed cottage overlooking the mountain peaks above Ullswater. The door was built of oak, very old and studded with metal spikes. I was just about to knock when it opened suddenly and an elderly lady stood there, blinking at me with surprise. She was, I estimated, in her late sixties, tall and straight and still trimly built. Her cheeks were lined, but it wasn't difficult to see that she'd once been a very beautiful woman. She was wearing a pleated dress in red and green tartan, with a cashmere scarf and a corduroy hat. She'd been in the process of pulling on a pair of gloves, and was plainly on her way out, but seeing me, she froze in her tracks and stared expectantly. I knew without a doubt that this was Helene Rössner, and felt my heart begin to pound. For months, this woman had been as real to me as my own flesh. Now, seeing her in person, I realised for the first time that she was not my creation, she was not a fragment of my own life but an individual in her own right.

'Mrs Vaslav?' I whispered.

'Yes?' Her voice carried just a trace of a foreign accent.

'I'm from the BBC. I wonder if I might speak to you for a moment? It's rather important.'

She hesitated. 'Well, I was just on my way to the village.'

'I can give you a lift, if you like. I've driven up from London, Mrs Vaslav. It's about Erich Spengler.'

Her eyes flickered and she studied me suspiciously. There was a touch of colour on her high cheekbones.

'No one's mentioned that name to me for over thirty years,' she whispered. 'Who are you, young man?'

'My name's Laurence Hemsworth,' I said. 'You *did* know Erich Spengler?'

'A long time ago.'

'When you worked for British Intelligence? As Dr Helene Rössner?'

Again, I was aware of that searching gaze. She was sizing me up. Shrewdly. Wisely. Deciding if she liked me.

'You appear to know a great deal, young man,' she grunted.

I waited, praying I wouldn't be turned away. But she finished pulling on her gloves and gave a thin smile.

'I do hope you're a slow driver,' she said, 'I detest speed.'

We cruised back down the road towards the lakeshore, and I felt faintly uncomfortable. It was a strange experience to be in the presence of this woman. Helene Rössner, I thought. It was hard to believe she actually existed. Had this frail old lady really gone through such torment on the North Face of the Eiger? I wanted to share her innermost thoughts and feelings.

The road nosed its way through banks of lush green foliage. Farmhouses snuggled among the pasture folds like scattered rice. Slivers of crimson danced over the hummocks of Gowbarrow Fell and Swineside Knott, and the wind carried the scent of sunwarmed pine, moorgrass and peat.

'Beautiful, isn't it?' Helene Rössner said.

'It's charming,' I agreed.

'The loveliest corner of England. It reminds me of the place where I was born.'

'In Switzerland?'

She smiled thinly. 'You *have* been doing your research.'

'I wondered why you didn't go back there at the end of the war. What brought you to Britain?'

She shrugged, her face expressionless. 'Memories,' she explained simply. 'I needed a fresh start.'

The road hugged the lakeshore, and in the campsites on the water's edge, holidaymakers in brightly coloured shirts were busy cooking lunch. The water looked indescribably blue, and tiny wisps of froth danced where waves had been lapped up by the breeze.

'Tell me about Spengler,' I said casually.

She smiled. 'He was an artist, a virtuoso on rock and

237

ice. When he moved up a mountain face, he was beautiful to watch, like a cat.'

'Was that how he was on the Eigerwand?'

'Look,' she said, pointing.

I peered through the windscreen. Above the road, in buttercup-scattered meadows, people were milling about in great confusion. I spotted huge white dogs being lined up by their collars.

'They're holding a hound trail,' she explained. 'They drag sacks of aniseed over the heather, then turn the dogs loose. First one back is the winner. It's quite a sight to see an entire pack stampeding over the hilltops.'

'Mrs Vaslav,' I said, 'you haven't answered my question.'

'I didn't understand it,' she declared.

I frowned. She was trying to fence me off. Why?

I said: 'Mrs Vaslav, last summer a Swiss mountain guide climbing the North Face of the Eiger discovered the body of a German soldier at the 'Traverse of the Gods'. Around his neck he carried a medal inscribed with the name Erich Spengler, and a locket containing your photograph.'

Her eyes filled with amusement. I had the feeling she was laughing at me. 'How fascinating,' she breathed.

'One body, Mrs Vaslav. But as you know, there should have been two. Spengler's and Henke's.'

'Young man, you're talking in riddles. Who on earth is Henke?'

I glanced at her quickly. Her eyes were glowing with a strange discomforting brightness. I knew she was lying, but for what reason?

'I've spoken to Dr Lasser, Major Shellburn and Kurt Hüsser,' I told her. 'I *know* what happened on the Eigerwand. What I don't know is how Spengler died.'

'The Erich Spengler I knew was killed on the Russian front,' she said in a calm voice.

My God, I thought, what's she trying to hide?

'I don't wish to appear offensive,' I said as carefully as I could, 'but I've talked to eye-witnesses, men who were present at the attack on the Jungfraujoch. I know you were there, and I know the role you played.'

She smiled again. 'Then perhaps you'd better explain it to me. That way, we'll avoid talking at cross-purposes.'

I frowned. 'I hardly know where to start.'

'Why not try the beginning?' she said.

So I went through the entire story piece by piece, beginning with her recruitment in Paris, going on to the events at the training school, Spengler's battle with Henke on the summit of the Calania Tower, and ending with the assault on the Eigerwand. Throughout it all, she peered straight ahead, listening intently, a strange little smile on her lips. When I had finished, she said: 'That's quite a narrative.'

'I think so.'

'I didn't realise I'd led such an exciting life.'

'You're not still denying it?'

'Of course,' she said. 'Mr Hemsworth, you're the victim of an over-fertile imagination.'

I felt a surge of anger. 'I got that story – or bits of it – from numerous sources. You can deny it until you're blue in the face, Mrs Vaslav, but I know you're lying.'

There was no change in her expression. She looked as calm and as demure as if we'd been discussing the weather.

The first house of the village slipped into view. A sign said: 'Pooley Bridge'.

'Will you let me out here,' she murmured. 'I want to go to the post office.'

I slid the car to a halt, my anger turning to alarm. When she eventually died, the Eiger's secret might well die with her.

'Mrs Vaslav,' I said as reasonably as I could, 'please tell me what happened to Erich Spengler. The world deserves to know.'

'The world deserves nothing,' she replied easily. 'It's always better to let the dead remain dead.'

She opened the door and clambered out, pausing to smile back at me. 'Good-bye, Mr Hemsworth,' she said, 'I'm sorry you've come such a long way for nothing. It's a fascinating story, truly, but it simply isn't true.'

I drove back to the Sharrow Bay Hotel, feeling tired, bitter and disgusted, and booked myself a room. I knew I could try again tomorrow, but she carried an air of determination that seemed impossible to penetrate. Then something happened which put the final seal on the whole remarkable episode.

I drove down to the local pub after dinner. It was a beautiful evening, very still, the air soft and warm. People sat at tables on the terrace, basking in the fading sunlight. I went inside and ordered a glass of beer at the bar. A pleasant-faced young man in a dark sweater nodded at me. 'Up from London?' he asked.

'Yes,' I said, 'I'm with the BBC.'

'Oh? On holiday?'

'Not really. I've come to see someone.'

'Who's that?'

'Mrs Vaslav,' I said.

He chuckled. 'She's quite a lady. Quite a lady.'

'You know her?'

'Only in a professional sense. I'm her solicitor. Did you know she was a famous spy during the war?'

'So I understand.'

He drained his glass and ordered another. 'Her husband sometimes pops in here for a drink on his way home from work,' he said. 'He's retired now of course, but he helps out at the community centre three days a week.'

I nodded, drawing circles in the moisture on the bar with my fingernail. 'Polish, isn't he?'

'No, German.'

I frowned. 'That's odd. I thought he was a Pole.'

'Not old Vaslav. German as they come. Speaks English well though. He used to be a distinguished mountaineer in his youth, but he lost an arm in the war and that put an end to his climbing days for good.'

I felt a faint sense of unease. 'Which arm?' I asked softly.

The young man looked surprised. 'Right, I think. Or was it left? To tell the truth, I can't be sure.'

He grinned. 'He gets a little crazy when he's tight,' he said. 'Keeps claiming he made the second ascent of the North Face of the Eiger. Quite untrue, of course. I looked up the records once. The second ascent was made by Terray and Lachenal in 1947.'

I felt my mouth dry up. It was just too remarkable to be a coincidence.

I finished my beer and drove swiftly back up the road towards Martindale, my mind in a turmoil. The hills seemed to shimmer in the summer evening. A few fleecy bits of fluff scudded westwards across an otherwise faultless sky.

I parked the car beside a muddy cart-track, and made my way on foot through a patch of spruce trees to the garden of Helene Rössner's cottage. The ground was soft and littered with peat bogs. Tufts of long, coarse grass tilted beneath my feet. The trees ended, and I peered through their branches at the quaint little cottage beyond. Helene Rössner was sitting on the lawn, reading. Behind her, the dipping sun cast crimson shafts across the bracken-clad hillslopes. Flies buzzed lazily on the soft summer air. Someone was working at the side of the house, pruning rose bushes amid the little clumps of carefully-nurtured shrubbery. He was dressed in gardening clothes, and as I watched, he straightened and strolled casually down the lawn. Helene Rössner looked up from her book and smiled at him as he sat down and squeezed her shoulder with his right hand. I felt my heart thumping. He was a thickset man in his late sixties or early seventies, white-haired, strong-jawed, with piercing grey eyes. His left arm was missing, the empty shirtsleeve pinned to his shoulder.

I opened my wallet and took out a picture of Spengler I'd had photo-copied from the 1935 Mountaineering Journal. It had been taken immediately after an assault on the North Buttress of the Admonter Reichenstein, and he was dressed in civilian clothes, his wool shirt open to the waist, his head tilted back in the sunlight, laughing, a feathered Bavarian hunting cap perched rakishly over one eye.

I held the picture to the light and studied it carefully. Time had taken its toll, but the resemblance was unmistakable. The man in the garden, Helene Rössner's husband, was clearly and irrefutably Erich Spengler.

I felt almost dizzy with excitement. For months, I had toured Europe, digging out facts, clues, witnesses, and all the time, the answer to the mystery had been right here. By some bewildering miracle, Erich Spengler had managed to escape the Eiger. The man Shellburn had left near the 'Traverse of the Gods' had, with his left arm gone and his strength badly depleted, fought his way off that Face for the second time.

My first impulse was to march out of the trees and confront them both with my discovery, but something held me back.

I had thought endlessly of Spengler and Helene Rössner, I had tried to re-create them on paper, to make them as real and as vivid as my imagination would allow, but seeing them here before me, two elderly people sitting in their garden in the warm flush of an English summer evening, I realised I had no right to interfere with their lives. They belonged here. I didn't. Against the fading sunlight, the lazy mewing of the sheep, the valley bursting with woodland, I was an intruder.

Had Spengler been captured by the Swiss and transported to England as a POW, or had he come after the war had ended? And why had he changed his name to Vaslav? Was it because of official pressures to preserve the legend of Swiss neutrality, or was there another, more personal reason?

As I made my way back through the trees to the car, I realised I would never know the answer. Their masquerade would remain a mystery until the end of time. Like the Eiger itself, sombre and eternal, I knew Mr and Mrs Vaslav, enigmatic to the last, would carry their secret with them to the grave.

WARLORDS

BY BOB LANGLEY

BRITAIN'S FUTURE?

Britain is on the verge of total collapse. North Sea oil has suddenly run dry. Rationing and unemployment spread like wildfire. And four elections in two months have plunged the nation into a terrifying chaos.

Across the Atlantic America decides it is time to step in and assist their one-time ally. BY FERMENTING NO LESS THAN A FULL-SCALE BLOODY REVOLUTION GUARANTEED TO BRING THE DYING NATION TO HER KNEES AND TO CHANGE THE COURSE OF WORLD HISTORY WITH ONE DEVASTATING, FINAL COUP DE GRÂCE . . .

Fast and furious, WARLORDS is a terrifying and disturbing vision of Britain at the mercy of the powerlords in the not-so-distant future!

ADVENTURE THRILLER   0 7221 5409 7   £1.25

SPHERE BOOKS FOR THE BEST IN ADVENTURE/THRILLER READING

THE WATCHDOGS OF ABADDON	Ib Melchior	£1.75 ☐
I, SAID THE SPY	Derek Lambert	£1.75 ☐
RAISE THE TITANIC	Clive Cussler	£1.50 ☐
VIXEN 03	Clive Cussler	£1.50 ☐
SHARKY'S MACHINE	William Diehl	£1.50 ☐
THE CRASH OF '79	Paul Erdman	£1.50 ☐
TUNNEL WAR	Joe Poyer	£1.50 ☐
SNOW FALCON	Craig Thomas	£1.50 ☐
FIREFOX	Craig Thomas	£1.50 ☐
THE TAMARIND SEED	Evelyn Anthony	£1.25 ☐
AIR FORCE ONE	Edwin Corley	£1.25 ☐
THE BENEDICT ARNOLD CONNECTION	Joseph DiMona	95p ☐
FIRESTORM	Robert L. Duncan	£1.10 ☐
HOLLYWOOD GOTHIC	Thomas Gifford	£1.50 ☐
THE SWEETMAN CURVE	Graham Masterton	£1.50 ☐
THE MITTENWALD SYNDICATE	Frederick Nolan	95p ☐

All Sphere books are available at your local bookshop or newsagent, or can be ordered direct from the publisher. Just tick the titles you want and fill in the form below.

Name _____

Address _____

_____

Write to Sphere Books, Cash Sales Department, P.O. Box 11, Falmouth, Cornwall TR10 9EN

Please enclose a cheque or postal order to the value of the cover price plus:

UK: 40p for the first book, 18p for the second book and 13p for each additional book ordered to a maximum charge of £1.49.

OVERSEAS: 60p for the first book plus 18p per copy for each additional book.

BFPO & EIRE: 40p for the first book, 18p for the second book plus 13p per copy for the next 7 books, thereafter 7p per book.

Sphere Books reserve the right to show new retail prices on covers which may differ from those previously advertised in the text or elsewhere, and to increase postal rates in accordance with the PO.